Green-Eyed Boys

Christian Jennings was a member of the Territorial Parachute Regiment and the French Foreign Legion before becoming a freelance journalist and television researcher. His account of his time in the Foreign Legion, *Mouthful of Rocks*, was published in 1990.

Adrian Weale is a military historian and journalist who has published a number of books on military subjects, including *Fighting Fit: The SAS Fitness Guide* and *Renegades: Hitler's Englishmen*. He is a former regular army officer who served in regimental and staff appointments.

CHRISTIAN JENNINGS &
ADRIAN WEALE

GREEN-EYED BOYS

3 Para and the Battle for
Mount Longdon

HarperCollins*Publishers*

HarperCollins*Publishers*
77–85 Fulham Palace Road,
Hammersmith, London W6 8JB

www.**fire**and**water**.com

This paperback edition 1996

3 5 7 9 8 6 4 2

First published in Great Britain by
HarperCollins*Publishers* 1996

A catalogue record for this book is
available from the British Library

ISBN 0 00 638448 X

Set in Meridien by
Rowland Phototypesetting Ltd,
Bury St Edmunds, Suffolk

Printed and bound in Great Britain by
Caledonian International Book Manufacturing Ltd, Glasgow

Contents

Illustrations

Members of A Company pose in the burial pit with the Argentine dead. *(Vincent Bramley)*

An Argentine body still smouldering hours after being phosphorus grenaded. *(Vincent Bramley)*

The burial pit. *(Vincent Bramley)*

Mount Longdon: view from the north-west. *(Mark Cox)*

3 Para's temporary mass grave at Teal Inlet. *(Vincent Bramley)*

HRH the Prince of Wales and General Sir Anthony Farrar-Hockley greet Hew Pike at the RAF Brize Norton as the battalion returns to Britain. *(Cassidy and Leigh)*

Hew Pike and Mrs Marika McKay, widow of VC winner Ian McKay, with other members of 3 Para who won awards in the Falklands honours. *(Des Fuller)*

Rifle and helmet on Longdon mark the spot where Ian McKay died. *(Tom Smith/Express Newspapers)*

MAPS

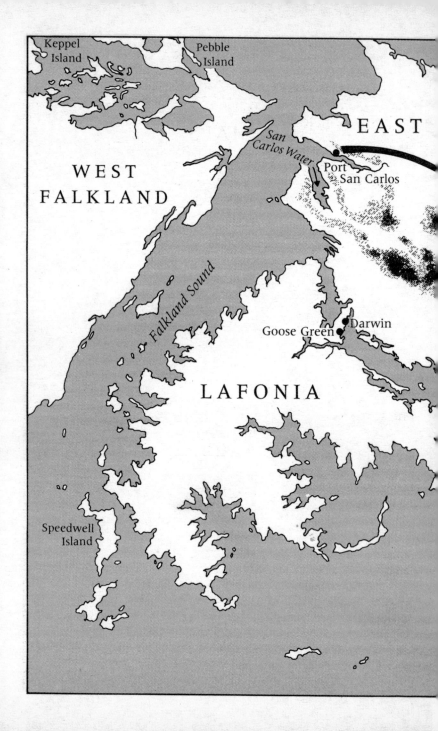

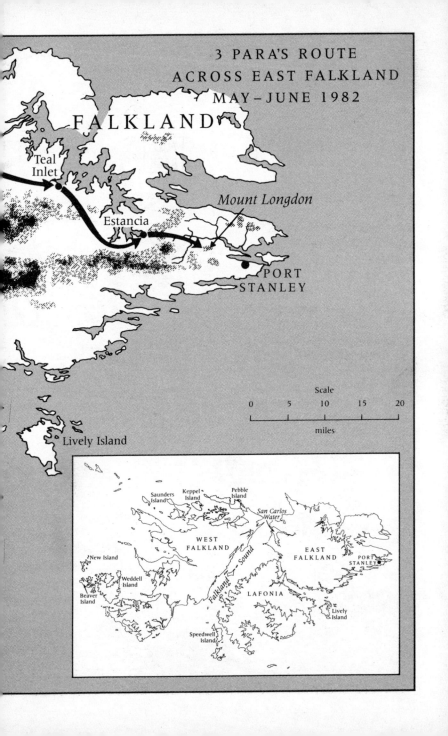

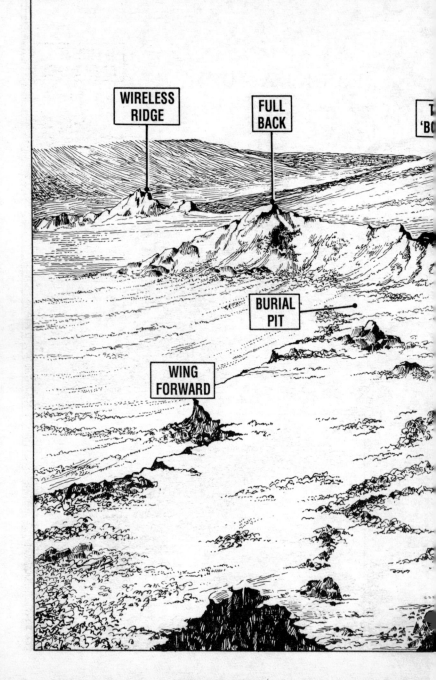

WIRELESS
RIDGE

FULL
BACK

BURIAL
PIT

WING
FORWARD

MAJOR UNITS OF 3 COMMANDO BRIGADE
OPERATION CORPORATE, APRIL–JUNE 1982

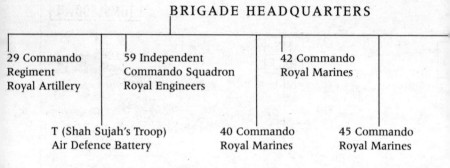

BRIGADE HEADQUARTERS

29 Commando Regiment Royal Artillery

59 Independent Commando Squadron Royal Engineers

42 Commando Royal Marines

T (Shah Sujah's Troop) Air Defence Battery

40 Commando Royal Marines

45 Commando Royal Marines

3 PARA'S ORGANISATION
APRIL 1982

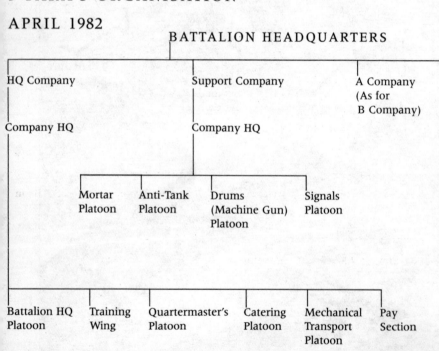

BATTALION HEADQUARTERS

HQ Company

Support Company

A Company (As for B Company)

Company HQ

Company HQ

Mortar Platoon

Anti-Tank Platoon

Drums (Machine Gun) Platoon

Signals Platoon

Battalion HQ Platoon

Training Wing

Quartermaster's Platoon

Catering Platoon

Mechanical Transport Platoon

Pay Section

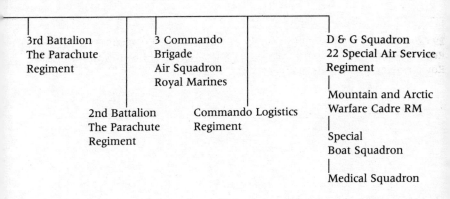

3rd Battalion
The Parachute
Regiment

3 Commando
Brigade
Air Squadron
Royal Marines

D & G Squadron
22 Special Air Service
Regiment

Mountain and Arctic
Warfare Cadre RM

2nd Battalion
The Parachute
Regiment

Commando Logistics
Regiment

Special
Boat Squadron

Medical Squadron

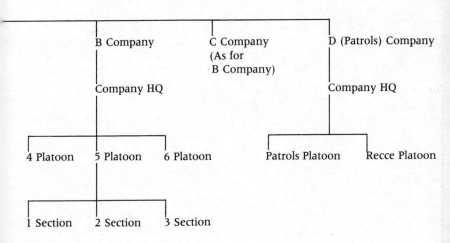

B Company

C Company
(As for
B Company)

D (Patrols) Company

Company HQ

Company HQ

4 Platoon   5 Platoon   6 Platoon

Patrols Platoon   Recce Platoon

1 Section   2 Section   3 Section

Acknowledgements

My thanks and acknowledgements are due to all the men from 3 Para who contributed to this book, especially to Sammy Dougherty, John Weeks and Thor Caithness, from whom I first heard the story of Mount Longdon more than thirteen years ago. Thanks also to Caroline Dawnay, for 'green-eyed' agenting, to Susie Dowdall, who facilitated the process of writing the book, and to Steve Boulton, for his investigative intuition.

CHRISTIAN JENNINGS
London, June 1995

I should very much like to thank the following, without whom *Green-Eyed Boys* would have remained impossible (please excuse the omission of decorations): Mike Argue, David Collett, Kevin Connery, Mark Cox, Sammy Dougherty, Brian Faulkner, Lee Fisher, Des Fuller, Dominic Gray, Dave Kempster, Tony Kempster, Tony Mason, Roddy de Normann, Chris Phelan, Jim Pritchard, Dave Robson, Ernie Rustill, John Weeks and Yvonne Weeks. In addition, those members of 3 Para (and other units) who preferred to remain anonymous are also gratefully thanked. Colonel Hamish Fletcher OBE and Lieutenant Colonel Ian Smith MBE, successive regimental colonels of the Parachute Regiment, treated me with great courtesy and forbearance, even though our discussions were ultimately fruitless.

Additionally I am particularly grateful to the following for their help: my literary agent, Andrew Lownie, who, as always, knew exactly what to do at every stage of the process and who handled negotiations and 'agenting' on behalf of both authors with his usual style and aplomb; Vincent Bramley, for his general assistance throughout the project; Tim Lupprian, for reading the manuscript and providing many helpful comments; Caroline Ballinger and

Sebastian Thomas for allowing us to stay in their New York apartment; Robert Lacey, for his very professional copy editing; and Richard Johnson, who has been the most understanding and tolerant of publishers.

Finally I want to thank my family. My mother and father, Carole and Ken Weale, and my parents-in-law, Rosula and Alan Glyn, have combined to look after my son Robert during the last phases of the writing of the book when everything was almost, but not quite, falling into place. I cannot, of course, thank my wife Mary enough for her support, tolerance and incisive editing.

ADRIAN WEALE
London, October 1995

The authors and publishers wish to thank the following for permission to reproduce copyright material: Reed Books for an extract from *Contact*, by A.F.N. Clarke (Secker & Warburg, 1983); Little, Brown for extracts from *Don't Cry for me Sergeant Major*, by Robert McGowan and Jeremy Hands (Futura, 1985); and Leo Cooper for extracts from *No Picnic*, by Brigadier Julian Thompson (Leo Cooper, 1985).

For the record, the opinions expressed in this book are those of the authors and of individuals who are directly quoted. They do not represent the views of the Parachute Regiment, the Ministry of Defence or any other official body.

The authors' approach to researching this book was to write to as many veterans of Longdon as they could find and to conduct interviews with them, usually on tape. The majority of those approached agreed to co-operate in full, some agreed to speak anonymously, and a few declined to assist. Parachute Regiment headquarters were briefed on the project but declined to give any formal assistance: the acting Colonel Commandant of the regiment (coincidentally Lieutenant General Hew Pike DSO MBE) ruled that:

> a. By agreeing to support a request for co-operation there is scope for the views portrayed in the book being accredited as those of the Parachute Regiment.

And:

   b. There is concern that the book will be perceived as a
   further 'investigation' of alleged war crimes.

The authors, naturally, disagree with these views.

Preface to the Paperback Edition

Following the publication in May 1996 of the first edition of *Green-Eyed Boys* a considerable amount of new information has come to the authors' attention. Much of this, although interesting, does not add materially to the story, but in a few important cases it does and consequently the authors and publishers have decided to take the opportunity to incorporate this new material into the paperback edition. We would very much like to thank Mark Cox for the help that he has given with regard to these corrections.

Introduction

In the summer of 1992, a number of stories were published in the British press recounting allegations made in a book by a veteran of the Falklands War of 1982. The ex-soldier, Vincent Bramley, had written an autobiographical account of his involvement in the campaign, during which he had been a junior non-commissioned officer in the 3rd Battalion of the Parachute Regiment In his book he described several incidents that he had either witnessed himself, or been told of, which were open to the interpretation of being 'war crimes'. The book itself had actually been on sale for over a year by this time, but nevertheless there was sufficient concern, both in the media and in official circles, for the Secretary of State for Defence, Malcolm Rifkind, to order an investigation by detectives of the Metropolitan Police.

Nearly two years later, in July 1994, the Director of Public Prosecutions announced that no charges were to be brought. Although by then there was a good deal of evidence in the public domain that a prisoner of war had been killed some time after the battle of Mount Longdon had finished, the decision was widely regarded, in the popular press at least, as a victory for common sense.

The DPP's decision appears to have been made on the eminently sensible basis that, twelve years after the events took place, there was little realistic prospect of producing evidence compelling enough to satisfy a British jury that British soldiers had committed serious offences during one of the most popular military campaigns of recent times. All very well, but it left unanswered the big question: what did actually happen?

In part, this book provides an answer. The basis of the inquiry, that questionable incidents occurred, was sound, and this book provides eye-witness accounts of them, but far more interesting than the bald retailing of these unpleasant events is the whole process of war in the modern age. The Falklands War was not much different from any other war in terms of the reasons for which it was fought. An important political principle, the right of peoples to self-determination, was at stake, and it seemed that the only way to preserve it, in this instance, was to fight for it. Although some people have made great sport in condemning it as the last gasp of British imperial 'gunboat diplomacy', in reality it was a thoroughly modern war. There is a good argument for saying that the Falklands conflict was a key event in the Cold War then being fought between the Western democratic and Soviet Communist power blocs: Mrs Thatcher's government demonstrated that the West had teeth and was not afraid to use them, that there were provocations to which no civilised government could turn a blind eye.

In fact, what discomfited many liberal intellectuals was the popular support that the despatch of the Task Force and the subsequent campaign elicited across the political spectrum, from Labour's then leader Michael Foot to the *Sun*, with its notorious but unforgettable 'Gotcha!' headline celebrating the sinking of the *General Belgrano*. And the sheer skill and professionalism of the British forces in the Falklands did not sit well with the 'intellectual' view of Britain as a declining, even decadent, power.

But only a fool would claim that nothing went wrong during the Falklands campaign: that it was somehow a perfect operation. There were mistakes of policy, of strategy, of tactics and of individual fieldcraft. These are inevitable in war and we must try to learn from them. The Falklands War of 1982 was the first serious international conflict fought by Britain's new all-professional post-National Service forces. This book represents a picture of how one highly-motivated élite unit approached the campaign, and how its extraordinary culture of aggressive self-belief and violence helped to win the most bloody battle of the conflict.

ADRIAN WEALE
August 1995

From his position in company headquarters, one tactical bound behind the rear elements of the assault platoons, John Weeks could clearly see his men gingerly patrolling forwards: 4 Platoon on the left, 5 Platoon on the right. As they crossed an open, grassy area, Weeks was surprised that they hadn't been spotted by someone, anyone, in the Argentine position amongst the rocks that loomed in front of them. It seemed that they might be able to get into the defences, amongst their enemy, without having to fight their way in.

But as B Company closed on the Argentine bunkers there was a loud percussive bang. A brief moment of silence was followed by the shocked shouts of Corporal Brian Milne, his foot blown off by an anti-personnel mine. Alerted by the noise, Argentine sentries began to fire on the advancing Paras; tracer ammunition flashed through the darkness, grenade fragments clattered amongst the rocks. The battle was on.

Time to rock and roll.

CHAPTER ONE

The Maroon Machine

Now all you recruities what's drafted today,
You shut up your rag-box an' 'ark to my lay,
An' I'll sing you a soldier as far as I may:
A soldier what's fit for a soldier.

KIPLING, 'The Young British Soldier'

The story of the Green-Eyed Boys is the story of the battle for Mount Longdon, the fiercest of the series of sharp infantry actions fought to control the high ground around Port Stanley during the Falklands War of 1982, an operation during which 3 Para – the Third Battalion of the Parachute Regiment – suffered twenty-three fatal casualties and about fifty wounded. The Green-Eyed Boys were the young soldiers of the battalion: too young to be thinking of long-term careers in the army, they were high on the culture of professional skill and aggressive élitism that they found in the Parachute Regiment, and they craved an opportunity to display their prowess. On Mount Longdon they found it.

The attack was planned by Lieutenant Colonel Hew Pike, and directed by his team of Sandhurst-trained officers, but it was the sergeants, corporals and privates who stormed the mountain, an apparently insignificant feature that had been turned, to all intents and purposes, into a fortress.

Even now, almost fifteen years later, there is a certain pride about these men. Today, most of the Green-Eyed Boys are civilians: they've put on weight, their lives are quieter, they will never go into battle for their country again. They are employed in every kind of job imaginable: from insurance salesman to trawlerman; from security consultant to civil servant; from banker to restaurant manager. But it was an experience so profound that they will still pause during their daily routines and think: 'Yes, I was on Longdon.'

For the outsider the military existence is nearly incomprehensible. The whole world of the military, so apparently familiar from films, books and television, is actually a world apart. We see soldiers occasionally, in and around garrison towns, on the motorways and on railway stations, but most of us have little notion of how they live, the way their lives are ordered, what they think about. Foreigners, particularly Europeans, often think of the British as a warrior nation, but few of us have any kind of military experience, even in comparison to Denmark and the Netherlands, for example, where national service remains compulsory. Fantasy stereotypes of the British Army being composed of blimps, thugs, bullies and supermen remain current even though they are derived from a largely fictitious picture of Britain in the Second World War. As a nation, we celebrate a military tradition more glorious than that of any other country, earned on battlefields stretching from Crécy and Malplaquet to Badajoz, Rorke's Drift and El Alamein. But the generations born after the Second World War have little idea of the horrors and tragedies to which we subject our soldiers in our name. Two of the 'men' of B Company who died in the assault up Longdon, Ian Scrivens and Jason Burt, were only seventeen years old: not old enough to vote; not even old enough to walk into a pub and buy a pint of beer. Ian Scrivens died in the arms of his sergeant major, coughing out his life with a lung wound that drowned him in his own blood as a medic only a few years older desperately massaged his heart in an attempt to keep him alive. Neil Grose, who died nearby, had just celebrated his eighteenth birthday.

Every Armistice Day, the ranks of parading British Legion veterans grow thinner, and the memories and understanding of war gained on a hundred battlefields from the Somme and Vimy Ridge to Kohima, the Mareth Line and Arnhem die with them. Very few British citizens have seen active service since Korea, and now that we live in a society without National Service, where war is scarce, we hardly comprehend the nature and relevance of a military existence. Before we can even begin to understand what was going through the minds of the soldiers of 3 Para during the battle of Mount Longdon, it is crucial to look at the organisation to which they belonged and the place they occupied within it.

The Parachute Regiment was originally conceived in the dark days of 1940 when the British Expeditionary Force had been expelled from France by the vastly superior 'Blitzkrieg' strategy of Hitler's Wehrmacht. The German paras – Fallschirmjäger – had played a key role: they had seized and held the modern Belgian fort of Eben Emael, and forced a crossing of the Albert Canal, a key strategic defence line. Winston Churchill, who took over as Prime Minister in May 1940, just as the military disaster in France was taking place, was impressed by the *élan* and fortitude of the German paras and directed that the British military should start training similar troops. At the end of June 1940, the first British soldiers – members of No. 2 Commando – were earmarked for parachute training at the newly formed 'Central Landing School' at Ringway airport outside Manchester.

The original airborne concept envisaged the paratroops as aerially-delivered commandos, raiders with a precise tactical objective, ready to hit the enemy and withdraw quickly, rather than as infantry soldiers with a novel and exhilarating means of getting into action. The first few British airborne operations reflected this: in February 1941 thirty-eight men of the 11th Special Air Service Battalion* successfully destroyed the Tragino aqueduct in southern Italy – although they were all subsequently captured – and a year later C Company of the 2nd Parachute Battalion attacked a radar station at Bruneval in France.

In between these first two airborne raids a German operation took place which successfully transformed the status of airborne forces. In April 1941 Hitler launched his attack against Yugoslavia and Greece, and on 20 May began the airborne invasion of Crete, using the 7th Fallschirmjäger Division of the Luftwaffe. This was the first large-scale airborne assault ever attempted, and it profoundly altered the British view of parachute operations. Although the Germans suffered enormous casualties – up to a third of the paratroops

---

* 'Special Air Service' was the original cover designation of all parachute units. The current SAS are descended from 'L Detachment of the SAS Brigade'.

were lost – nevertheless, by a combination of audacity, determination and British tactical incompetence, they were able to overwhelm the numerically superior and better-armed Commonwealth defenders. Churchill himself wrote on 27 May 1941: 'We ought to have 5000 parachutists and an airborne division on the German model, with any improvements that might suggest themselves from experience.'[1]

The airborne concept had changed, at least as far as the British were concerned. Although there has always remained a place for a small-scale parachute-capable raiding unit – a role now fulfilled in the British forces by the SAS and Special Boat Service – the lesson of Crete was that it was possible, by gaining local air superiority, to inundate a defended area with paratroops who would then fight as infantrymen, using conventional assault tactics. When all is said and done, when the bombers have dropped their last bomb, the artillery have fired their last shell and the tanks have clattered to a halt, wars are won by foot-soldiers, by the 'poor bloody infantry'. It is the infantryman with his rifle, bayonet and pack who physically occupies a few square feet of ground and denies it to the enemy by killing him, capturing him, incapacitating him or scaring him away. In 1941, the idea of utilising airborne infantry seemed to the British to be a thoroughly modern way to go about winning wars, and the idea was adopted with gusto: in November 1941 the 1st Airborne Division was formed, comprising a Parachute Brigade and an Airlanding Brigade who used gliders to reach their objectives. (Oddly enough, the Germans' reaction to their victory in Crete was precisely the opposite. They were so shocked by the level of casualties sustained by their lightly-armed paratroopers that they abandoned large-scale parachute operations for the remainder of the war.)

There was some disappointment within the fledgling parachute units at the change in their role. Major Tony Hibbert, who had joined No. 2 Commando, has described the mixed feelings which greeted the arrival of the new commanding officer of the '11th SAS Battalion' in the summer of 1941:

> He envisaged us as highly disciplined, superbly trained
> attacking infantry, the only difference being that we would
> be delivered to the battle by air instead of by sea or by

road. This meant that we'd need a totally different course of training and also a different type of recruit: so, sadly, quite a few of those wonderful first chaps who'd been with us for over a year were returned to unit within weeks of his [Colonel Down's] arrival.[2]

Despite this, within a year or so of getting down to serious training as airborne infantry, the CO was confident that he was commanding 'the most highly trained fighting unit in the British Army',[3] and although this was a somewhat ambitious claim to make – after all, by this stage a number of regular infantry battalions, commandos, armoured and cavalry units had been in action in the deserts of North Africa for more than a year – it is a measure of the *élan* and *esprit de corps* of the paratroops that they believed it.

Even though the Parachute Regiment (as the parachute battalions formally became in August 1942) was being trained in an infantry role from mid-1941 onwards, there were a number of ways in which it was distinguished from normal infantry regiments which served to emphasise, for the Paras at least, their élite status. The most obvious, and perhaps the most superficial, was the way they dressed. The perilous economics of wartime Britain had forced all the armed forces into adopting strictly utilitarian uniforms which, for the vast majority, meant wearing the nondescript 'battledress'. Battledress was composed of a pair of heavy serge trousers and a short, waist-length jacket which buttoned together in the middle to create a sort of khaki 'boilersuit'. Generally the only splash of colour came from the regimental and divisional patches worn discreetly on the shoulders; headgear was, except when pre-war stocks of regimental side-hats and forage caps were available, made of the same shade of khaki. But the new *corps d'élite* which were forming in the British Army in the first half of the war needed some way in which to express their distinctiveness: they found it by issuing their soldiers with French-style berets to wear with their uniform. The Royal Tank Regiment selected a jet-black beret with their silver regimental badge; the Commandos a green beret; David Stirling's SAS in North Africa opted for a tactical sandy colour. But the Paratroopers, disdaining any spurious notion of camouflage, settled on maroon – a colour originally suggested by the novelist Daphne du Maurier, the wife of Major

General Browning, the Inspector of Airborne Forces. On their right shoulders they wore their blue parachute wings, and beneath it the emblem of Airborne Forces, designed in May 1942 by the artist Major Edward Seago, camouflage officer of Southern Command. On a maroon patch it showed a sky-blue Bellerophon, the first recorded instance of an airborne warrior, whose exploits are recounted in Greek mythology, mounted on the winged horse, Pegasus, ready to swoop down and destroy the fire-breathing monster Chimaera.

The maroon beret quickly achieved a near-religious status amongst the Paras, but it was helped along by other unique items of uniform. First amongst these was the camouflaged 'Denison' jump-smock. In the early days of parachuting there was much concern about the negative aerodynamic effects of the various projections and protuberances of standard uniforms. Early experiments had shown that paratroops needed to jump with their personal equipment and weapons bundled up in a separate container attached to the soldier in a way that prevented the static line, parachute canopy and rigging lines from fouling. Once the parachute had opened, the container was lowered to dangle a few metres below the parachutist, safely out of the way for the landing. The Denison smock, its camouflage pattern and cut loosely modelled on those issued to the German Waffen-SS and Fallschirmjäger, was designed with large pockets so as to be an additional means of carrying personal kit as well as to smooth the outline – and thus, it was assumed, the descent – of the military parachutist. Throughout the entire war it was almost unheard-of for non-airborne soldiers to be issued with camouflage clothing and, again, the camouflaged jacket achieved cult status within the Parachute Regiment as one of the most easily identifiable signs of the true Para.

But far more important than the outward symbols in defining the early culture of the Parachute Regiment was the fact that all the soldiers were volunteers. They were, almost by definition, more highly motivated than soldiers of non-élite units: fitter, more focused, more aggressive. United by an attraction to the idea of combat (if not necessarily the reality), their behaviour mirrored that of the young fighter and bomber crews of the RAF, and the Navy men fighting the battle of the Atlantic: 'Let us eat and drink; for tomorrow we shall die.'[4]

From the very beginning, the Parachute Regiment displayed a firm grasp of the principles of creating a separate military tradition with élite status, and found that their all-volunteer composition was the perfect breeding-ground for that idiosyncratic British mix of amateurism and ruthless professional excellence. This came to be epitomised by the likes of Major John Frost from 2 Para, who led his men in fighting retreat from Oudna in North Africa while blowing his hunting-horn, and, later in the war, by Major Digby Tatham-Walker advancing over the Arnhem bridge carrying an umbrella.

By the time the Parachute Regiment was committed to the first British airborne infantry operations in North Africa at the end of 1942, their nascent élitism was firmly established. By November of that year there were four Parachute Brigades in existence, and 1, 2 and 3 Para each launched battalion parachute operations in support of the 1st Army's push towards Tunis, jumping respectively at Souk el Arba, Depienne and Bone. As winter came on, airborne operations were precluded by the weather, and the battalions fought on as infantry against their hard-bitten German opponents. For six months they fought more battles than any other unit in 1st Army, undertook three airborne assaults, captured 3500 prisoners and inflicted over 5000 casualties, for a loss of 1700 to themselves. The retreating Afrika Korps had been tenacious and desperate, and the weather had been described by one brigade officer as: 'Mud, mud, mud, everywhere . . . rain and howling wind. Sunny Africa.'[5]

It was during this campaign that the Paras received the nickname 'Red Devils' from the Germans, but they earned the respect of conventional soldiers on their own side for the skill and determination with which they conducted themselves. The name derived not, as is popularly believed, from the colour of their berets, but from their habitual heavy covering of red Tunisian dust and mud, which was a regular feature of the fighting in North Africa in 1943. The authority to adopt this name as an unofficial sobriquet came from Major General Browning, on 15 January 1943:

> To all Para Units. General Alexander directs that 1 Para Brigade be info that [they] have been given name by Germans of 'Red Devils'. General Alexander congratulates the brigade on achieving this high distinction.[6]

The brigade earned two battle honours in North Africa, at Oudna and Tamera, and went on to win another one at Primosole bridge, during the capture of Sicily, before returning to Britain together with the rest of the 1st Airborne Division in the autumn of 1943 to prepare for the invasion of Europe. The invasion of Sicily was a success, and the targets of the Primosole bridge and Ponte Grande were captured, not without heavy casualties. Three hundred men were drowned when their gliders landed short in the sea, and at Primosole bridge, where all of the 1st, 2nd and 3rd Battalions were dropped, only 295 officers and men, out of 1856, landed accurately enough to carry out the attack.

The two operations which most firmly defined the airborne soldier in the public imagination took place within four months of each other in the summer of 1944. The seaborne invasion of Normandy on 6 June 1944 employed British and American airborne troops to secure the two flanks of the invasion bridgehead. The 6th Airborne Division's tasks involved capturing two strategic bridges over the Caen canal and the River Orne, as well as seizing a heavy-gun emplacement at Merville which potentially threatened the entire British sector of the invasion beaches. Although the divisional drop, which took place on the night of 5–6 June, was carried out in less than ideal conditions, all of the division's immediate objectives were achieved at the cost of comparatively light casualties. Glider-carried troops were actually the first into action, their aircraft landing within a few yards of the bridges codenamed 'Pegasus' and 'Horsa', the first parts of occupied France to be liberated, whilst members of 9 Para stormed the heavy-gun emplacement at Merville, losing almost half their assault force in the process. In the following days and weeks the division, commanded by Major General Richard Gale, organised an aggressive flank guard for the invasion forces being built up, ready to break loose into occupied France.

The next major airborne operation, and perhaps the key to the airborne myth, was the attempt by the 1st Allied Airborne Army to seize the road bridge over the Rhine at Arnhem in Holland and hold it until ground-force elements from Field Marshal Montgomery's 21st Army Group could arrive. The background to the operation lay in the strategic situation in the late summer of 1944. After the breakout from the Normandy bridgehead, Montgomery had handed over command of the land element of the invasion forces to the American Supreme Commander, Eisenhower, whose strategy for the campaign envisaged a 'broad front' advance. Montgomery disagreed with this policy, believing that a single thrust on a weak area of the German defences could unhinge the defending forces and bring a quick victory. A compromise between the two men was reached when Eisenhower agreed to authorise the Arnhem operation (codenamed 'Market-Garden'), which, if successful, would have outflanked the main German defensive positions along the Rhine.

The operation began with a massive para drop on 17 September 1944. The United States elements, the 82nd and 101st Airborne Divisions, captured the majority of their objectives (the 82nd Airborne had to fight for four days to take the Nijmegen bridge, but captured their other target bridge at Grave very quickly), but the British drop, by the 1st Airborne Division, ran into immediate problems. Instead of meeting the demoralised second-rate garrison troops that they had been led to expect, the British Paras found their opposition consisted of two Waffen-SS Panzer divisions that were refitting in the area. A number of reputable intelligence sources, including signals intelligence (Sigint), aerial reconnaissance and the Dutch resistance, had warned that the two enemy divisions were east and north-east of Arnhem, but the information was ultimately discounted by Montgomery in his haste to end the war quickly on his own terms. The 2nd SS Panzer Corps comprised the 9th and 10th SS Panzer Divisions, named 'Hohenstaufen' and 'Frundsberg' respectively, which were based on the modern and effective Panzer IV tank, and manned by real Germans (the majority of Waffen-SS divisions were manned by 'ethnic' Germans from Central Europe, and by out-and-out foreigners: the combat record of these units was patchy at best). For the Paras, armed only with small-arms, PIAT* rocket-launchers and light air-portable anti-tank guns, the presence of these troops signalled disaster. Only 2 Para, under the command of Lieutenant Colonel John Frost, made it to the Arnhem bridge, and they were only able to seize one end of it in the face of heavy

---

* Projector Infantry Anti-Tank. An early bazooka-type hand-held anti-tank weapon.

German opposition. 2 Para held onto their end of the bridge, waiting for relief that would never come, for three days and four nights, while they were steadily ground down by the superior strength of the SS units. By the time they were overrun, only 130 officers and men were in a fit state to attempt to make a break, and virtually all were captured (although some subsequently did escape). Other elements of the British Airborne Division were evacuated from a shrinking perimeter on 25 September as the operation was abandoned. Of the 10,095 men from the 1st Airborne Division who landed at Arnhem, only 2018 managed to cross the Lower Rhine back to safety.

The strategy and planning of the Arnhem operation were deeply flawed, not least because senior officers ignored clear evidence of enemy strength in the area, but at a tactical level the Paras had performed excellently, impressing even the hardened SS veterans of the eastern front, some of whom later claimed that the Paras were the hardest enemy they had ever fought. The gallantry of the British was recognised in the award of five Victoria Crosses, and although an operational failure, Arnhem was to become a yardstick of gallantry for future generations of British paratroopers. In the airborne museum in the Dutch town there is a photograph which sums up the British airborne fighting spirit: a scruffy, exhausted paratrooper in a Denison smock, hair matted and cropped, is being led off to captivity by the SS. The British soldier is shown turning to the SS photographer and flicking him two fingers of total defiance, his eyes filled with unbeaten pride.

The last and most successful airborne operation of the war took place on 24 March 1945, when the British 6th Airborne Division and the American 17th Airborne Division were dropped on the Wesel area to secure and deepen Montgomery's bridgehead over the Rhine. With lessons learnt from the Arnhem failure, the operation was more modest in its objectives and more sensible in approach. As a result, all of the objectives were taken and the link-up with ground forces achieved within twenty-four hours. For the remainder of the war in Europe, 6th Airborne Division acted as infantry, spearheading the drive across northern Germany until they met the Russians at Wismar on the Baltic coast at the beginning of May.

When the war in Europe ended, the British Army was in possession of two divisions of battle-hardened paratroops (1st Airborne Division had been reformed after Arnhem), but the decision was swiftly made to disband one of them. As a result the 1st Airborne Division was brought back from Norway, where it had been undertaking occupation duties, and broken up, with some of its units earmarked to join 6th Airborne Division, which had been selected to go to the Far East to take part in the projected assault on the Japanese home islands. In the event, only the 5th Parachute Brigade had made it out to the Far East theatre by the time the atomic bombings of Hiroshima and Nagasaki brought the war to a precipitate close, and instead the division was ordered to Palestine to perform a role that has remained almost a tied appointment for Britain's airborne forces: as the strategic reserve for operations outside Europe. They remained in the Middle East until the British withdrawal from Palestine in 1948, having become engaged in 'peacekeeping' operations against Zionist terrorists. With the withdrawal came the decision to disband the division and reduce the strength of Britain's regular airborne forces to a brigade, to be named 16 Parachute Brigade – the 1 and the 6 being taken from 1st Airborne Division and 6th Airborne Division in a typically bizarre feat of military logic.

With the disbandment of 6th Airborne Division, the regular Parachute Regiment was reduced to the strength that it retains to this day: three battalions. Even so, changes in the command structure for airborne forces have continued throughout the post-war period, although there has only been one significant airborne operation – and that only at battalion level. Apart from the parachute assault by 3 Para on the El Gamil airfield during the Suez invasion in 1956, Parachute Regiment battalions have fought EOKA (Greek-Cypriot nationalists fighting for union with Greece) in Cyprus, Indonesians in Borneo and Communist insurgents in Aden and the Radfan, as well as supplying troops to the SAS for patrolling in Malaya and deploying to such varied locations as Belize, Jordan and Oman for training and garrison duties. Closer to home there have been regular internal security tours by the Parachute Regiment in Northern Ireland, several of which have turned out to be less than happy experiences all round.

The structure of the modern airborne infantry battalion evolved during the 1960s and 1970s, when it became apparent that, unless the Soviet hordes came storming across the inner German border intent on finishing the job that Stalin had left off from in 1945, the most likely employment for the Paras would be in low-intensity counter-insurgency operations and 'confrontations' rather than in all-out war. The basic composition of the parachute battalions has always been much the same as that of regular infantry battalions, but the airborne role, which demands greater flexibility from units, has imposed a more fluid structure on the Paras together with, perhaps, a greater readiness to change. What has evolved is an infantry battalion with a headquarters and administrative element, three rifle companies, a patrol company organised into reconnaissance and patrol platoons, and a support-weapons company that deploys mortars, anti-tank weapons and a medium machine-gun platoon.

So that is the structure of a parachute battalion. But who are the soldiers? What makes them tick? The British Army of the 1940s and 1950s – when the Paras were in their heyday – was a genuine citizen army, composed of people from all walks of life and reflecting a broad spectrum of political opinion, from extreme left to extreme right. The first 'official' British Army fatality of the Second World War was a member of the British Union of Fascists,[7] for example, whilst Communists and their fellow-travellers were commonplace in the service throughout the war. Because military experience was so widespread under the conditions of National Service, the notion that the military constituted some form of élite within society would have been regarded as bizarre and nonsensical. Certainly, some formations which were composed entirely of volunteers – Commandos, Airborne Forces and the SAS spring immediately to mind – had a kind of élite status within the army itself, but there was no real sense in which this carried over into civilian life. The present situation is very different.

Since the early 1960s, all recruits to the British Army have been volunteers, and this has created an institution that is profoundly different from the citizen army of the National Service era. The most memorable army recruiting slogan of recent years has urged young men (and women) to 'Join the Professionals'; yet despite the hopes and pretensions of the upper echelons, the great mass of the 'professionals' have, in a variety of crucial ways, divorced themselves from the behaviour and norms of wider, civilian, society. In the days of National Service, the discipline and rigour of life in the forces, although in many respects harsh, were by necessity tempered by the fact that the majority of servicemen were there because they had to be, not out of choice. In the absence of war, compromise between the leaders and the led was an unacknowledged *fact* of life which ensured a reasonable *way* of life for all concerned. The cultural echoes of this are still audible in the comic stereotype of the small-minded corporal figure – the 'Little Hitler' – whose petty-minded adherence to obscure rules and regulations can disrupt the smooth flow of existence.[8] When conscription came to an end, new recruits to the army were people – overwhelmingly men – who had consciously opted for the rigour of military life, and perhaps even relished it; for them service life had become a goal in itself, not simply a rite of passage that had to be endured.

So what then is the reality of life in the modern, professional army? What is it that attracts young men and women to volunteer for a job in which ultimately they may, like the Green-Eyed Boys of 3 Para, find themselves storming a hilltop fortress in the teeth of a defensive barrage of small-arms and artillery fire unparalleled since the Korean War, sustained only by a spirit of 'snot and aggression'?[9]

Although there were slight variations from training depot to training depot, the basic training of the average British infantry soldier followed a fairly standard pattern throughout the 1970s and 1980s; and although some aspects have been altered to reflect official concern about bullying which arose in the mid-to-late 1980s, it continues much the same today. Soldiers receive a period of seven weeks' instruction in the very basic military skills, followed by a further fourteen weeks of more advanced tactical instruction in specialist infantry techniques. But no matter what sort of character a soldier is, it is the first five weeks of his basic training that stick most vividly in his mind.

'The first five weeks' is an institution in itself within the army. This is the period of time that it is reckoned is needed to receive an average civilian 'off the street' and turn him into a soldier who can be safely allowed to move around, in uniform, without causing serious embarrassment to the army. (It should be emphasised that nobody would expect a recruit at this level of training to be able to function as a soldier, but he should be able to *look* like one at least.) During this phase, the new recruit will receive a first, dramatic, military haircut; be issued with uniform and shown how to maintain it; and be medically examined.

Then the fun starts. For the entire first five weeks, the only time in which a recruit is likely to be left unsupervised is when he is in bed asleep, usually sharing a room with eleven others. During the 1970s and early 1980s this was carried beyond the point of harassment, and the NCOs – usually corporals – responsible for the immediate supervision of new recruits were given a tremendous amount of latitude by their superiors.[10] Aside from helping to teach the rudiments of drill, map reading, weapon handling, first aid, fieldcraft and so on, recruit-squad corporals would also take control of such activities as room cleaning, clothes washing and 'shining parades' (when recruits polish their parade boots under supervision). When the recruits need to go anywhere, whether to a classroom for a lesson or to their breakfast, for example, they are marched there together as a squad. Other restrictions would normally include the recruits being confined to barracks and being banned from drinking alcohol or visiting the Junior Ranks' NAAFI* except for the (supervised) purchase of essential items like boot polish, washing powder and starch. The sheer unpleasantness of the entire process is doubled for Parachute Regiment recruits, because the necessity of training at high intensity for the rigours of 'P-Company', increases both their fatigue *and* the quantities of dirty, sweaty clothing and equipment that need to be cleaned during their rare off-duty periods.

P-Company – the pre-parachute-training selection test – is the ordeal that separates Parachute Regiment recruits from the rest of the infantry. In the early 1980s it took place during week eight of training, and it represents an experience that no regular Para ever forgets. Supposedly based on the physical training programme devised for the Arnhem operation in 1944, P-Company is a series

---

* Navy, Army and Air Force Institute. The body that provides shop, canteen and bar facilities to military establishments.

of marches, runs and other physical tests intended to demonstrate that the potential Para has sufficient endurance, determination, fitness and aggression to undergo the rigours of airborne life. The tests include a ten-mile forced march (a 'Tab' in airborne parlance – probably an acronym for 'tactical advance into battle'), a stretcher race carrying a simulated casualty, a 'confidence course' which involves running about on a rickety scaffold over thirty feet high, an assault course and 'milling' – a minute of no-rules boxing against a similarly-sized opponent.

The whole process of training and then joining a unit adds up to a gigantic culture shock for almost all new recruits. Although the average working-class youth of the late twentieth century would appear to be fairly streetwise and sharp, in reality that is only the case within their own *milieu*. What most instructors find is that recruits are naive, homesick, anxious and eager to be told what to do. They are vulnerable to the pressures of an environment that is completely and utterly alien to them, and they quickly learn how to fit in (those who don't, by and large, are out). Dave Robson, who was the Mortar Platoon colour sergeant in the Falklands, remembers that when he first joined 3 Para's Support Company, several of the other privates had been in the battalion for ten or twelve years, and had fearsome reputations.[11] Importantly, many young soldiers begin to ape the posturing and attitudes of their instructors and superiors in a manner similar to children at a junior school copying the 'big boys'.

A bizarre personality cult can come to surround certain individuals who are regarded as 'real soldiers'. In B Company of 3 Para, the two successive company sergeant majors prior to the Falklands conflict, Sammy Dougherty and John Weeks, were both the subject of some adulation from the younger members of the battalion. In their eyes, Weeks and Dougherty were 'soldier's soldiers': both are tough men with sharp minds, not prepared to suffer fools of any rank gladly, and both would be surprised to find themselves the subject of personality cults. Another such was Stewart McLaughlin, a corporal in B Company who had trained with the SAS and who was subsequently to spearhead the assault on Longdon.

In the strange, anxiety-laden atmosphere of a tough fighting unit, young soldiers find comfort and security in doing a small range of things well: they are trained to be fit and to operate weapons and equipment that kill people, and if they do this well they receive praise from men they admire. It is only natural that their new values extend into all aspects of their behaviour, giving them an outlook alien to the normal social mores. It was not until the ultimate test came for 3 Para, a real shooting war, that this culture was to be allowed its full expression.

CHAPTER TWO

Airborne Infantry

First mind you steer clear o' the grog-sellers' huts,
For they sell you Fixed Bay'nets that rots out your guts –
Ay, drink that 'ud eat the live steel from your butts –
An' it's bad for the young British soldier.

KIPLING 'The Young British Soldier'

The prosperous but ugly town of Osnabrück lies in the German
Land of Nordrhein-Westphalia, between Münster and Minden, and
astride the main E30 autobahn which heads east through Hanover
towards Magdeburg and Berlin. A provincial and uninspiring place,
it became home from home to many young British men and women
after the Second World War, as one of the principal garrison towns
of the British contribution to the defence of West Germany against
the Soviet Union: the British Army on the Rhine. In 1945, Field
Marshal Montgomery's 21st Army Group had found itself occupying
the bulk of the north-western corner of Germany and, in the absence
of a peace treaty, they had stayed there – first as victors over the
evils of Nazism, then as defenders against the threat of Soviet Com-
munism. The British Army took over old German barracks and built
themselves new ones, settling in for a stay which, in some ways,
came to bear a superficial resemblance to the Raj in colonial India:
the natives were kept at a distance (except when employed as servants) and their culture was eschewed; polo and cricket were played;
and a social hierarchy grew up in a closed society which maintained
– by subsidy – an artificially opulent lifestyle.

This was fine for those able to adapt, but many British soldiers,
then and now, hated Germany. The main reason was the language:
few British squaddies arrived for the first time in Germany knowing

more German than they had managed to glean from old war films and 'Commando' comics. In consequence, the young soldiers grew isolated from the outside world and came, of necessity, to rely on the companionship of their colleagues to an overwhelming extent. For various reasons, but largely due to the physical location of the barracks, Osnabrück Garrison developed a particular reputation for this isolation. Laughingly referred to by some as 'Swindon on the Rhine' because of the small-town tedium of garrison life there, it was also known to many soldiers as 'Osnatraz', or 'the Traz': the town from which there was no escape. It was to there, in January 1978, that 3 Para received a surprise posting.

Taken out of their parachute role, the battalion was dispatched to serve as mechanised infantry, readying themselves to counter the tanks of the Soviet 3rd Shock Army who were expected to come pouring across the inner German border in the event of World War III. For 3 Para, Germany marked a return to earth after several hard tours of Ireland and a series of postings abroad, characterised by Major David Collett, later to take over A Company, as '3 Para's world tour'.[1] In the fifteen years leading up to Germany, the battalion – or elements of it – had served in Bahrain, Aden, Libya, Ghana, Malta, Cyprus and the Sudan, without necessarily seeing any action. Now in Osnabrück, under the command of Lieutenant Colonel Keith Coates, they would be in the same role as the despised 'hats',* on standby for 'Active Edge' alerts – simulated scrambles into war deployment positions – but essentially vegetating in the line infantry role that many had joined the Parachute Regiment specifically to avoid.

To Sergeant Des Fuller, the posting to Osnabrück and the whole BAOR lifestyle was anathema:

> The first we heard of it was through John Pettinger's girl-friend, who worked on the military telephone exchange in Aldershot . . . Everybody's reaction was 'uuuurrggh!' I hated Germany with a vengeance because we weren't in our para-chute role and from a soldiering point of view it was totally bloody boring. We'd be sitting around in the backs of trucks

---

* Any soldier who does not wear the maroon beret of airborne forces is a 'crap-hat', or 'hat' for short.

for days, or running around in NBC* suits hiding in woods. Word would get round that there was to be a call-out on, say, Tuesday, so when Tuesday comes, the alarm goes off, you grab your kit, jump on the trucks, go off into the woods about ten kilometres behind Osnabrück, dig in, put your NBC suit on, and sit there for four nights watching the lights of the married quarters from your hole.[2]

The battalion in Germany was made up of three rifle companies, Support Company and the various elements which comprised battalion headquarters and the administrative echelon ('Patrols Platoon' was in Support Company at this time), but their round of activity had changed enormously. The routine of training in Osnabrück was circumscribed to some extent by agreements between British unit commanders and the local civil authorities. This often meant, for example, that field training would not take place over weekends, and that all British soldiers who were on exercise on Fridays would either return to their barracks or remain *in situ* on their exercise areas in a non-tactical mode, barbecuing and drinking. Although this enabled the local people to take advantage of their own countryside without having to risk bumping into groups of British soldiers rampaging around in armoured vehicles, it also introduced an air of unreality – and even crap-hat softness – into the training. Members of the Parachute Regiment have always argued that the rigours of airborne soldiering by their nature produce enhanced readiness and efficiency, and many felt that the Osnabrück experience could only damage 3 Para.

By the end of the 1970s, the British Army as a whole had adjusted itself to the demands of post-colonial soldiering. The 'brush-fire' wars of the fifties and sixties in South Arabia and the Far East were a thing of the past, and the army's major commitments were confronting the Warsaw Pact forces in Europe, as part of NATO, and dealing with domestic counter-insurgency in Northern Ireland. The reality was that maintaining forces sufficient to fulfil any 'out-of-area' emergencies that might arise, as well as maintaining garrisons

---

* Nuclear biological chemical suits: protective clothing worn with a gas mask, gloves and overboots. Wearing it for long periods is an uncomfortable and demoralising experience.

in Hong Kong, Cyprus and Belize, was becoming an expensive luxury, however much this illusory world role might appeal to politicians. The very existence of British airborne forces was predicated on a commitment to operations outside the NATO area in the remnants of the Empire, but many in Whitehall were keen to see the back of both the Paras and the colonies; in effect, posting 3 Para to a line infantry task in Germany could be seen as an experiment. Was the Parachute Regiment more than just a highly specialised infantry regiment with attitude? It is a question that, arguably, still remains unanswered.

More or less oblivious to the whys and wherefores of their situation, the 'Toms' of 3 Para set about making the best of a bad lot. Within the Parachute Regiment there has always, and probably quite naturally, been competition between the three regular battalions for 'supremacy' within the regiment. At one level this consists of the officially sanctioned sporting and military competitions which exist throughout the army as a means of fostering *esprit de corps* and promoting military excellence, but there is the unofficial side as well, in which the more visceral aspects of military existence are celebrated. Colour Sergeant Dave Robson of 3 Para's Mortar Platoon remembers 1 Para as 'being considered the bee's knees'[3] after Bloody Sunday in 1972 for having chalked up what were seen, within much of the army at least, as 'good kills' in the controversial incident in Londonderry. On 30 January 1972, 1 Para was on riot-control duty in the Creggan and Bogside districts of Londonderry. After being ordered to break up a group of stone-throwing youths, the Paras believe that they were fired upon by terrorists and returned the fire, killing thirteen civilians, none of whom could subsequently be conclusively linked to any terrorist group. 1 Para's more lyrical members eventually commemorated this tragedy in a song that retains some popularity in Parachute Regiment circles:

We shot one, we shot two,
We shot thirteen more than you,
With a knick-nack paddywack, give a dog a bone,
Paras thirteen, Provos none.

Chorus: Bring out, bring out,
Bring out your dead,
We're going to make the streets run red,
When the red, red beret goes bob-bob bobbing along,
There'll be no more paddies when we start singing our song . . .

Things can change quickly: Bloody Sunday took place in 1972, but Robson reckoned that in 1973, when 3 Para hit Belfast like a ton of bricks, they were the dominant battalion. Under their CO, Lieutenant Colonel John Lorimer, the battalion was encouraged to fight fire with fire, taking on both Republican and Loyalist paramilitaries with uncompromising aggression. A.F.N. Clarke, a platoon commander during that tour, captured the spirit of the battalion in an account he wrote of a raid on a Loyalist drinking club:

> Hookey hits the door with a flying kick and bounces back into the street. Fury doubled, he and Brian attack it with crowbars and finally break in where the noise of screams from the women and yelling abuse from the men, mixed with flying bottles, glasses, chairlegs and whatever else is available, hits you like a wall. Some guy tries to crown me with a broken whisky bottle. I try to get my baton into a swinging position and eventually have to club him with my SLR.
>
> Hookey's biting a bloke's nose virtually in half, and Brian's swinging lustily with his baton, yelling all the while. Two of my men manage to get to the rear of the club and the physical resistance begins to falter under the viciousness of the onslaught. More soldiers come in from the street, but there's still a little fighting going on. I cock my rifle and the place goes quiet.
>
> 'Right, you bastards. Men on the floor, spread, women over the right-hand side and for Christ's sake, shut up.'[4]

Others who were to accompany the battalion to the Falklands had their own memories of their antics on that tour. Chris Phelan was then a very junior private soldier:

> Some of the things we did in the Ardoyne . . . that was unbelievable . . . My patrol lance corporal was Frank Wiley,

the famous Frank Wiley ... and the corporal, he was a monster, they used to call him 'the vulture'. He was big, and mean, and everything you would dream of a Parachute Regiment corporal being ... and he was old, like thirty, and he looked mean, he was a really nasty bit of work, he really was. But Frank Wiley, my brick commander,* horrendous, some of the things he bloody did was unreal. Being a junior soldier you just do as you were told. One particular night, we'd stopped this individual, on the road, and he'd gone on to him, and said do the P-check, go through the system. He said to this lad, 'Where you going then?'

He said 'I'm going to the gym ... boxing.'

'Boxing, eh,' said Wiley. 'You a boxer, eh, are you? PHELAN!!! You box, don't you?'

'Urr ... yes, Corporal ...'

'Get over here, give me your rifle. RIGHT ... three rounds with him.' So there we were, me and this Irish lad, sparring at the side of the road.'[5]

Pole position continued to be exchanged throughout the rest of the 1970s as the battalions took their turn chalking up successes in Northern Ireland and elsewhere. Each unit had a particular reputation or forte: 2 Para could claim a glorious record from the Second World War, and maintained an air of élitist superiority towards their colleagues, whilst 1 Para built on 'Bloody Sunday'. But the Toms of 3 Para decided that they would emphasise their current no-bullshit operational skills. 'They used to call us "Gungey 3", because we were always in the field,' remembers John Weeks, by 1978 a sergeant in B Company of 3 Para. 'Baggy smocks, baggy trousers. 2 Para were always the drill pigs and 1 Para were the "Home Guard", the sports battalion.'[6]

By 1978 the concept of going into battle by parachute was almost unthinkable, and there could be no worse blow for a parachute battalion than to be consigned to a 'hat' infantry role. The self-image of the soldiers of 3 Para was threatened because they were operating in a capacity which essentially left them no different from any other

---

* In Northern Ireland, patrols were generally made up of three 'bricks' of four men each.

infantry unit. Even so, the unit continued training hard, drawing on the tactical expertise and military proficiency of the long-serving cadre of officers and NCOs who had learnt their soldiering in the small post-colonial wars of the sixties. Among the officers, it was not uncommon to find a certain idiosyncrasy of personality expressing itself. Private Lee Fisher has fond memories of one company commander:

> Major McGregor was the best officer I ever met. When he joined he gave this speech – it was the best speech I ever heard. The first thing he said was 'I am not a murderer.' I think what had happened was he'd been undercover and going down this street in Ireland and seen somebody who was wanted at a bus queue and he'd like stuck his Sten gun out the window and gunned him down.* He was in the MRF, that was it. He was an excellent OC.
>
> I remember once in Germany, we used to have to go and clean the block, the OC's office, the CSM's office, the colour sergeant's office, and it had to be done by morning, after we'd finished work ... I went over in the evening to clear up and I'd done the colour man's office and the sergeant major's and I went to the OC's office and there's this bloke on the floor, crawling around, and a bergen full of stuff just all over the place, and I said: 'Are you taking the piss or what? You can't do that here,' and he looked round and it was the OC, sorting out his kit. And I went 'Oh! Sorry, sir' and he says, 'Don't worry Fisher, you carry on,' so I carried on sweeping, but there's this wig on the floor and I said 'What's that?' and he said 'Fisher, you never know when you may need a disguise.'[7]

The character of most infantry battalions is defined by the senior NCOs, and 3 Para was no different in this respect. The NCOs and

---

* McGregor had in fact been a passenger in a car driven by Sergeant Clive Graham Williams, who was tried for, but found not guilty of, the attempted murders of three men whom he claimed had fired on his vehicle in Belfast in June 1972. McGregor was charged with firearms offences but the charges were dropped before the trial. Both soldiers were members of the Military Reconnaissance Force (MRF), an undercover intelligence-gathering unit.

warrant officers who took the battalion to the Falklands began to assume their posts while the battalion was in Osnabrück, and it was there that they began to mould the teams which would fight through the Longdon position. The spirit of the British Army is derived, to a large degree, from the continuity of tradition created by the 'family' unit. In a battalion like 3 Para, it was normal for non-commissioned members to spend their entire careers there, moving around between the companies and occasionally going for a two-year stint at the depot or in a training job with the Territorial Army or overseas. Consequently, in the late seventies there were still a handful of men who had jumped at El Gamil airfield during the Suez invasion, and *they* would have joined when the battalion was manned, to a large extent, by veterans of the Second World War. Ernie Rustill, company sergeant major of D Company in the Falklands, enlisted in the army in 1963 and joined a platoon in 3 Para whose sergeant was a former member of No. 6 Commando and had served in North Africa during the war. Such was his experience, Rustill remembers, that: 'When the battalion was in Libya, he used to parade us in the evenings and say, "Who wants to go out into the desert and learn desert navigation?" Over half of us would volunteer.'[8]

The majority of senior NCOs in Germany were like Rustill: men such as Brian Faulkner, 'Blue' Harding, Thor Caithness, John Weeks and Sammy Dougherty were part of the first wave of the all-professional army created by the end of National Service. They had served through the 1960s and seventies in the last outposts of the Empire, garrisoning fly-blown territories and occasionally taking on nationalist- and Communist-inspired insurgent movements as successive British governments withdrew from colonies and protec-torates they could no longer afford to maintain.

Rustill's first operational experience was in the Radfan, hinterland to what was then believed to be the key strategic port of Aden, into which 3 Para were sent, under their then CO, Lieutenant Colonel Anthony Farrar-Hockley, in the spring of 1964. The original plan had been to parachute a company onto a position marked by an SAS patrol and then to link up with a Royal Marine commando unit, but the SAS were compromised and two members of the patrol were killed and then decapitated by the insurgents. Following this, B Company was deployed from Bahrain for a sweep operation, and subsequently the whole battalion was sent in. Rustill remembers the inspirational role of 'Farrar the Para', a veteran of the Second World War and the Battle of the Imjin River in Korea, and probably the leading British soldier of his generation:

> He was our CO in 3 Para then, and was a real airborne soldier. I was in C Company, and we were off on a long, hard march across the djebel to resupply the forward companies. There was 'Farrar', this short, squat figure with this full jerry-can across his shoulders, ready to lead the way. Where he led, 3 Para would follow – if necessary over a cliff.[9]

An American journalist from *Time* magazine accompanied them: 'He went back and said that we were the fittest unit in the British Army, and probably, therefore, the world.'[10]

Hand in hand with the tactical lessons dealt out by the wild colonial boys came the discipline. The British Army of the 1960s and early seventies lived and trained in a hard school. Des Fuller, a sergeant in B Company in 1978, remembered the experience of arriving in 3 Para in October 1968. Only thirteen men out of the original sixty in his recruit platoon had made it to the end of basic training. Fuller had passed out successfully, but would never forget his experiences as a member of the Junior Parachute Company being trained by Sergeant Arthur Richer, a veteran of the regiment from World War II. As junior soldiers – Fuller had joined in 1966 – they were paid pocket money of a pound a month, some of which would be held in safekeeping by their NCOs. Richer used to come into the barracks every Monday morning and distribute to the boys in his platoon packets of Kensitas cigarettes that he had bought with their money.

Fuller remembers being the first junior ever to be 'jailed' at the depot in Aldershot. An officer called 'Black Jack' Crane, then the officer commanding the Junior Parachute Company, inspected the boy's lockers one morning and discovered that Fuller's toothbrush had a film of dried toothpaste clinging to the bottom of the bristles. He was promptly fined five pounds, a huge sum, and a punishment which Fuller boldly refused to accept. He was put in jail instead.[11]

'I remember the RSM at the time,' says Fuller. 'Nobby Arnold, the ugliest man in the Parachute Regiment . . . he once put a bicycle and a pace-stick in jail for being disobedient.'[12]

By the time he was posted to Osnabrück, thirteen years after he had joined, Fuller's service was typical of many senior NCOs in the battalion. He had served in Malta, Cyprus, Ghana and Northern Ireland, had completed a HALO ('High Altitude-Low Opening' – military free-fall parachuting) course with Patrol Company, a Signals cadre, a mountaineering course, and had twice passed out as a ski-instructor.

Like Fuller, Chris Phelan, who joined up in 1971, has mixed memories of his training at the adult soldiers' depot when he arrived after 'Junior Leader' training at Oswestry:

> The depot was frightening for me . . . because there were a couple of older guys . . . and there were a couple of minor pilfering incidents within the platoon. Of course they had a kangaroo court – when the corporals weren't there – and they broke his hand, broke his fingers, you know . . . [and] somebody got stabbed in the neck with a bayonet – this was all within our first week there, you know – I was shitting myself. All the stories you'd heard as a Junior, about what happens down there . . . it was a very nervy time, very apprehensive.[13]

Captain Dave Robson, who was a sergeant in Support Company in 1979, remembers joining Mortar Platoon as a young soldier at the beginning of the seventies:

> You should have seen it. You had blokes who'd been in as privates for ten or twelve years, who'd go out on the piss, fight, break the place up, and then come back to the block still raring to go. I tell you, as a young Tom, you slept with your helmet on.[14]

But for the men who had just arrived in 3 Para when it was posted to Osnabrück, the South Arabian deserts and the Borneo jungle must have seemed an age before. The battalion was consigned to a programme of training designed to fit them in to the large, conventionally-roled formations that made up the 1st British Corps in Germany, with little outlet for 'airborne initiative' and the skills and capabilities that many felt gave the Paras a unique edge over their 'hat' counterparts.

Osnabrück represented a period during which the Parachute Regiment was being forced to conform with the rest of the army. One of the most obvious changes was to the uniform. From the earliest days of the regiment, the Paras had worn the unique camouflaged Denison smock. The bulk of the army only began to wear camouflaged clothing in the late 1960s, adopting the familiar 'DPM' (disruptive pattern material) which is still worn today, but the Paras retained their distinctive gear until the end of the 1970s. Lee Fisher, then a junior private in B Company, remembered the first man to be sighted wearing a DPM para smock:

> It was Dennis O'Kane and I think he'd just come from the Depot and got it there, and we were jeering and hooting at him, calling him a hat and all sorts. He was livid, he really bit, and he was saying: 'You can fucking laugh but you'll all have 'em soon.' And he was right, we did.[15]

The one way in which 3 Para were still able to make their presence felt, despite the efforts to make them conform, was their sheer *élan*. It is a fact that in much of the rest of the army at that time, the culture of soldiering for soldiering's sake was a minority preoccupation. Certainly there were men throughout the combat arms who kept themselves extremely fit and their tactical skills honed, but for many Paras these were the be-all and end-all of their existence. The majority of Parachute Regiment soldiers maintained a level of fitness not far short of what they had had to achieve when they passed P-Company, and most took a professional pride in their individual military skills beyond that seen in line-infantry regiments. Their airborne status still allowed the Paras some privileges in terms of equipment that weren't normally granted to their 'hat' counterparts in BAOR. One of the most basic, and most surprising, was that 3 Para's soldiers were issued with rucksacks whilst the 'hats' had to make do with the 'large pack', a flaccid concoction of canvas that attaches to the shoulder yoke of webbing equipment.[16]

Rucksacks have always been an important item of equipment for British airborne soldiers because they enable them to 'tab', the form of high-speed marching developed by the Paras to cover ground at

speed whilst carrying heavy loads. The action requires an exaggerated swing of the arms and a thrusting forward of the thighs to
generate sufficient momentum to cover six miles per hour. It is at
the depot, and particularly on P-Company, that young Paras first
learn to tab, but it remains a feature of their training throughout
their careers. A rucksack is essential for tabbing because it keeps the
load fairly stable; by contrast, the webbing 'large pack' was
renowned for falling off at every opportunity. In Osnabrück, tabs at
platoon, company and even battalion level became a regular feature
of life and always seemed to end on the same stretch of road, as the
Paras stomped triumphantly past their 'hat' neighbours.

Despite the supposed shame of their unaccustomed role and their
inauspicious surroundings, there was, nevertheless, much to be
enjoyed about the Osnabrück posting. For many of the younger
soldiers it was their first extended sojourn in a foreign country, and
was therefore of considerable novelty in itself. On a more practical
level, alcohol and cigarettes were duty-free within the barracks, and
thus available at ridiculously low prices, and the German government had a far more liberal view of the 'dangers' of the sex industry
than its British counterpart.

Chris Phelan remembers:

> What does stick in my mind in those days was drinking a
> lot. For some reason, I don't know, we didn't get paid that
> much . . . you could spend it all Friday and Saturday night,
> and it was gone . . . a good night downtown . . . We'd all be
> boasting, but really, we would be drinking perhaps seven or
> eight pints and we'd be shitfaced.[17]

Jim O'Connell, then a private with the Anti-Tank Platoon,
remembers a typical Friday in Germany in 1979:

> What I remember about Germany was it was about cheap
> beer; and cheap beer and young soldiers don't mix. We'd
> have a whip-round on the Friday evening amongst our-
> selves, then it would be off to the NAAFI and returning with
> a car-boot full of cheap local lager, which would be carried
> up into the barrack-rooms, and drunk all weekend. Often
> we'd be there till the Sunday evening . . . [18]

For more adventurous souls, eating and drinking downtown supplied a certain exoticism, and there was also the opportunity to visit the town's red-light area. Since the end of the Second World War, every German garrison town worthy of the name has had a red-light district to some degree. The German government has traditionally sought to control the sex industry through regulation rather than prohibition and, in consequence, a clean, safe and legally-run brothel or sex show was never difficult to find. For soldiers who were interested, there was plenty of opportunity to get laid without tiresome language barriers interfering with their chat-up technique, and weekends of enjoyable depravity were no more than a train ride to Hanover or Hamburg away.

The pay-off for the pleasures of Germany came on Monday mornings. Company 'orders' would be held when miscreants from the weekend would be summoned in front of the company sergeant major or OC and invited to explain their misdemeanours. At their most formal, these 'orders' are invested with the authority of a summary court-martial, with powers to inflict legally enforceable fines and detention in jail, but more often they take the form of a 'bollocking' or, to the cynics, an 'interview without coffee'. Sammy Dougherty, B Company's sergeant major for most of the Osnabrück tour, became accustomed to seeing Private Dominic Gray appearing in front of him every Monday, usually accused of one transgression or another:

> This one Monday, he didn't show so I called him in anyway and asked him what was wrong. He said: 'Sorry, sir, I couldn't go out 'cos I was skint,' so I said, 'If you're short, you can always come to me and I'll see you right.' So the next Friday comes round and Gray comes in and says, 'You know you said you'd see me right, sir . . .' and I says, 'Sure,' and gave him some cash, and sure enough, the next Monday morning, there he was.[19]

It was during this time in Germany that a small sub-group began to develop within the battalion. With their attention focused inwards by their isolation from 'normal' life, some of the more intelligent and thoughtful junior ranks began to analyse what they admired most about themselves and their peers. Certainly a high degree of professional skill was a prerequisite but, more than that, an arrogant insouciance was essential as well. Those who soldiered in a regulation manner, closely observing military discipline, were loosely known as 'blue-eyed', a term which implied keenness, zest for career advancement and acceptable, orderly behaviour on and off the battlefield or training area. But the members of the sub-group saw themselves as the fundamental opposites of this regulated type, eschewing the letter of military law and its tightly regulated existence in favour of a free-wheeling, earthy lifestyle, where loyalty to their fantasy ideal of the 'airborne warrior' demanded an attitude towards outsiders of contempt bordering on loathing. There was no clearly defined line between the two factions, but it was understood by the protagonists that a fundamental difference existed, and that this difference was most clearly expressed, in peacetime at least, not just by solid professional achievement while soldiering, but also by grotesque and extreme behaviour while socialising together in their time off. As a whole, this amorphous group had no particular name, but a very small clique within the battalion's B Company began to describe themselves as 'green-eyed'. What was the significance of this? It is difficult to say: probably it denoted a contrast with blue-eyed career-mindedness. These 'Green-Eyed Boys' were focused on the military existence and the dominant colour that forms its backdrop (this is not such an outlandish notion: within the army, many things with overt military connotations are described as 'green'; the SAS divide operations into 'black', covert, and green, overt), and possibly it is also an allusion to the green of 3 Para's recognition colour within the airborne forces.

The Green-Eyed Boys' behaviour manifested itself in a variety of ways. In the field, they strove to project an aura of professionalism and competence by a number of means. These included adapting their equipment to give off subtle signals, to those in the know, that the wearer was far more than just a common-or-garden infantry soldier. In place of a set of '58-pattern webbing, for example, the Toms would wear SAS-style 'belt order', based around the jungle issue '44-pattern gear used by Special Forces. To this might be added a Gurkha *kukri* or an equally fearsome fighting knife of different provenance. No physical test was too hard for the Green-Eyed Boys at least to try, and no weight too heavy to carry. But this essentially admirable attitude towards field soldiering has to be contrasted with their behaviour in barracks.

In the drunken discussions that took place during the long weekend boozing sessions in the block, and in the Junior Ranks' Club, the Green-Eyed Boys vied to nominate heroes to whose reputation they could seek to attach themselves. Although they naturally admired the exploits of their predecessors in the Parachute Regiment, and before that in the British Army as a whole, there was a tendency to look elsewhere for their role models. At this time, the trashy military novelettes of Sven Hassel and Leo Kessler were enjoying a vogue amongst the more literary-minded soldiery, books that celebrated the fictional exploits of unruly German soldiers on the eastern front during the Second World War. Sex, alcohol and violent combat were their stock in trade, and these held a great deal of appeal to the Green-Eyed minority. Also popular, and much more realistic and up-to-date, were the films and books about the Vietnam War. At the end of the 1970s, the United States was just beginning the period of post-Vietnam navel-gazing that has continued to this day. Michael Cimino had directed *The Deer Hunter* and Francis Ford Coppola *Apocalypse Now; Dispatches*, the brilliant book of Vietnam War reportage by the American journalist Michael Herr, was published in 1977. Vietnam was the source of the Green-Eyed Boys' jargon: 'zapping', 'wasting', 'gooks', 'spooks', 'grunts' and 'lurps' were common currency amongst a group of men who largely hailed from the respectable working-class homes of middle England and had been no further east than Hanover. The most committed of the Green-Eyes took their research further: one, Sammy Dougherty's friend Dominic Gray, a highly intelligent and well-read man, still has a photograph of the World War II German tank ace, Hauptsturmführer Michael Wittman of the Waffen-SS, on his wall: 'a warrior with the face of an angel,' as Gray has described him.[20]

One outbreak of Green-Eyed behaviour which took place in Osnabrück consisted of a vogue for urinating and defecating on one another. During the weekend drinking marathons, Gray remembers:

> We'd get some guy's respirator out of his webbing and crap in it, then stick it back in the pouch and leave it in his locker.

He wouldn't find it until he next got his respirator out, usually when he was on exercise . . . [21]

The boozing sessions were, in a very real sense, self-destructive. The men would behave increasingly badly, and the room and its fittings would be systematically rubbished. As Friday evening wore into Saturday morning, the shiny linoleum would be covered with empty beer-bottles and cans, some of which would be overflowing with cigarette ends, others with the urine of those drunken men who hadn't bothered to make their way to the ablutions down the corridor. Their behaviour would depend on who was present at the drinking session, but if the room chosen was normally occupied by one of the less popular members of the platoon or company, it was likely that his locker might be vandalised and his kit trashed. Yet this was the same accommodation that the men were responsible for 'parading' for inspection at least once a week.

For every Green-Eyed Boy in 3 Para, there were twenty normally adjusted soldiers, trying to make the most of their careers for themselves and their families. And even the most hard-core Green-Eye had a more human side. John Weeks took over from Sammy Dougherty as B Company's CSM in Tidworth, Wiltshire, in 1980, and his wife Yvonne has very different memories of the fearsome Dominic Gray: 'Really, butter wouldn't melt in his mouth. He was the best babysitter we ever had.'[22]

Luckily for the morale and well-being of the battalion, the tour of Osnabrück came to an end in June 1980 and the unit was posted back to the UK, 'in role' as a Parachute Battalion in 5 Infantry Brigade. The battalion was accommodated at Candahar Barracks in Tidworth, but it was already preparing for a deployment on an 'emergency' tour to Aughnacloy in County Fermanagh, Northern Ireland. This was their sixth tour of duty in the province since 1970, and their approach, and that of the Parachute Regiment as a whole, had been forcibly changed by circumstances since the 'glory days' of John Lorimer's command in 1973, when they had ruled the Shankill and the Lower Falls with their own form of street government. By 1980, with 'Police Primacy' into its third year, the army in Northern Ireland was operating far more circumspectly than it had in the early seventies, and there was much less room for the heavy-handed wild-west tactics which some felt had become the hallmark of the Parachute Regiment. The killings on Bloody Sunday in Londonderry and the murder of sixteen members of 2 Para at Warrenpoint in August 1978* had been the visible signs of a stressful relationship with Ulster which had lasted ten years. Its critics argued that the Parachute Regiment was completely unsuited to the subtleties of domestic counter-revolutionary warfare, while its champions felt that if the muscular soldiering methods of the regiment had been accepted as the norm, rather than an exception, the fight against the Provisional IRA would have been won long before. Certainly they had achieved some good results, but these had been at the expense of the almost total alienation of the Catholic populations in the areas in which they had been based. 'They soldiered too hard,' remembers a senior officer from another unit who served in Ulster at the same time. 'If they saw a hedge, their instinct was to go through it, and that was the same way they treated the local populace. They wanted to crush them categorically, rather than infiltrating into their midst and cutting them out selectively.'[23]

Many within the battalion didn't enjoy the rural aspect of service in Fermanagh. Lee Fisher recalls: 'It wasn't as much fun as the city. There wasn't as much going on. Just boring patrols.'[24]

Back in England, the battalion's brief was to return to the airborne role, ready for deployment outside the NATO area – an event which was to happen much sooner than most imagined. Tidworth is a garrison on the edge of Salisbury Plain, just north of the A303 where it lurks unsuspected between the towns of Amesbury and Andover, hard by its twin garrison of Bulford. For 3 Para, it represented a return to a more familiar form of military life than that experienced in Osnabrück. Although there were brief training commitments overseas, life was a return to the principles which many believed the battalion was there to serve: back to basics.

Their military existence was that of any garrison in England, the normal routine of army life – barrack guards, training and trivial

---

* 2 Para was the resident infantry battalion based at Ballykinler in County Down, supporting the South Armagh roulement battalion. In a cleverly-worked ambush, the Newry/Dundalk Provisional IRA succeeded in killing a company commander and fifteen other ranks of 2 Para just outside the small village of Warrenpoint. Also killed was the Commanding Officer of the Queen's Own Highlanders.

fatigues, interspersed with exercises on a number of training areas around the United Kingdom, from Sennybridge in mid-Wales to Lydd and Hythe on the Kent coast. The airborne role demanded that the battalion should parachute, so some of their exercises would begin with the unit being inserted by C-130.* These drops always followed a formula and routine. The men selected to jump drive to the emplaning airfield – normally RAF Lyneham near Swindon, or South Cerney in Gloucestershire. They will have packed their equipment containers before leaving barracks, and will often spend several hours at the RAF station before taking off. This is a tiring period of boredom and anxiety for most of the men, many of whom find military parachuting a frightening process.

A heavy meal is served in the RAF cookhouse, after which the soldiers proceed across the base to the hangar where they draw and fit their parachutes. Some of the men, especially those with the GPMGs,† mortars and 84mm Carl Gustavs,‡ carry personal equipment containers in excess of seventy pounds. With a main and reserve parachute fitted, another twenty-eight pounds are added, the entire weight suspended from the shoulder straps of the main parachute harness. The troops are checked off by the RAF Parachute Jump Instructors, and by their own battalion PJIs, and then wait around the hangar, gossiping, smoking and sleeping, before the order comes to put their parachutes and equipment back on and move out to the C–130s parked outside on the tarmac.

Only after a noisy, bumpy, smelly and nauseating flight would the Paras experience the relief of actually jumping from the aircraft. By then, many would be soaked in vomit from airsickness, and sweating with exertion, anticipation and anxiety.[25]

In between exercises and organised training there were often long periods when the soldiers didn't have a great deal to occupy them – and boredom is a great enemy of the maintenance of good order and military discipline. One former Para who subsequently joined

---

* The C-130 is the standard transport aircraft used by the RAF for parachute operations. It can carry sixty-four fully-equipped Paras or ninety-two with minimum equipment.

† A belt-fed 7.62mm 'general-purpose machine-gun', known as a 'Gimpy' and used by both sides in the Falklands.

‡ An anti-tank rocket launcher.

the SAS has related how, as a member of the Parachute Regiment, he 'got a quarter of the amount of work done in twice the length of time. I spent hours lying on my pit in the battalion, smoking, wanking and wondering how I could avoid the "jif-jobs"* that my platoon sergeant would come up with.'[26]

In this atmosphere practical jokes and other spoofs became common currency. A private from A Company of 3 Para, who joined the battalion at the end of the seventies, remembered his first 'wind-up' by the other members of the platoon. The Easter weekend was approaching, and with it block leave for the battalion. Men were preparing for ten days off, arranging trips up and down the country. Rail warrants were being issued and training was winding down. A notice appeared on the company noticeboard asking for volunteers to go on a 'knife-fighting course' in Taiwan. Several names were already listed by the time the new private got to it and eagerly added his. He didn't take any notice of the fact that the departure date for the course was Easter Sunday, and when the day came he sat on his bed in the block, bergen packed, webbing ready and dressed in the full 'Number 2' uniform specified on his joining instructions. Full of anticipation, he waited until well after midday, but was surprised that nobody joined him. He went along to the guard-room, through the deserted barracks, his bulled boots squeaking on the polished lino. The guard sergeant was nonplussed. Knife-fighting? Taiwan? He didn't know anything about it. The unfortunate private related the story, before suddenly realising what had happened and that, to his horror, he had missed his entire leave.

The return to the UK certainly allowed 3 Para's soldiers to let their hair down and relax, and it is from this era that many of the Green-Eyed Boys' favourite horror stories of anti-social behaviour date. Lieutenant Mark Cox was present at a Tidworth pub when a detachment of French Army paratroopers from the 3ème Regiment Parachutiste d'Infanterie Marine d'Assaut (3 RPIMA) was visiting 3 Para on an exchange. Cox and his French counterpart, whom he was hosting, watched in fascinated horror as two teams, one British, one French, conducted a 'vomit boat race' in an effort to consolidate Anglo–French airborne solidarity. The members of each team of

---

* Unpleasant or unwelcome assignments.

eight lay on the floor and, when the signal was given to start, the first player stuck his finger down his own throat to induce the vomiting reflex. When this took place, he carefully ejected the contents of his stomach into the mouth of the man next to him, who would, either reflexively or with the aid of his own finger, do the same to the next man, and so on.[27] History does not relate who won.

At The Rat-Pit, a spit-and-sawdust bar in a Para pub in Aldershot (the spiritual home of the Paras, just half an hour from Tidworth) whose walls were lined with photographs of Paras past and present, as well as signed trophies of women's underwear, Vince Bramley from Support Company was the occasional observer of rounds of 'Freckle', a game with simple and unforgettable rules. A group of paratroopers would gather round a table and a beer-mat would be placed in the middle, onto which one of the assembled company would defecate. A second beer-mat would be placed on top of it, and as the men sat round the table, the turd-and-cardboard sandwich would be hit soundly with the bottom of a pint glass. The man who had the most 'freckles' lost, and bought the next round of drinks. At the end of some evenings, pints of urine and vomit would be drunk in one-off bar challenges, before the men left the pub and undertook the serious business of picking up members of the local female populace or 'hogs' from the Women's Royal Army Corps.

It is against regulations to bring women into the barracks, but in 1981 there were few fences or walls at Tidworth, and it was an easy matter to dodge the guard patrols, which would in any case be made up of friends and colleagues who would probably turn a blind eye. Non-commercial sex in Tidworth (or Aldershot, Andover or Amesbury for that matter) was a great deal easier to come by than it had been in Germany, for the simple reason that both parties were speaking the same language, and, strange as it may seem, army units often attract groupies prepared to 'do a turn' for one or more of 'the lads'. Occasionally, women who agreed to accompany one of the men back to the barracks would end up consenting to sex with several of his friends as well. A former member of 2 Para remembers one Saturday night in early 1981 when he came back from town, drunk and eating a kebab, to find a queue of five or six men at one of the doors of the barrack block in Rhine Barracks in Aldershot. Inside, on his friend's bed, lay a completely naked woman:

> She was giving this mate of mine from Mortars a blow-job, while another bloke was giving her one from behind.* Three or four of the lads from B Company were waiting at the end of the bed, having a fag, sharing a couple of cans and waiting their turn. It was quite normal. The lads who didn't pull downtown knew that if they were lucky, there was always a chance of walking into somebody else's room and getting a four- or fives-up on some bird.
>
> Another time, a mate from Patrols was shagging this woman in the billet, when she starts talking. She's lying face-down, and he's whapping it to her doggy-style. Suddenly she asks him to turn round, so that she can see his face when she comes. Without going off his stroke, he reaches into the back pocket of his jeans, takes out his MOD 90 [military identity card] and holds his picture in front of her face.[28]

Sometimes even the most minimal effort at seduction proved unnecessary. A Para based in Aldershot remembers being woken in his bunk-bed in the block in the early hours of one morning by a small fat girl who asked him: 'Do you want a blow-job?' Although he declined her generous offer, he noted that one of the seven other men he shared the room with had no such qualms.

In tandem with the heterosexual rampages of the young Paras came rather more louche entertainments. During the late seventies and early eighties, 3 Para's Mortar Platoon developed a reputation within the wider army as a hotbed of homosexuality. Rumours circulated that members of the platoon frequented Heaven, the gay nightclub in Charing Cross, allowing themselves to be picked up by elderly gay men whom they would subsequently rob or fuck as the fancy took them. Although the stories are, without doubt, wildly exaggerated, there is certainly one substantiated incident of the court-martial of a member of 3 Para for similar behaviour, but surprisingly this provoked a certain amount of indignation within the

---

* A procedure known in the army as 'spit-roasting'.

battalion. A former Para remembers: '[He] was a good hard soldier. He reckoned he wasn't a poof 'cos he was a "giver" rather than a "taker".'[29]

John Weeks agrees: 'He was a male prostitute. He got done for it, but don't get me wrong, [he] was a very, very hard man. He never interfered with anybody in the battalion, he went up for his weekends as a single guy and did what he wanted to do.'[30]

By the seventies, Support Company was where all the long-serving private soldiers, the 'eighteen- and nineteen-year Toms', tended to end up. Because the specialist platoons within the company required a certain amount of technical aptitude of its members, be it in firing mortars or laying down sustained machine-gun fire, the unit considered itself as being slightly apart from the rest of the battalion. Former Private Lee Fisher from the Patrol Platoon recalls: 'Support Company was full of men fucked up by three or four years in the rifle companies.'[31]

Although the rumours of out-and-out homosexuality are exaggerated, nevertheless in such a self-consciously macho battalion as 3 Para there was a strong homoerotic subtext to some of the soldiers' behaviour. No Para's photograph album is complete without at least one picture of a night out drinking in drag, and women's clothing and lingerie were readily available 'from stock' if one had the right contacts:

> Yeah, Mortars would always be able to fix you up. You'd go down to Mortars to get kitted up when you were going out, and it would be like, 'What do you want, heels or flatties? What colour lipstick do you want?' Sometimes they wouldn't have the right size, so you would go somewhere else . . . the Anti-Tanks were just as bad.[32]

Mostly such behaviour remained at the level of innocent fun, but it could become unpleasant. A newly-joined young officer in the mid-1980s was taken drinking by his platoon during his first weekend with the battalion, as a gesture of welcome, but the evening ended with him being held down whilst oral sex was administered to him by another member of the platoon.[33] Despite the stereotypes, soldiers are generally realistic enough to tolerate discreet homosexuality amongst their comrades, and such an incident, while far from common, was by no means unique.

In 1981, B Company was the heart of the Green-Eyed culture. Its commander, Major Mike Argue, had started his military career as a gunner in the Royal Artillery and had gone on to serve as a trooper in 22 SAS Regiment, including time in Dhofar in Oman during the war there in the early 1970s, before being commissioned into the Parachute Regiment. Despite this, he was not particularly popular with the men of his company, and he didn't get on at all well with his company sergeant major, John Weeks, who thought him arrogant and rigid. The antipathy between the two men was obvious to others in the battalion. To be fair to Argue, other company commanders sympathised with him for having such a strong and wilful CSM. Certainly David Collett, who took over A Company shortly before the Falklands crisis, feels that 'they're both very similar characters',[34] strong-willed and assertive. The tension between them was exacerbated by a company training deployment to Oman at the beginning of January 1982 which brought some of their conflict out into the open. Argue had of course been there before with the SAS, while Weeks's experience of the Middle East was limited to the tail-end of 3 Para's final tour of Bahrain. Argue knew the terrain, he was familiar with the customs of the people, and he spoke their language (he has since been described to one of the authors as 'one of the British Army's best Arabists'[35]), and 'Exercise Rocky Lance', as the deployment was called, should have been an ideal opportunity to mould the company together.

In Oman, the men carried out some four weeks of tactical training in the desert and the djebel, practising harbour and patrol drills, actions on enemy contact, tabs carrying large amounts of equipment in their bergens, and section-, platoon- and company-level attacks. The soldiering was hard, due to both the hot weather and the unforgiving nature of the country, and the problems the men experienced tactically and physically were not entirely helped by the divisions that were becoming apparent at Company HQ.

Argue and Weeks disagreed over serious matters, such as whether it was safe to use live hand-grenades on the ranges, and trivia, like the siting of an improvised shower which, in Argue's view, needed to be protected from the view of passing Arabs. For the three young platoon commanders, Andy Bickerdike, Jon Shaw and Mark Cox, it was an unsettling experience, not improved by the presence of various Green-Eyed pranksters: the irrepressible Dominic Gray decided one night to crap into one of the company's water bowsers, an action that led to him spending a night in the desert, hiding from reprisals.[36]

Young officers, virtually fresh from Sandhurst, as all three platoon commanders were when they went to B Company, are in a very difficult position when they join a unit for the first time. Although vested with all the authority of 'the Queen's Commission', they are, despite (or rather because of) their training, military toddlers, largely unsure of themselves but painfully aware of their own inexperience in comparison to many of the soldiers and NCOs they are required to command. In his own view Mark Cox was the least competent of the three, and he probably had the hardest task, commanding 5 Platoon, which featured as platoon sergeant the Ulsterman John Ross, a man capable of running rings round him, together with Corporals Stewart McLaughlin and Graham Heaton, and Privates Gray, Kempster and Gough. In Oman, Cox remembers a night march that took 5 Platoon to the top of an escarpment as dawn was breaking. The rising sun had brought out the extraordinary colours of the desert: purples, oranges, greens and blues. Overwhelmed, he turned to Ross, his right-hand man, and exclaimed, 'Look at that, Sergeant Ross, isn't it beautiful?'

To which the baleful Ulsterman replied: 'It's gopping, sir.'[37]

CHAPTER THREE

Rumours of War

Then it's Tommy this, an' Tommy that, an' Tommy 'ow's yer soul,
But it's 'Thin red line of 'eroes' when the drums begin to roll.

KIPLING, 'Tommy Atkins'

The drums began to roll for the Green-Eyed Boys in March 1982. Two and a half years earlier an Argentine wheeler-dealer named Constantino Davidoff had bought the remains of three whaling stations on the small South Atlantic island of South Georgia from the Edinburgh-based company Christian Salvesen. He visited his purchase briefly in December 1981 before returning to Buenos Aires to make arrangements to dismantle the stations the following year. On 17 March 1982 an Argentine freighter, the *Bahia Buen Suceso*, arrived off the deserted port of Leith to begin the task, and Davidoff's forty-one civilian workers started work two days later, unloading equipment and setting up living accommodation to keep them sheltered during the harsh South Atlantic winter that was, even then, drawing on.

Davidoff's operation would have caused no excitement whatsoever had his men not failed to observe one formality required by their visit to South Georgia: they did not get a landing permit from the British Antarctic Survey research station at Grytviken, twenty miles down the coast. There is some debate still over whether or not this was a calculated move by the Argentines: certainly they were aware of the requirement, but their excuse, which has some validity, was that they had neither the time nor the means to make the journey. Their ship, chartered from the Argentine Navy but crewed by civilians, had left them as soon as their kit was unloaded, although it would not have been too difficult for them to make the journey cross-country. Even so, two days after their arrival, a British scientist surreptitiously observed that the scrap-men had hoisted an Argentine flag above their living quarters, and he also heard the sound of rifle shooting in the area. He immediately reported this back to his base.

At Grytviken, the British Antarctic Survey team leader, who doubled as the magistrate on the practically uninhabited island, sought the advice of his superior, Rex Hunt, the Governor of the Falkland Islands, 800 miles away. Hunt's decision was to report the matter to London, and to order the BAS team to tell the Argentines by radio to lower their flag and send a representative to Grytviken. The flag was grudgingly lowered, but no Argentine appeared at the BAS base. The matter then began to take on an international dimension.

Governor Hunt was fully aware that the Argentine government disputed British sovereignty over South Georgia as well as the Falklands themselves, and was alive to the possibility that the Argentines were launching a 'provocation' against the British. Misinterpreting the information that the BAS had heard shooting from Leith, he reported to London that Argentine *military* personnel had come ashore, and gave his opinion that the Argentine Navy were attempting to establish a presence on the island.[1] From that moment, Britain and Argentina began to move inexorably towards conflict.

The British reaction to Hunt's note was a formal diplomatic protest to Argentina which demanded that the *Bahia Buen Suceso* return to South Georgia and remove the entire Argentine party, or else 'the British government would take whatever action seemed necessary'.[2] London backed up this stiff protest by despatching the patrol ship HMS *Endurance* from Port Stanley, capital of the Falklands, with a party of twenty-two Royal Marines under the command of Lieutenant Keith Mills.* As far as the Argentine government was concerned, this escalated the situation to an entirely new level: the pride of the military regime was affronted, and a naval ship exercising nearby was ordered to proceed to Leith to land a group of Argentine Marines.

---

* Mills is known within the Royal Marines as 'Fairly Famous' as a result of his participation in this episode.

Unbeknownst to the Foreign Office in London, their overreaction to a mild territorial infringement had given the Argentine government an excuse to launch an operation that they had been planning since the previous December: the invasion of the Falkland Islands.

The Falklands invasion was the initiative of Admiral Jorge Anaya, the naval member of the three-man junta that had ruled Argentina since 1976, and its longest-serving member. He had spent time in London as Naval Attaché during the early 1970s and, perhaps because of this, perceived Britain to be ruled by weak, vacillating governments; his judgement was that if Argentina seized the Falkland Islands by force, the British government would not risk military action in an attempt to win them back, and they would become Argentinian by *fait accompli* whatever subsequent discussions took place in the United Nations and other diplomatic forums. Anaya was a fervent believer that the Falklands should be 'returned' to Argentine sovereignty, and was equally clear that the navy should play a leading role in this objective. When General Roberto Viola resigned the Argentine Presidency in December 1981 in favour of General Leopoldo Galtieri, Anaya apparently briefed the new president that recovery of the Falklands was a significant national priority.[3]

The Argentine claim to the Falklands rested on two basic points: the Falkland Islands are on the supposedly 'Argentine' section of the South American continental shelf; and Argentina had ruled the islands between 1826 and 1831. Both of these facts were undoubtedly true, but more or less meaningless in terms of modern international law. Since 1833, despite the relative proximity of the islands to mainland South America, they have been ruled and settled by Britain. The population is almost exclusively of British origin, and is overwhelmingly in favour of remaining a British colony. The Argentine claim simply does not recognise the principle that territorial disputes are nowadays usually resolved on the basis of self-determination by the population of the area in question. Whatever the historical rights and wrongs of the situation, any Argentine claim to the islands stumbled and fell on the wishes of the Falklanders to remain British; inevitably it would have continued to do so in any sensible tribunal to which the Argentine government had appealed.

Anaya's planning team devised an operation centred around naval assets but using elements from all three Argentine armed services. It wasn't a particularly difficult task: the Falklands were garrisoned by a 'Naval Party' of British Royal Marines not normally stronger than fifty 'all-ranks', supported by the survey ship HMS *Endurance*, and the British had neither heavy weapons nor any hope of rapid reinforcement. The order was given to go ahead with the operation in the last week of March, and D-Day was set for 1 April 1982.

The Argentine plan was straightforward enough. Specialist commandos would seize the Royal Marines' barracks at Moody Brook outside Stanley, whilst a smaller team was tasked to capture the Governor and his official residence, Government House. Following this *coup de main* a Marine battalion would land outside Stanley and take control of the town and the nearby airport, allowing army reinforcements to be flown in from the mainland to establish an Argentine garrison. The intention of the Argentines was to avoid British casualties if possible, in the expectation that Britain would accept a bloodless loss of face far more easily than it would a pitched battle.

The Argentine fleet set sail on 'Operation Blue' on Sunday 28 March, leaving Puerto Belgrano on a course which would take them along the Argentine coast to a position south of the Falklands. A fierce storm blew up on the twenty-ninth which lasted for two days and set back the timetabled landings by twenty-four hours; the first Argentine troops would now set foot on the islands during the night of 1–2 April.

The British government was alerted to the possibility of serious Argentine military action the day before the ships sailed. British diplomats in Argentina reported unusual troop movements and intense activity at Puerto Belgrano as the fleet prepared to depart, and reports from GCHQ, the government's signals intelligence (Sigint) agency in Cheltenham, suggested a wider mobilisation of Argentine naval assets. By chance, the crisis had erupted as the Royal Marines garrison in the Falklands was changing over, and consequently there were double the normal number of soldiers present (sixty-nine Royal Marines and eleven sailors from HMS *Endurance*). Even so, this was a pitifully small force with which to mount a credible defence of the islands, and in London it was realised that if Argentina went ahead and launched a full-scale invasion, the Falklands would be lost.

The commander of the Falklands garrison, Major Mike Norman of the Royal Marines, was told during the afternoon of Thursday 1 April that an Argentine landing appeared to be imminent. He called his men together for an initial briefing:

> I gave them the good news that tomorrow we would start earning our pay. They took it remarkably well but the sailors from *Endurance* became very wide-eyed. Most of them were keen to get on with it and, although we were all military men, they took it as a personal affront. There was a 'Who the hell do they think they are!' attitude, although we all knew that we couldn't really stop them.[4]

Norman had only a very limited stock of 'defence stores' – a few coils of barbed wire – but he sent a team of Marines to lay this out on a potential landing beach near the airfield. The airstrip itself was temporarily blocked by the simple expedient of parking earth-moving vehicles on the runway. At 11 p.m. Norman gave his final orders for the defence of Port Stanley, and shortly afterwards his men were dropped off at their positions by truck.

Even as Norman was briefing his Marines, the first Argentine troops – also Marines, of the Amphibious Commando Company – were landing at an unnamed and unguarded beach close to Lake Point, about four kilometres south of Port Stanley. For the next six hours, the Argentine commandos carefully infiltrated north towards their two targets, Moody Brook barracks (which had been abandoned by the British) and Government House, now being used as a headquarters and the focal point of Major Norman's defensive plan. Just after 6 a.m., the defenders heard the sound of firing and grenade explosions coming from Moody Brook as the Argentines 'cleared' the empty buildings, and ten minutes later the first probes were made at Government House.

Earlier in 1982, an Argentine tourist claiming to be an architect had managed to obtain a copy of the plans of Government House from Governor Hunt, who said that 'like a fool, I gave them to him'.[5] It is likely that these had formed the basis of the original attack plan.

But when the Argentine assault began on Government House, it was not the originally-tasked army unit that took part but a detachment of sixteen members of the Amphibious Commando Company under Lieutenant Commander Giachino. Giachino, who had not seen the architect's drawings, led a small five-man party into what he thought was the main building in order to demand Hunt's surrender. In fact he and his squad were attacking the empty servants' quarters, which were in an outbuilding. Following this error, Giachino had to take his squad out into the courtyard at the rear of the main building. Here, as they prepared to try to break into the house they were met by well-directed machine-gun and rifle fire from the forty-five defenders located inside. Giachino was hit and knocked down, still holding on to a grenade from which he had pulled the safety pin, and several of the other Argentines, one of whom was also wounded, fled back into the servants' block. Seriously wounded, Giachino shouted for help, but a medic who came forward was wounded by a British grenade and had to withdraw. Shouting and brandishing his hand-grenade, Giachino slowly bled to death from his wounds in the courtyard of Government House while his men waited for reinforcements.

Even as the Commandos launched their farcical attack on Government House, Amtracs* of the 2nd Marine Infantry Battalion were leaving the hold of the *Cabo San Antonio* heading towards the landing beach of Yorke Bay. After a short skirmish on the outskirts of Stanley, where a group of British Marines fired their 84mm Carl Gustav at the lead vehicle (they missed, despite subsequent optimistic claims), the Argentines had occupied the town by 8 a.m., and Government House was surrounded. It was then only a matter of time until the Governor would be forced to order the Marines to surrender. By 9.30 a.m. the Falkland Islands were under Argentine control.

The occupation of the Falklands cost Argentina one dead and a handful of wounded (two seriously); there were no British casualties. In the very limited time available to him, Major Norman did not have sufficient resources to mount an effective defence of Port Stanley or Government House, but he probably could have taken

---

* US-designed amphibious armoured personnel carriers.

the opportunity to leave the town and set up some form of defence in the countryside. Commenting on the battles in the hills around Stanley after the islands were recaptured, many officers suggested that well-trained soldiers – and the Royal Marines are amongst the finest fighting troops in the world – could have held the high ground 'until they died of old age'. By choosing to centre his defence on Government House, an indefensible site of purely symbolic value, Norman ensured that any fighting that took place would be a purely token exchange. The reality of the defence of the Falkland Islands on 2 April 1982 is that Naval Party 8901 offered only a gesture of resistance.

The initial reaction in Britain to the loss of the Falklands was one of extreme confusion. It became apparent to the British government that an actual invasion was about to take place during the evening of 1 April, and the US President, Ronald Reagan, agreed to telephone his Argentine counterpart, General Galtieri, in an effort to persuade him to call it off. Galtieri refused to take the call. At 3.15 a.m. on Friday 2 April, Brigadier Julian Thompson, commander of 3 Commando Brigade, was telephoned by Major General Jeremy Moore, his Royal Marines superior: 'You know those people down south: they're about to be invaded. Your brigade is to come to seventy-two hours' notice to move with effect from now.'[6]

At other military locations throughout Britain, duty officers and night-time operations staff were receiving similar messages. But the exact situation remained obscure: communications with Hunt and his staff were out, and as the Argentine forces took control of the islands a *de facto* news blackout was in force.

As the drama taking place in the Falkland Islands began to echo around the world, a normal day was unfolding in Candahar Barracks in Tidworth, home of 3 Para. Although the battalion was taking its turn as the 'spearhead' unit, theoretically ready to move anywhere in the world at twenty-four hours' notice, the Paras themselves were split up doing the normal routine of training, guards and duties around the camp. Lee Fisher, a lance corporal in the recently reformed D (Patrols) Company, was learning the rudiments of sniping on a course run by the battalion's training wing out on Salisbury Plain. Vince Bramley, a lance corporal in the Drums Platoon, was on an assault pioneer course with the Royal Engineers in Aldershot, learning how to dig field defences and gaining his first hands-on experience with military explosives. Others, like Captain Tony Mason, who had recently returned from the Junior Division of the Staff College (a twelve-week course held at Warminster for all captains), were getting on with the time-consuming and tedious business of administering the daily lives of a platoon of exuberant young men who were not necessarily over-enamoured of the thought of another weekend in Tidworth. Mason had considered his twelve weeks in Warminster 'an enormous pain in the arse',[7] and was looking forward to the start of Easter block leave in a week's time.

The news which began to break on radios during the morning was a source of considerable puzzlement to most members of the battalion, not least because very few of the soldiers had any idea where the Falkland Islands were. 'Why have the Argentinians invaded Scotland?' thought Lee Fisher. 'It's a long way to go for them. Of course, I wasn't actually sure where Argentina was, let alone the Falklands.'[8] His reaction was echoed by Chris Phelan, a sergeant in the battalion's Training Wing who was in the process of getting divorced and was thus living in the Sergeants' Mess: 'Initially it didn't really sink in, it flashed up on the news a few times but I've got to say I didn't know where the Falklands were – I thought they were in Scotland or the Outer Hebrides or somewhere.'[9]

As the day wore on, the decision was made by United Kingdom Land Forces (UKLF) command to put 3 Para on standby for possible employment in connection with the crisis. Brigadier Ayrey of Headquarters UKLF telephoned the battalion's second-in-command (2ic) at 5 o'clock that afternoon to ask: 'Are you ready to go?',[10] and an hour and a quarter later Lieutenant Colonel Pike, 3 Para's commanding officer, gave the order – 'Exercise Fastball' – designed to bring the battalion onto a war footing.

The first that the soldiers heard was during the early evening of 2 April. At a quarter past six Major Martin Osborne, then commanding the administrative headquarters company, contacted British Rail requesting them to put out chalkboards at stations informing members of the battalion that they should return to Tidworth, and at 7.30 a batch of recall telegrams were sent out via Bristol GPO. According to Lee Fisher: 'We were getting ready for the weekend and they said, "Nobody's allowed to leave camp," and everyone was – BOOF! – gone, "Let's get out of here quick . . ." everyone went to the pub, The Drummer Boy.'[11]

Others reacted slightly more dramatically. Private Early of A Company heard the news of the recall while he was on the London–Edinburgh express train, and pulled the communication cord to stop the train; his comrade Private Burns flagged down and commandeered a police panda car. But despite the standby, the immediate reaction, of some at least, was that 3 Para would not actually be called upon to do anything. Tony Mason, discussing the situation with his Anti-Tank Platoon colour sergeant, Steve Knights, came to the conclusion that: 'We thought it was basically a Royal Marines operation – they lost it, they were going to have to go and get it back.'[12]

In fact, at 8.30 p.m. on 2 April, 3 Para's first 'O' Group* of the Falklands campaign was taking place in battalion headquarters in Candahar Barracks. Captain Giles Orpen-Smellie, the intelligence officer, had managed to put together a sketchy briefing on the islands from the few sources immediately available to him, and Major Stratton, who was still in place as 2ic, talked about what he considered the three most likely operational scenarios for the battalion's employment: an airborne assault, an 'airlanding' operation and an amphibious assault. Moving on to more prosaic matters, it was decided that the band would take over guard duties in the camp while the battalion was preparing to go.

Tony Mason, having finished his normal workload for the day, had returned to his married quarters in Tidworth only to be summoned back to the barracks by a telephone call from support company headquarters:

> The whole mobilisation process was fairly rapid. There was a telephone call I had at home on Friday night asking me to come in to work . . . I came in; and I left in the early hours of the morning having put together, I suppose, the basis for mobilisation.[13]

* Formal meeting at which detailed operational orders are passed down the chain of command.

Others who had been called in had less to do. Vince Bramley of the Drums Platoon turned up at the platoon stores only to find himself, and his mates, sitting around for four hours with nothing to do. Eventually Geoff Deaney, the drum major,* appeared with Mike Oliver, the lieutenant commanding the platoon, and sent them home, telling them to reappear for work the next morning at 8 a.m.

On the wider scene, it had been concluded that Brigadier Thompson's brigade needed reinforcements, and that 3 Para was the ideal unit to slot into the Commando formation. As the night of 2 April wore on, Thompson's staff in Plymouth were developing plans to get the brigade, with its stocks of rations, ammunition and other stores, en route to the Falklands via Ascension Island. Hew Pike, 3 Para's commanding officer, had been 'warned' by Major Hector Gullan, a Parachute Regiment officer on the staff of 3 Brigade, to attend a briefing on Sunday 4 April at the commando brigade headquarters in Plymouth. In turn, when the soldiers of 3 Para showed up for work on Saturday morning, they were told that the CO would brief the battalion on the parade square at 0945 hrs.

Meanwhile, at Depot Para – the training unit for the entire regiment – in Aldershot, the Sergeants' Mess was gearing up for its Easter Ball. Des Fuller remembers:

> We all had to turn up at about 10 o'clock Saturday morning
> – all the senior NCOs on the Entertainments Committee –
> to put up the decorations, hang the 'chutes and tart the place
> up a bit. We were all there whingeing and talking about it,
> and the RSM there was Ron Lewis, and we were all going
> up to the RSM and saying, 'How are we going to get there?'
> and he was just telling us all to 'Piss off, you're here and this
> is where you're staying.'[14]

Fuller and his colleagues, having finished decking out the mess, had a drink in the bar; then he went home to watch television.

At his briefing, Hew Pike didn't detain his men long. With the battalion formed into a hollow square, RSM Lawrie Ashbridge called them to attention and then Pike spoke:

---

* In reality a sergeant.

Gents, just to let you know the full implications and developments. We will be going to Southampton on Wednesday or Thursday to embark on a ship yet to be named. We will then sail south. There will be a lot of running about and a lot of changes between now and then, so please be patient. You will have tomorrow off and then, by Monday the fifth, you and I will have a better idea of the coming events. Good day.[15]

As the soldiers of 3 Para dispersed for their last free weekend in Tidworth – the last, in fact, that many of them would ever have – Des Fuller was being disturbed from his afternoon in front of the television:

A Land-Rover turned up at the house with a telegram, or a message of some sort, saying that we'd got to report to the depot at ten o'clock tomorrow morning – which was a Sunday. I knew what it was for, at least I hoped I knew what it was for . . . it had to be something to do with the Falklands. So I went and had a rip-roaring evening, got blasted out of my brain, turned up at the Depot on the Sunday . . . told that 2 and 3 Para were looking for volunteers. 'They want you back in battalion if you want to go – it's voluntary.' I put my name forward and, Monday morning, turned up at the Depot and there's a Land-Rover taking me down to Tidworth where 3 Para were . . . I was dropped off at the Mess, given a room and told to report to Lawrie Ashbridge, the RSM. Lawrie told me I was going to B Company so I went down there and met Mike Argue – I knew Johnny Weeks – I knew quite a lot of the guys in B Company.[16]

The atmosphere in the battalion by then was 'go', according to Fuller. The previous morning, Hew Pike had flown with his ops officer to Headquarters Commando Forces at Hamoaze House, Devonport, where Brigadier Thompson gave a briefing to his commanding officers. Intelligence reports were still extremely sketchy, but Thompson was able to produce the colourful Marine Major Ewen Southby-Tailyour, who had, during a tour of the Falklands some time before, made a detailed survey of the coastline with the intention of writing a yachting guide. Southby-Tailyour briefed the assembled officers on the terrain and conditions of the islands, and was followed by a naval lieutenant with recent experience of South Georgia. Thompson was then able to give an outline of forthcoming events and activities, and also to lay down his requirements for unit training and preparation during the voyage south.

Faced with the complex task of preparing their battalion for combat operations, Pike and his staff encountered an attitude at UKLF that some felt amounted almost to obstruction. Kevin McGimpsey, the Adjutant, was told at one stage that '3 Para is presently "peanuts" and right at the bottom of the list of priorities,'[17] by a staff officer at the headquarters, even though they had by then been seconded to 3 Commando Brigade and were likely to be the first major army unit to leave. At the same time as this problem was being attacked, another surfaced. As they mobilised, 3 Para had two foreign officers serving with them: Major Buck Kernan of the US Army was commanding C Company, and Captain Ray Romses, a Canadian, was attached to B Company. Both were keen to accompany the battalion to the Falklands, but both needed clearance from their own governments, which were maintaining – officially at least – a stance of neutrality between Britain and Argentina. In the outcome, despite strenuous efforts by both men (Kernan even pleaded with the Chief of Staff of the US Army), they were denied permission to travel with their unit, and replacements had to be found. To the slight unease of several officers within the battalion, Kernan was replaced by Major Martin Osborne from HQ Company.

On the Monday and Tuesday preparation continued within the battalion as it prepared to go to war. Two significant items of kit arrived at Candahar Barracks, both of which were high on the 'wish-list' of all British infantry battalions at the time. The first of these was windproof clothing: combat gear made of a higher-quality and more tightly woven camouflaged material. Routinely worn by special forces units and also issued to troops deployed in Arctic regions, windproof smocks were seen as a prestige item by most soldiers, and were difficult to get hold of. Although 300 sets of Arctic equipment came from the reserves held by the Commando Logistics Regiment, many of the windproofs taken south by 3 Para were actually from the stores of 1st Battalion, Prince of Wales's Own (1 PWO), a unit of tough Yorkshiremen based two miles from Tidworth in Bulford, who at the time were the army's 'in role' Arctic-warfare-trained battalion with the ACE Mobile Force.* To the fury of many officers and soldiers of the PWO, they were prevented from going to the Falklands because of their NATO commitment, even though they were clearly well suited to the operation.[†] Together with the windproofs came a quilted jacket and trousers, known as a 'Chairman Mao' suit, which was designed to be worn under combat clothing, as well as other cold-weather gear, including hats, gloves and socks.

More important than the new clothing was a new communications system called 'Clansman'. Up until then the battalion had been using the temperamental and unwieldy A41 'Larkspur' system, and the issue of the robust, reliable and portable Clansman was to prove a boon during the campaign. Even so, it took a considerable struggle with the powers that be at HQ UKLF to obtain issue of the radios: it was almost as if the new equipment was actually the personal property of the staff officers with the power to release it. Watching in some amazement as the new kit appeared, Corporal Johnny Cook of the Drums Platoon was heard to remark, 'It makes you wonder how long that fucking stuff has been sitting on some twat's shelf.'[18]

Two members of the battalion not involved in the frantic preparations in Tidworth were Captain Bob Darby and Colour Sergeant Brian Faulkner, who was temporarily without portfolio as the result of a disciplinary 'misunderstanding'.[19] Attached to the Quartermaster's department, they were hastily dispatched with a team of Royal Navy and Royal Marines officers to take control of the P&O liner *Canberra*, then enjoying a stopover in Gibraltar while in mid-cruise. With typical linguistic violence, the vessel had been 'STUFT' (Ship Taken up from Trade) by the Ministry of Defence, and Darby and Faulkner assisted the crew as the bewildered and disgruntled passengers were disembarked (Faulkner managed to earn himself punitive 'extra duties' because RSM Ashbridge spotted him not wearing a belt – and therefore 'improperly dressed' – on a TV news

---

* Allied Command Europe Mobile Force. A multi-national brigade designed to protect the northern and southern flanks of NATO in Europe.

† Adrian Weale served as a platoon commander in 1 PWO in 1986–87, when this still rankled with veterans of the period.

broadcast). As the enormous liner – later to be nicknamed 'the Great White Whale' by the troops aboard – sailed for England to meet the elements of 3 Commando Brigade that she was to carry to the Falklands, Bob Darby was appointed 'Ship's Adjutant', and Faulkner took over 3 Para's allocation of accommodation and hold space and started work on the loading plan for the battalion.

While the battalion's heavier support weapons were packed into their purpose-built containers for the journey, the soldiers were sent to zero their personal weapons at nearby ranges along the Bulford–Tidworth Road, and at Perham Down Barracks just outside Tidworth. The rifle companies had already taken the opportunity to run through section, platoon and company attack drills so that the soldiers were thinking along the right lines if, as seemed likely, there was no further chance to practise on dry land, but in truth training opportunities were limited in the rush to get moving. The time was now approaching when they would move out of the barracks and head for Southampton to meet the *Canberra*. On Wednesday, the word came down from Battalion HQ that they would move the next day, boarding the ship on Thursday the eighth and departing on Friday when the brigade units which had embarked had everything sorted out to their satisfaction. This was, not unnaturally, a time of considerable tension for the soldiers, some of whom, like Jason Burt, Neil Grose and Ian Scrivens of B Company, had yet to see their eighteenth birthdays.

David Collett, A Company's newly-installed commander, remembers that there was still, even at this stage, a distinct air of unreality about proceedings:

> Once they said we were going, we actually realised that we probably would go. Once they went off and got the *Canberra* . . . But still, that was just sailing, it didn't mean we were actually going to war. A lot could have happened. I really wanted to go, I think we all did really . . . I mean it's a soldier's training to want to go and fight . . . it's the natural thing – 'specially if you're in the Paras! There was no problem with anybody not wanting to go, it was all the other way. The Paras had a problem with all their outlying staff wanting to get back in.[20]

Vince Bramley described the journey thus:

> After dinner on Thursday 8 April we climbed on to the fleet
> of coaches for the two-and-a-half-hour journey to South-
> ampton. The last goodbyes were short and sad and the lads
> just sat for the first few minutes of the journey, deep in their
> own thoughts.[21]

At the time that 3 Para was despatched to the Falklands, it was
organised as a standard 'in-role' parachute battalion. This means, in
effect, a unit of approximately 700 all-ranks, under the command
of a lieutenant colonel: in 3 Para's case, Hew Pike, in 1982 a thirty-
eight-year-old graduate of Sandhurst.

Hew Pike had had the classic Parachute Regiment career; the son
of a lieutenant general,* he had been commissioned directly into
the regiment in 1962 at the age of nineteen, serving with 3 Para in
the Middle East, Africa and Guyana, as an ADC in Britain and Norway, with 1 Para in the Middle East and UK, and with the Territorial
Army in 44 Para Brigade (V). After attending the army's Staff College
in 1975 – a sure sign that an officer is destined for higher things –
Pike was posted as 16 Para Brigade's last brigade major (in effect
Chief of Staff) before the brigade was disbanded in 1977, an appointment in which he earned the MBE. Thereafter he returned to 3 Para
as OC A Company before taking over as commanding officer in
1980.

By the time his battalion was 'warned' for service in the South
Atlantic, Hew Pike was acknowledged as one of the leading battalion
commanders of his generation. He was – and still is – both popular
and highly respected within the Parachute Regiment, where his
talent as a leader inspired fierce loyalty from the soldiers he commanded. His record as a staff officer was also exemplary, but, in
common with every other serving officer in the armed forces at
the time, his experience of operational command at company and
battalion level was restricted to the low-intensity counter-
insurgency campaigns of the 1960s, seventies and eighties. Northern
Ireland, where Pike cut his teeth as a battalion commander, was

* At the time of writing, Hew Pike is himself a lieutenant general, and Deputy
Commander-in-Chief of the UK Land Command.

acknowledged by the beginning of the 1980s to be a campaign where the majority of immediate tactical decisions were made 'on the ground' by corporals, sergeants and lieutenants. Conventional warfare in the Falkland Islands was likely to prove an altogether more demanding experience.

Pike's second-in-command in the Falklands was Major Roger Patton, occupying an appointment that many find both difficult and sensitive, not least because the 2ic's tasks are vaguely defined in peacetime and remain so until the CO is absent, dead or incapacitated. Even during the occasional periods when a 2ic temporarily assumes command, his courses of action remain constrained by the need to fit in with his boss's policies at all times. In reality, the role of second-in-command is a dead-end job until an 'operational' task appears, and even then he is likely to feel surplus to requirements, at best, whilst the CO directs the action. Patton took over as 2ic just before the battalion left for the Falklands, as his predecessor, Major Stratton, was sent to the headquarters of 3 Commando Brigade. Below the CO and his 2ic, battalion headquarters consists of a small number of officers and NCOs who act as the CO's staff to implement his operational plans. In peacetime, the most important of these is the adjutant, a senior captain (normally in his late twenties) who acts, in effect, as the CO's personal assistant but also has particular responsibility for personnel and disciplinary matters (in staff terms he is a battalion-level G1 officer). At the time of the Falklands crisis the post was held by Captain Kevin McGimpsey. Working hand in glove with the adjutant is the regimental sergeant major, a warrant officer class 1 (WO1), who is, in reality, almost as influential within a battalion as the CO. The RSM will be one of the two or three most experienced non-commissioned members of the battalion, having usually completed at least eighteen years' service before assuming the appointment, and he will almost certainly have served outside the battalion in training units or with the TA. Lawrence Ashbridge, 3 Para's RSM in 1982, was a veteran of Northern Ireland's undercover war, having served with the secretive 14 Intelligence Company in the province during the 1970s.

The remaining commissioned members of battalion headquarters – the intelligence officer, the operations officer and the regimental signals officer – are all posts filled by captains who are normally in their mid-to-late twenties, learning the rudiments of staff work before fulfilling a staff appointment outside their parent battalion. After the CO, the senior operational officer members of a battalion are the company commanders: officers in the substantive or acting rank of major, and normally aged between twenty-eight and forty (at that time, an officer could become an 'acting' major at the age of twenty-eight, but could only assume the substantive rank 'in the year in which they are thirty-two', having passed the necessary exams). In 1982, parachute battalions differed from the rest of the infantry in that they possessed an extra fighting company, having five instead of the usual four, the fifth being a specialist patrols company.

The three rifle companies in the Falklands – A, B and C – were commanded by, respectively, David Collett, Mike Argue and Martin Osborne. David Collett and Mike Argue both had experience of active service with 22 SAS Regiment in Oman in the 1970s, but Osborne was a different kettle of fish, having started out in adult life as a journalist on the *Leicester Mercury* and gaining his commission via the TA. He took over C Company at the last minute as the battalion was about to depart for the Falklands: up until then he had been in charge of the largely administrative 'HQ Company', and before that he had commanded Support Company, where at least one of his officers was unimpressed by him: '[He] was a total fucking wanker who I despised and loathed,' according to his Anti-Tank Platoon commander, Captain Anthony Mason, and the fact that he had taken over a rifle company was 'something of a joke really'.[22]

Each company consisted of three platoons of approximately thirty men, formed from three sections of eight and a small platoon head-quarters. Support Company, commanded by another SAS veteran, Major Peter Dennison, was completely different. Although classed as a fighting sub-unit, it was composed of specialists trained in the use of mortars, anti-tank weapons and the General Purpose Machine Gun (GPMG) in the sustained-fire role, and organised into three platoons. (To the secret shame of many of its members, the 'Machine Gun' Platoon was actually the 'Drums' Platoon – in the infantry, drummers are fighting soldiers and not bandsmen, who act as stretcher-bearers in wartime.)

D (Patrols) Company, led by Major Pat Butler, was somewhat

smaller than the other companies, but no less important. The Parachute Regiment's patrols companies are a hangover from Malaya and Borneo, when 'parachute squadrons' were formed to supplement the strength of 22 SAS Regiment. 3 Para's Patrols Company was reformed in 1981 when the unit resumed its parachute role, and under Butler, his 2ic Captain Matt Selfridge* and Company Sergeant Major Ernie Rustill, it was broken down into four-man patrols very much along SAS lines.

The building blocks of the rifle companies are the sections, teams of eight men commanded by a corporal – a 'full-screw' in army slang – with a lance corporal ('lance-jack') as his second-in-command. Despite the small size of an infantry section it can, nevertheless, deploy quite formidable firepower. In 1982, British infantrymen were armed with a 7.62mm calibre self-loading rifle (SLR), a British variant of the Belgian FN 'FAL' (fusil automatique léger – light automatic rifle). The 7.62mm bullet is a powerful and accurate projectile, and British soldiers were trained to be able to use their weapons accurately to a range of 300 metres, at which the round would still have a devastating effect on its target (in reality, a 7.62mm round is potentially lethal at ranges of two miles or more, but it is not possible to aim it at this distance). Unlike the FN version of the rifle (which was in use by the Argentine Army), the British SLR does not fire in bursts, because, it is argued, this compels soldiers to conserve their ammunition and shoot more accurately. There is still considerable debate as to which is the best option. Also available was the 9mm Sterling submachine gun (SMG), usually carried by radio operators and others who would be hindered by the weight of a heavy rifle. SMGs fire low-velocity pistol ammunition in bursts with a range of up to 200 metres. Although popular with filmmakers, they are only really effective at close quarters, and to soldiers they feel worryingly flimsy in comparison to the reassuring bulk of a rifle.

In addition to the seven rifles in a section was one GPMG. The British GPMG, firing the same 7.62mm round as the SLR but in

---

* Selfridge died tragically after the Falklands War in a hideous parachuting accident which took place in front of his parents and fiancée. He is thus commemorated by the Green-Eyed Boys as 'Matt the Splat'.

bursts via a belt feed, is also based on a Belgian FN design, and is intended to provide each infantry section with its own built-in fire support. The fully-automatic capability of the 'Gimpy' means that effective fire can be brought down on the enemy at ranges of up to 800 metres or, if tracer ammunition is used, 1100 metres. The volume of fire delivered is more than sufficient to demolish a brick wall, shatter rocks, or riddle a soft-skinned or lightly armoured vehicle. It has a notional rate of fire of 850 rounds per minute, but in practice it is not possible to fire anything like this quantity, for the simple reason that the gun would melt down: the friction of bullets travelling down the barrel and the heat from the propellant gases are more than enough to make parts of it red-hot in a very short space of time.

In battle the basic routine for a section was to split down into two teams, a 'rifle group' led by the section commander, and a 'gun group' commanded by the 2ic.* These two teams are then able to provide support for each other during manoeuvre, with the gun group giving the rifle group fire support in the last stage of a section assault, when, in all likelihood, the section would have further broken down into pairs, working on the 'buddy-buddy' system and covering each other.

To supplement the rifles and the machine-gun, each section would carry a variety of other weapons including the L2A2 high explosive grenade, which detonates creating a lethal cloud of high-velocity metal fragments out to a radius of five metres, and the 66mm Light Anti-Tank Weapon, a short-range high-explosive rocket launched from a disposable tube. The '66' is a controversial weapon because, although it can have a devastating effect on a target, it is exceedingly difficult to aim and fire accurately without a good deal of practice. Even more controversial, but for different reasons, is the No. 80 White Phosphorus Grenade. White phosphorus is banned from being used as a weapon by the Geneva Conventions, and the No. 80 (also known as the 'Willie Peter') is officially a smoke grenade. The reality of the WP grenade is that it can shower an enemy position with fragments of burning phosphorus

* The introduction of the SA-80 family of weapons has altered this somewhat; each section now has two 'LSWs', and in any case the SA-80 rifle has fully-automatic capability.

which cannot easily be put out, due to the fact that the chemical oxidises very easily in air, and, like lumps of burning Vaseline, will stick to the clothing and skin of any soldier on the receiving end; it does create an effective instantaneous smoke screen, but for most users that is very much a secondary benefit. It is a weapon that is both highly lethal and psychologically terrifying for those on the receiving end, and the restrictions on the use of WP have not actually had any noticeable impact on its employment, by all armies, since the Second World War.

Three infantry sections are formed into a platoon commanded by a lieutenant or second lieutenant with the assistance of a sergeant. In addition to the section weapons, the platoon 'headquarters' also deployed an 84mm Carl Gustav anti-tank rocket launcher, a more accurate and, supposedly, more effective weapon than the '66', with at least twice the range and an easier sighting and firing system.

The rifle platoon is the lowest level at which officers are involved in commanding soldiers, and the platoon commander is the key interface between officers and soldiers. By the time of the Falklands War, cost-cutting and economies meant that young officers were taking over infantry platoons after only about six months' training at Sandhurst. Well into the 1970s the Standard Military Course at Sandhurst lasted for two years and included a considerable academic input alongside the purely military disciplines, but this was swept away during the financial crises of the seventies, and even military and tactical training for officers was pared to the bone. The training syllabus for young subalterns thus had to include the basic military skills – fieldcraft, weapons, signals etc. – along with the tactics of platoon operations, administration, military law and the intangible qualities of leadership, in roughly the same period that a normal soldier was allocated to receive his entire course of basic training. The absurdity of this policy was heightened by the foolish practice of incorporating vast quantities of parade-drill into the syllabus at the expense of more relevant training.* At the end of this course

---

* On the Standard Graduate Course in 1985 – three years after the Falklands War – drill still formed the largest single element of the officer-training programme. Most students at Sandhurst attributed this to the malign influence of the Brigade of Guards and their desperation to have some 'useful' – or at least observable – role within the wider army.

the best advice that instructors could give their charges was that they should 'listen to their platoon sergeant': it is to the credit of most young officers in the British Army that they do precisely this.

The platoons of Support Company are generally commanded by older and presumably wiser officers, and the soldiers are also normally more experienced and mature. Captain Tony Mason, commanding the anti-tanks, had been in the Parachute Regiment since 1973. He had served with 2 Para, as an ADC to General Howlett in Germany, and as a recruit instructor at Depot Para, before taking over the 3 Para Anti-Tank Platoon. In comparison to the platoon commanders in, for example, B Company, all of whom were serving their first tours with the battalion, he was a man of considerable experience. 3 Para's Anti-Tank Platoon was armed in 1982 with both the 120mm Wombat recoilless anti-tank gun and the Milan guided-missile system: both are formidable weapons. The Wombat is essentially a tube on wheels which launches an anti-tank shell with a range of about a kilometre against static targets; the Milan, which was just coming into service with the British Army in 1982, is a highly sophisticated wire-guided missile with a range of up to 1950 metres.

The Mortar Platoon, commanded by Captain Julian James, deployed the standard British 81mm infantry mortar, the battalion's only integral indirect-fire weapons. The 81mm mortar is a powerful weapon with a maximum range of over 5000 metres when firing high-explosive rounds. An 'in-role' Para battalion has eight 'tubes' in its mortar platoon, and a good crew should be capable of firing at least twelve bombs per minute at the rapid rate.

The 'junior' platoon in Support Company was the Drums or Machine Gun Platoon, commanded by Lieutenant Mike Oliver with Sergeant Geoff Deaney as his 'drum major'. This platoon utilised the same GPMGs as the rifle sections, but deployed in the 'sustained-fire' (SF) role as a direct-fire support weapon. In sustained fire, the machine-gun is mounted on a heavy, hydraulically buffered tripod rather than its lightweight integral bipod and, in consequence, can fire longer bursts with a greater degree of accuracy. The tripod mounting is designed to allow the gun a certain amount of 'play' as it recoils after each shot. As a result, the rounds from each burst do not land in precisely the same spot but instead create what is described as a 'beaten zone', an elliptically-shaped area that is repeatedly swept by 7.62mm bullets. Firing longer bursts, the guns are prone to overheating, and SF crews therefore carry two spare barrels fitted out for rapid changeovers. Accuracy with the SF tripod fitted is such that, provided the fall of shot can be observed, the guns are effective to at least 1800 metres.

Totalled up, the fighting strength of 3 Para in 1982, including the rifle companies, Support Company and Patrols Company, was about 500 officers and men. In addition to the combat element, there were the support troops: REMFs.* Headquarters Company is the administrative sub-unit within the battalion which looks after all those soldiers who are not on the strength of the combat companies, including the cooks, signallers, medics, drivers, storemen, clerks and pay staff. In a battalion these are a mixture of regimental personnel and others attached from, for example, the Army Catering Corps or the Pay Corps.† At Southampton docks, amidst cheering crowds and the sound of bands playing, the 651 members of 3 Para stalked up the gangways carrying their personal kit and weapons. It was time for the long voyage south.

---

* Rear Echelon Mother-Fuckers.
† Now subsumed into the Royal Logistics Corps and Adjutant General's Corps.

CHAPTER FOUR

Going Down South

When the 'arf made recruity goes out to the East
'E acts like a babe an' 'e drinks like a beast,
An' 'e wonders because 'e is frequent deceased
Ere 'e's fit for to serve as a soldier.

KIPLING, 'The Young British Soldier'

Lee Fisher and his friends from Patrol Company were leaning on the stern rail of the SS *Canberra* playing 'spot the war-widow'. It was 7.30 in the evening of 9 April and they were watching the Royal Marine and Royal Navy wives who had gathered on Southampton dock to wave goodbye to their husbands. 'Spot the war-widow' involved loud speculation about which of the women assembled on the dock would have lost their spouses by the time the Falklands had been retaken and how much they would value – and, indeed, deserve – any physical consolation provided by the victorious heroes of 3 Para.

Fisher was standing with about fifteen of his friends, including Private 'Taff' Goring, and a mixed group from the Patrol and Support Companies. It was an emotional moment. The P&O liner was loaded with some 2500 men of 3 Commando Brigade, made up of 3 Para and their various attachments, as well as 42 and 45 Commandos of the Royal Marines, many of their logistic elements and a horde of 'odds and sods', including representatives of the British press and their MOD minders. The dock-workers had struggled overtime to get the huge liner ready for sea, and prepared for the demands of transporting an entire brigade to war across 8000 miles of the Atlantic. The work had included adding a helicopter deck to the stern of the ship, as well as boarding up the floors of many of the lounges and rooms so that they wouldn't be ruined by the men's boots. In addition, there were many tons of stores to be loaded, not least of which was the food which the men would require three times a day over the next six weeks. The crew of P&O seamen would remain on board while their ship became a floating barracks of the Task Force which, as Alexander Haig, the United States Secretary of State, engaged in his round of shuttle diplomacy, was being dispatched by Margaret Thatcher to liberate the Falklands.

This all meant little to the men of 3 Para, who by now understood that they were, as individuals, very small pawns in a very large game of international diplomatic chess. They also knew as they stood at the rail that any decisions to be made about their future were, as always, entirely out of their hands. They had been recalled to the ship at 4 o'clock that afternoon, and 400 of them had been detailed to line the side of the vessel as it pulled out of harbour. While the officers of the battalion had struggled with the logistics of sending their men to war, the other ranks had been kept preoccupied with such details as the nature of the footwear required to board the liner. P&O were worried that the men's DMS* boots would scuff and damage their decks, and so a small but intense battle had been fought between P&O and the military hierarchy, who were adamant that the finest fighting men in Britain were not going to be seen going off to war in gymshoes and suede desert boots. A compromise was eventually reached: the men would board the ship in boots, but keep soft shoes 'handy'.[1] At the meeting of the Military Force Commanders' 'O' Group on 9 April, led by Colonel Tom Seccombe, the senior military officer on board, various matters had been raised. These would, effectively, occupy the minds of the commanders over the next six weeks, and were divided between clear military concerns, such as training and states of readiness, and the problems posed by the logistical nightmare of maintaining the good order, health and welfare of a brigade of troops for a month and a half on board a cruise-liner.

The brigade commander, Brigadier Julian Thompson, was concerned that 3 Para (and his other units) would eat and drink too much and soften without any exercise, and would thus not be in

---

* 'Direct-moulded sole'. It was also believed to stand for 'Dem's my shoes'.

any fit state to fight a war at the other end. Hew Pike had ordered RSM Lawrence Ashbridge to restrict the supply of beer to two cans per man per day, an arbitrary ration adopted by many units in Northern Ireland, to the irritation of the troops (who inevitably sought to circumvent it). On the other hand, majors and above were to be allowed to keep alcohol in their cabins. After some discussion, it was decided that, due to the tiny number of women on board, the ladies' lavatories on the ship could be used *by the men*. After this radical reordering of priorities, Hew Pike's CO's 'prayers' at ten past two that day were inevitably anti-climactic: the main concerns expressed were over the cleanliness of the men and their accommodation, and the need for the officers to be careful about leaving their weapons in their rooms, as it was possible that some of the P&O stewards were Irish.[2]

Meanwhile, the men lined the decks, the band of the Parachute Regiment played 'The Ride of the Valkyries' on the quayside, and many of the soldiers' wives and children had driven down to see them off. For some, the farewells had been more private: in the married quarters around Tidworth or at home with relatives. The families of many soldiers and Marines found it hard to believe that their men were actually going to take part in a shooting war. For a few, the final glimpse as the liner pulled away from the quay would be the last time they saw their loved ones. The men settled into their accommodation, which, because of the large numbers present, was very cramped. Lee Fisher and a number of other men from Patrol Company were berthed well down in the ship, and Fisher was surprised that from their billet they couldn't see the toss and fall of the ship's movement against the water. He was informed that this was because they were actually below the waterline, which led him to reflect that 'You couldn't see the fish either.'[3] Fisher had unloaded all his equipment, consisting of his bergen, a kitbag, his webbing and a suitcase, into the space on and under his bunk, while the other men were crammed into the claustrophobic cabin in a stack of equipment and weapons.

Accompanying the 3rd Battalion on the ship were 42 and 45 Commandos of the Royal Marines, and the rivalry and resentment between the two formations was evident and palpable. The Royal Marines, as another military élite, maintained their sense of superi-

ority in much the same way as the Parachute Regiment. Both formations were keen to claim the high ground, each believing,
predictably, that they were operationally and historically superior
to the other. The Paras joked that it was the Marines of Naval Party
8901 who had lost the Falklands in the first place, and that it was
only natural that they should need the help of the Parachute Regiment in reclaiming them. The Marines riposted by saying that the
Paras were simply a bunch of dimwitted landlubbers who had no
idea of real soldiering, and that they were stupid enough to jump
out of aeroplanes. All the old jokes about Paras and birdshit being
the two things that dropped from the sky were wheeled out, as were
the songs:

> Para, Para in the sky,
> Living proof that shit can fly,
> If you've got a low IQ,
> You can be a Para too!

> Para, Para flying high
> Drops like birdshit from the sky,
> Thick as fuck and tough as heck,
> Hope you break your fucking neck.

It was inevitable that there should be rivalry between the two
formations, but if pressed, both sides would admit that there was
no other unit, apart from the Gurkhas, with whom they would
rather be fighting side by side. In the final analysis, general opinion
was that the Marines were more 'conventional' than the Parachute
Regiment, despite their role as amphibious soldiers. Both sides had
plausible claims about their own abilities, and the technicalities of
their relative proficiencies could be, and were, argued about *ad
nauseam*, but as they lined the decks of the ship as it departed, the
two groups felt common cause and sympathy with each other.

The *Canberra* pulled out of Southampton at 8 o'clock in the
evening of 9 April, and sailed down the Solent, bound for the English
Channel and the open sea. On board, the process of 'rumour control'
took hold, as everybody tried to work out from the wealth of intelligence material and gossip exactly what was going to happen. Among

the men of 3 Para, there was a feeling of being on exercise. Nobody sincerely believed at this point that the battalion would be going to war, and although there was a great deal of fighting talk, it was felt that diplomacy would win the day, and they would return to England. Sergeant Des Fuller remembers the atmosphere on the boat as being one of ' "Let's go and smack them one." It was all very gung-ho.'[4] As a supernumerary sergeant in B Company, his role was to provide a training cadre, along with the company quartermaster sergeant (CQMS), Tony Dunn. But as the *Canberra* moved out into the Atlantic, he found himself with little to do, so he set about making a model of the islands. At five past five that day, Pike held his daily 'O' Group, at which it was reported that a Russian trawler was following the Task Force, carrying out an intelligence-gathering mission. The need for medical training was stressed, and it was decided that the men would be taught how to deal with gunshot and blast injuries. A church service was announced for 10 o'clock the following day, at which the battalion padre, Major Derek 'The Cleric' Heaver, expected a turnout of some twenty men from the whole battalion. Pike gave orders that only regulation DMS boots were to be worn on this operation, forbidding any of the men from wearing Arctic mountaineering boots or Northern Ireland patrol boots (though few would have preferred the flimsy NI boot, even over the badly-made and unwaterproofable DMS, when actually dealing with the terrain of the Falkland Islands). There was concern over the supply of milk on the boat, and the men's tea ration was cut to half a cup per meal, while in the interests of cleanliness and hygiene spitting was formally forbidden on the Promenade Deck.

But by far the most important topic on the agenda at the 'O' Group was that of pilfering. P&O expected losses of company property from the ship to run at 25 per cent, and Pike briefed the RSM to be prepared to deal with a massive wave of theft of ship's goods by the men. Indeed, as the SS *Canberra* moved southwards forty miles off the Brittany coast, and as Alexander Haig met General Galtieri in Buenos Aires for the first time, some of the more ruthless and opportunistic members of the battalion had already liberated their first piece of P&O property: a steam iron severed from its plug outside one of the launderettes.[5]

By 10 o'clock the following day, the eleventh, the ship was half-way down the Bay of Biscay, the Promenade Deck was already beginning to crack under the pressure of the men's boots, Hew Pike had lost his kit-box of personal possessions and the problem of iron-theft was escalating. By the middle of that afternoon, P&O, who were also accusing men from 3 Para of stealing a ship's plaque, decided to solve the problem by handing over four steam irons to be used by the entire battalion.

The thoughts of the senior military officer, Colonel Tom Seccombe, were more concerned with the future of the Falkland Islands. He briefed the commanding officers on his belief that even in the unlikely event of Britain having to retake them by force, it would be a UN force of occupation who would look after them afterwards.[6] The men from 3 Para just wanted to get on with it:

> We on board would often say, 'Fuck the bloody twats sat there arguing. Let's get it over and done with.' . . . The general attitude of the troops was, 'Support the actions. We love Maggie for giving us the chance to kill some spicks. Let's just hope we get back in time for the World Cup and summer leave.'[7]

Over at A Company, Sergeants Chris Phelan and Mac French had been attached to the unit from the battalion training wing, as supernumerary instruction sergeants. Chris Phelan remembers:

> I can't remember being sort of anxious or anything like that, or worried that we're going to war and that, because it wasn't until I got onto the terra firma at the other end, after being pissed about in those landing craft for hours on end, and the Pucaras and the helicopter got shot down . . . and they were actually firing . . . it was: 'We're at war, fuck me, this is happening, really happening!' Because up until then it was just like going on exercise.[8]

Sergeant Des Fuller from B Company was meanwhile making his model and enjoying his cabin. He remembers the accommodation on the ship as excellent; the NCOs were allocated to the first-class cabins, and had P&O waiters serving them five-course breakfasts. This situation could be interpreted as part of the British squaddie's dream, of a process which was known in the Royal Marines as 'proffing'. If you had 'proffed', luck and chance had allocated you a cushy number, an easy billet, or a slack job. It had much to do with the British Army's concept of skiving and leisure. The nature of a military organisation is such that it creates extremes of activity and extremes of boredom. When the men were not busy, they still had to be kept occupied, even though they might have nothing productive to do, and consequently their corporals and sergeants would find them a variety of tasks to carry out. Skiving became a way of effectively avoiding being caught – 'jiffed' or 'rubber-dicked' – for any of these pointless time-filling exercises. In reverse, the military concept of leisure tended to be a negative one. You enjoyed yourself because of what you were *not* doing, rather than what you were doing. If you were not on a freezing night-march across the Brecon Beacons carrying sixty pounds of sodden kit and an 84mm Carl Gustav rocket-launcher, then you were already well off. If you were actually involved in doing anything at all which was physically more pleasant than what others were doing, then you had done well by yourself.

3 Para soon settled into the on-board routine. For the men, life was less comfortable than for the NCOs, and was dominated by five preoccupying elements: food, gossip, accommodation, training and waiting. In fact, conditions were not at all dissimilar to being on an exercise, except that the battalion was at sea on a cruise-liner. 'Rumour control' – the gossip grapevine – dominated the men's lives. On board was a large quota of journalists from British radio, television and newspapers. These included Bob McGowan from the *Daily Express*, with photographer Tom Smith, Alistair McQueen from the *Mirror*, Max Hastings from the *Evening Standard* and Robert Fox from the BBC, amongst many others. The 'hacks' were viewed with suspicion. On one hand they were the source of prized information, but too many soldiers had found themselves being held up to ridicule by the press in Northern Ireland and elsewhere to be happy in their presence. There is a widely held but completely false belief in the British Army that the US Army in Vietnam was stabbed in the back by a disloyal and sensationalist media that undermined support for a campaign that was actually being won; in consequence of this there was enormous suspicion of the motives of all of the press pack.

In carrying out their jobs, the journalists were obviously required to get the soldiers to talk about theirs, and this conflicted with the desires of the officers. The basic facts about the progress of the Falklands crisis which the men received came from the BBC World Service, from intelligence briefings (mostly derived from the World Service anyway) and direct from the journalists. By the time information had percolated down to their level, it had the inevitable spin of 'rumour control' put on it. As the ship sailed on towards the Falklands, this informal gossip-service was going to be responsible for many grossly exaggerated rumblings of misinformation. For instance, it was rumoured on 12 April that the island of South Georgia was to be retaken by an airborne drop involving all the parachute-trained members of 42 Commando, a ludicrous concept.

Food and drink were a major preoccupation. To feed all of the men on board was an enormous task, and the 'scoff queues' for the cookhouses assumed a life of their own. The men would line up for an hour for each meal, the queue stretching around corners and along corridors, and up and down the stairs from two different decks. While they waited the men would go off and find beer. Three days into the trip, the ability of the men to exceed their ration of two cans per day was already proving problematic for the RSM,[9] as men like Lee Fisher found their way round this obstacle to their enjoyment:

> Our allocation was two cans per man per day, which for a Paratrooper is like a cup of tea, so right away we decided to do something about it. While we were in the food queues, one of us would go off to the bar and say that he was picking up the beer ration for eight other people, before staggering off to his accommodation with sixteen cans of beer, a trick that would be repeated by all the rest of us.[10]

Then there were the letters from home. The Task Force generated an enormous amount of mail from the UK, the vast majority of it unsolicited letters from people who would simply write 'A Para, the Task Force' in the place of an address. These were dropped to the ships, along with videos, newspapers and so forth, by C-130s* and

---

* Four-engined turboprop-driven plane used as a general transport and Para-troop-drop aircraft.

Nimrods sent out from the nearest NATO bases. On arriving on the ship, the unsolicited mail was distributed among the men together with the letters from wives, girlfriends and families, sometimes sacks of mail to a platoon. The men would work through the unsolicited envelopes, picking those which had photographs inside them, and storing away for future reference the ones that appealed to them. Those which didn't found another fate.

The 'pig-board', or 'grot-board', is a tradition not unique to the Parachute Regiment, but with all the unsolicited female photographs arriving in the mail, it was much in favour on the *Canberra*. The prize photographs, both attractive and ugly, would be pinned up for the general appreciation of the men. The soldiers would reply to those letters and photographs which found approval. The rest were either pinned up or thrown away. In his book *Excursion to Hell*, former Lance Corporal Vince Bramley describes how one morning the men were told not to throw any rubbish over the side, as the Russian spy-trawler following the ship was picking up their detritus for 'intelligence analysis'. Bramley and his Green-Eyed colleagues promptly pitched several sackfuls of 'grot' photographs over the side, feeling that this, if anything, would put the Soviets off from breaking *détente* and invading England.[11]

Meanwhile, military training continued at a frenetic pace. The main areas available for exercise were the decks of the ship, around which the men would move in section and platoon groups, sometimes tabbing, sometimes running, always building up their fitness. They carried out map-reading lessons, medical instruction (which was subsequently to be a significant factor in the survival of many casualties), weapons training and signals classes.

> It was a lot of lessons, verbal lessons, it was a *lot* of weapon handling, that was the main thing that we did, we handled weapons all day every day. We ran round the decks like lunatics and there was a lot of recognition training: enemy kit and equipment. As the intelligence picture was built up, it was the old dissemination, it was disseminated and went down [to the junior ranks].[12]

For some, there was a harder edge to their preparations. Over in 5 Platoon, Corporal Stewart 'Scouse' McLaughlin was teaching his men knife-fighting. McLaughlin was feared and respected in equal parts by the men of his section, who included Privates Dominic Gray, Ben Gough, Grant Grinham, Tony Kempster and 'Lippy' Linton. In some respects a wild-man, McLaughlin was nevertheless a highly proficient section corporal, with finely developed military skills. An occasional bare-knuckle boxer from Wallasey in Merseyside, McLaughlin had joined the Parachute Regiment in 1971, originally being posted to 2 Para. But after an incident in Singapore, where he had fought with a corporal who had stolen a martial-arts 'rice-flail' from him, McLaughlin was repatriated, court-martialled and sentenced to a period of detention in Colchester Military Prison. On his release he was transferred to 3 Para, where Dominic Gray remembers him gaining an immediate reputation for uncompromising aggression towards outsiders. Another corporal, Steve Hope, was popularly regarded as a thug and a bully, liking nothing better than picking on the younger soldiers as they were returning from a night out in town. Privates Dominic Gray and Kevin Connery both had experience of his antics:

> He'd grab your chinky takeaway and stuff it down the back of your neck, and then taunt you into having a fight. One night he actually overturned the scoff-wagon [a takeaway burger van] outside the barracks, just as all the lads in our [McLaughlin's] section were queueing up. He turned the whole thing right over. Scouse went apeshit. 'Did you go hungry, lads?' he kept repeating, 'Did you go hungry?' So he went off to find Steve Hope, and the two of them had a set-to in the armoury. Hope was a nasty bastard, but Scouse punched the living shit out of him. Things were quieter after that.[13]

John Weeks, McLaughlin's company sergeant major, remembers:

> I thought, in the right situation, in the field as a corporal, he was a brilliant guy. In barracks he was fucking useless. He would have had his problems when he got into the Sergeants' Mess 'cos he would've thrown his mitts at the wrong time . . . that was his problem.

Gray and Tony Kempster remember McLaughlin's tactical acumen. He had applied to do SAS Selection in 1978, but on

ABOVE Sergeant Des
Fuller (*right*) poses
next to encouraging
Republican graffiti in
Belfast in the 1970s.

RIGHT Lieutenant
Colonel Hew Pike
(*right*) with the
battalion PT instructor,
Sergeant Ray Butters.

Members of 3 Para in Northern Ireland, late 1970s. Holding the binoculars is Corporal Gary 'Louis' Sturge.

Members of 6 Platoon, B Company, in Oman, 1982. Lieutenant Jonathan Shaw is crouching second from right.

LEFT Private Peter Hedicker assisting the press on the deck of SS *Canberra* during an equipment demonstration on the way to the Falklands.

BELOW At the heart of the Green-Eyed culture: 5 Platoon, B Company. *Left to right, back row*: Nigel 'Lippy' Linton, Terence 'Muldoon' Mulgrew, Terrence Bowdell, Glyn 'Scouse' Lloyd, Mark 'Boots' Meredith, Christopher 'Money' Masterman, Michael 'Babycakes' Southall, Andrew 'Sights' Steadman. *Middle row*: Peter 'Aker' Hindmarsh, Corporal Stewart 'Scouse' McLaughlin, Corporal Ian 'Beetle' Bailey, Philip Proberts, 'Taff' Edwards, Sergeant John 'JR' Ross, Lieutenant Mark Cox, Corporal Graham Heaton, Lance Corporal Lenny Carver, Tony Kempster, 'Hutch' Hutchinson. *Front row*: Nicholas Hillier, Francis O'Regan, Stuart 'Doc' McAllister, Darren 'Ben' Gough, Dominic Gray, Steven Phillips, Grant 'Grin' Grinham, Gary Juliff.

Lieutenant Colonel Hew Pike (*left*) at Ascension Island with fellow battalion commander Lieutenant Colonel 'H' Jones of 2 Para.

Beach-landing drills at Ascension. Walking with the rifle is Sergeant Ian McKay.

'Endurance', the final march across the Brecon Beacons, he slipped and broke an ankle. There was still some way to go, and McLaughlin was carrying a rifle, belt-kit and a fifty-five-pound bergen, but he completed the march. Although he was not able to take part in the rest of Selection, 22 SAS were so impressed with his determination that he was seconded from 3 Para to Hereford, waiting six months to join the next course through – a most unusual concession for the SAS to make. Despite this, he was eventually returned to 3 Para for hitting an instructor.

On the *Canberra*, clearly not satisfied with the level of training his men were receiving at the hands of their instructors, McLaughlin decided to school them in the somewhat outdated and irrelevant techniques of hand-to-hand fighting with edged weapons. Tony 'Fatty' Kempster remembers being ordered by McLaughlin to 'hone his fighting skills' by taking on another member of the section with a sheathed bayonet.

McLaughlin was a character whose peacetime soldiering exploits were legendary. Dominic Gray tells a possibly apocryphal story about how McLaughlin 'ordered' some of his men to go drinking with him one afternoon before the start of an exercise. McLaughlin's notable exploits on licensed premises included once strangling a Rottweiler, but, curiously for a large, hard man, he didn't have any tolerance for alcohol. 'We were more afraid of him,' says Gray, 'than we were of the officers and senior NCOs. So we got into his BMW, and drove off to a pub near Tidworth. After two or three pints, he was completely pissed. He couldn't take his drink at all.' When the men emerged from the pub, McLaughlin was, as Gray puts it, 'howling'. They all climbed into the BMW and set off across Wiltshire to return to Tidworth. On the way, they stopped near a field of cows, and McLaughlin took a bayonet from his glove compartment. Climbing over the barbed wire, he approached a small heifer and sawed through the arteries and veins of its throat, before ordering the men to help him drag the carcass back to his car and load it in the boot. Stumbling and sliding in the grass, the four men managed to get it in. With the back hooves sticking out at a crazed angle, the drunk foursome roared off to the married quarters in Shipton Bellinger where McLaughlin lived. 'The boot was deep in blood,' remembers Gray, 'so we took the calf out and dragged it into his kitchen, where Scouse cut out some of its insides, and half-hung it from the ceiling.' Then he went upstairs and brought down his young son, putting his head and shoulders inside the eviscerated body-cavity, inviting him to smell and taste the blood.[14]

On another occasion, McLaughlin accidentally cut open his arm while on exercise, providing his section with an opportunity to practise wound-suturing on him. 'And if it wasn't neat enough,' remembers one ex-member of his section, 'he'd fucking make you *do it again*.'[15]

Despite his hard-man image, McLaughlin was caring and protective of the soldiers in his section, and a good friend to those he respected. Lee Fisher, who used to take McLaughlin out to shoot rabbits on Salisbury Plain on the back of his motorbike, remembers him lending young soldiers his driving licence so they could hire cars from a garage near Tidworth although they were under twenty-one. He thought about his soldiering and, in a painstaking and methodical way, always tried to do his best.

By 8 o'clock on the morning of 13 April, the ship was just south of Gibraltar, and the main problem to exercise the minds of the senior military personnel at their daily meeting was the men's habit of waiting for the showers completely naked in the passageways. This was not deemed to be offensive to the women on board, but rather it was feared that it would be titillating for homosexuals amongst the P&O crew. By the following morning's meeting, graffiti was beginning to appear on the ship's panelling, and it was also noted, somewhat misguidedly, that the landscape of Ascension Island, which they would reach in a few days' time, was thought to be like southern Italy.[16]

On Saturday 17 April the ship arrived off Freetown, the capital of Sierra Leone. The men on board had military instruction in the morning, but during the afternoon they crowded the rail to watch the local people who had come down to the port to look at the ship. These included an expatriate British family waving a Union Jack; their large-breasted daughter, wearing a flimsy summer dress, stirred the hormones of the thousands of men on board who had been kept cooped up away from their women. Try as the family did to appear patriotic, the cries from the men of 'Tits out for the lads,' and 'Come up here and wave *my* flagpole,' left them unimpressed.

For their part, the Paras and Marines were unimpressed by the locals who rowed out in bumboats to try and sell native artefacts to them. Contact with the locals was banned because of the – probably irrational – fear that they might spread infections. Lee Fisher from Patrols remembers 'somebody dropping a chair on the back of one of these boats, which just cut it in half and sank it'. Vince Bramley describes the scene:

> The Intercom announced that anybody dealing with the bumboats would be charged, as they carried a high risk of malaria and other diseases. It was at this point that some lads below turned the fire hoses on the natives, which had a very good effect on them. The water was powerful and easily reached the boats bobbing beneath us. Crashing into the boats it soon began to fill them. The Negroes frantically tried to paddle away from us, but the hoses followed them. Two boats sank to their rims, sending us into fits of laughter. The group in another boat tried to paddle their half-filled and sinking vessel. The blacks were now angry and shouting, 'You bad white men, you bloody bastards.'
>
> As they struggled in the water with all their worldly goods, a lad from the deck below us shouted, 'We remember your sneaky attack on Rorke's Drift. Now swallow that.'[17]

On board *Canberra* was another native of Sierra Leone, in the person of Private Lansana from C Company. The CO was approached with a request that Lansana be allowed to go ashore and enjoy a reunion with his parents, and for a while it looked as though the West African rifleman might be afforded a chance to do so. The idea was, however, vetoed when it was discovered that Lansana's father had recently been involved in an attempted *coup d'état* to topple the President.

That night, the seventeenth, all was quiet on the boat as it lay at anchor, the only notable incident being that Lieutenant Mark Cox from 5 Platoon inexplicably failed to turn up for his dinner appointment with the deputy captain of the ship, a chore performed nightly by a junior officer from 3 Para or the Marines.[18] Cox, who admits to a certain dilettante approach to soldiering, had already been advised by fellow B Company subaltern Jon Shaw to pay more attention to his drill and discipline with his men. 'I'd never been able to see the point of polishing my shoes at Sandhurst, and I'd failed P-Company three times, dropping off through injury,' admitted Cox.[19] An intelligent and well-educated man, he was still somewhat naive about the slightly more macho attitudes he was expected to adopt as a Parachute Regiment officer; he had caused a certain amount of embarrassment to his fellows at the Parachute Regiment depot by making model aeroplanes in his free time whilst going through P-Company.

A day later, the ship had left Freetown and was steaming south in tropical weather towards Ascension Island. At 5 o'clock in the morning of the nineteenth, the *Canberra* crossed the equator, and the temperature that day climbed to 82 degrees Fahrenheit. Training was now starting as early in the morning as possible, with each sub-unit taking to the decks for thirty minutes' running, the aim being to get all physical training over by lunchtime. The men's fitness was improving as they pounded the decks in full kit, and in the heat of the afternoons they would attend lectures and training classes held in the cool of the ship's air-conditioned lounges. They took advantage of their time off to sunbathe on the upper decks, where one man, described by Lee Fisher as 'a real body beautiful, oiled from top to bottom', lay toasting himself, 'with suntan oil even between his toes'.[20] During one of these sessions, a self-conscious Royal Marine injured himself after executing a neat swallow-dive into the newly-emptied swimming pool, provoking much delight amongst the assembled Paratroopers who had watched his carefully posed preparations.[21]

As training continued in the afternoon heat, so in the evenings the men adjourned to their bars for drinking and singing sessions. There was plenty to drink, despite the two-can limit, but the other staple of a Paratrooper's night out – women – was sadly missing, unless one counted the tiny number of female P&O staff, who, it was assumed, would not be available. Left to their own devices sexually, a private from A Company of 3 Para remembers how the men had to learn the protocol of shipboard masturbation from the Royal Marines:

On navy ships, these blokes said, the toilet doors didn't lock from the inside in case the ship was attacked and somebody got stuck in one of the cubicles. So what the Marines would do was to tape the door shut from the inside with a strip of black masking tape. They were so open about this that you would see blokes leaving cabins, off for a Jodrell,* carrying their copies of *Razzle*, *Fiesta* or *Readers' Wives*, and with bits of tape stuck round their arms.[22]

Masturbation was certainly a fertile field for Green-Eyed activities, and rumours still circulate about an inter-unit wanking contest that is alleged to have taken place on the *Canberra*. Two lines of men, one Marines and the other Paras, faced off in a secluded part of the boat. The agreed rules barred visual pornographic stimulation, and nor were they allowed to shut their eyes, thus ensuring that titanic efforts were required to achieve a climax whilst staring at the frantically pumping form of some hulking, tattooed mortarman standing opposite.

The homosexuals among the crew were having a field day, surrounded at very close quarters by two and a half thousand of the toughest men in Britain, all of whom spent at least half their day in a state of advanced undress on account of the weather, and the rest of the time in a feverish male sweat as they pounded the decks and carried out their training programme. One gay P&O steward was persuaded by Green-Eyed members of 3 Para that the only man with whom he *really* stood a good chance of sexual contact was Stewart McLaughlin. Overjoyed at the prospect of getting to grips with a real Para, the steward was ecstatic to find the Liverpudlian corporal drinking illegally in one of the out-of-bounds crew bars on the night of the eighteenth. With McLaughlin were Private Tony Kempster from B Company, Private Hunt from Mortars, and one other. The P&O man duly made his approach. There are two accounts of what happened next. The battalion log states that the foursome were drinking with a crewman who knew Hunt's parents, and that relations between them deteriorated until McLaughlin beat the steward up. The account from Kempster and Gray is that the

---

* Rhyming slang: Jodrell Bank = wank.

P&O man made a pass at McLaughlin, who hit him in the face and tried to stuff him out of one of the portholes.[23]

A number of officers and journalists had taken to adjourning for morning coffee in two offices on the Promenade Deck belonging to Helen Hawkett, the ship's accountant, and Lauraine Mulbery, the senior assistant purser. Robert Fox, the BBC radio correspondent, remembers:

> The girls' offices became known as the 'coffee trap', and a strange coterie began to congregate there, with Helen and Lauraine, Martin Osborne, Pat Butler and Adrian Freer of 3 Para being the founders and the membership committee. Pat, Martin and myself came to be called third, fourth and fifth girl, though in what order of precedence we never worked out. The friendships formed in the coffee trap were the most cheerful and lasting of the expedition.[24]

But for one of the officers present, Martin 'Fatty' Osborne of C Company, there was much more on the agenda than percolated coffee.[25]

Just before arriving at Ascension Island on 20 April, the men from 3 Para had their morale boosted when they heard that their sister battalion, 2 Para, under the command of Lieutenant Colonel 'H' Jones, would be leaving Aldershot to join them. This was good news, and the men felt that the odds had now been shortened in their favour by the addition of 2 Para's 650-odd men, although intelligence reports flooding in were confirming that the Argentinians had already landed some 9000 troops, heavily supported by artillery and guided missiles, on the Falkland Islands. Dashing the battalion's expectations of an island with the terrain of southern Italy, Ascension turned out to be a lump of volcanic rock set some 1500 miles due west of the coast of Angola.

> The sight of the mid-Atlantic island was the biggest shock for most troops. We had had a vision of palm trees and golden beaches. In reality, the island was nothing more than ninety square kilometres of ash, dust and rock.[26]

Arriving at Ascension Island, the men embarked into the lifeboats and cross-shipped to the assault craft HMS *Fearless*, on which they waited to go ashore for their allocation of training. They were to be moored off the island for nearly two weeks, and during their time ashore the companies practised live-fire drills, landing-craft assaults and fitness training across the red dust and volcanic rock of the island. Although the time spent on the *Canberra* had enabled most of the men to get relatively fit, and to improve their basic military skills, they had not been able to practise any company- or platoon-level tactics which would help them to shake out on the ground.

For the Anti-Tank Platoon, Ascension Island meant a live shoot on one of the ranges set up inland, where they managed to loose off their entire normal annual allocation of training ammunition in one go. The range faced out to sea, and beyond the end of the target area, which was being hit by GPMG- and mortar-fire, was a bird sanctuary. Private Kevin Connery, with the Anti-Tank Platoon under the command of Captain Tony Mason, remembers the moment the Wombats opened up.

> We had a massive allocation of ammunition, and the Wombat is a bloody great 120mm weapon. All these rare birds had settled back down after their stonking by the mortars and the machine-guns, before we let rip with all the guns opening up at once. There was this massive cloud of red dust that covered us all from head to foot, and right down at the end of the range, this sodding great cloud of feathers.[27]

Sergeant Phelan's time at Ascension was more painful:

> Do you know what I remember about that? Getting my bloody arse burnt by the sun! We'd tabbed around the island for five miles, whatever, stretch our legs, and they had ranges there, so we fired, did group zeros,* and all the normal sort of kit that you would do. We came back and we did landing drills on the landing craft . . . This is the Royal Marines . . . this is what they do. Load of shit! You know, drawbridge down, run like hell! What's hard about that? And then we had an hour's R 'n' R. All kit off, you know, underpants on, and into the water. And where you'd been sunbathing with shorts on, and you had underpants on,

---

* i.e. They 'zeroed in' the sights of their weapons.

there was a gap, wasn't there, so I was, like, well-done, for
an inch all the way around me legs, and couldn't move for
about three days.[28]

The military training of the men aside, there were two other areas
which preoccupied the CO and RSM of 3 Para on Ascension. The
first was a tactical concern: the Task Force commander was worried
that the Argentinian navy might be attempting to use midget submarines to sink the ships in the British fleet. This meant that at night
the *Canberra* would often weigh anchor and zig-zag, while on deck
men equipped with lanterns were tasked with keeping an eye out
for the tell-tale washes of any enemy craft. Simultaneously, men
would be listening out for any knocks or bumps on the hull of the
ship which might signal the presence of frogmen attaching limpet
mines.[29] Lee Fisher remembers:

> The only time we hoped that we wouldn't be going was
> when we found out the Argentinians had U-boats. We were
> in the middle of the Atlantic in the brightest-lit vessel ever
> built: a white cruise-liner with 'shoot at me' written on the
> side! When we used to do the boat drills at three in the
> morning, you'd all get there and it would be packed, obvi-
> ously, and for a couple of Marine Commandos and 3 Para
> there was, like, three lifeboats. I was thinking: 'We're not
> all going to make it. On the next one I'll take me bayonet
> in case it's real, 'cos I'm getting in one of them boats!'[30]

The second problem concerned administration and discipline. The
regimental medical officer had noticed that not only was there a
problem with athlete's foot, but that the number of men going sick
on training days was averaging twenty-five, compared to only four
per day on Sundays. Additionally, the RSM was concerned about
an incident which had taken place during a drinking session in the
mess on the night of the twenty-second, when a member of the
press had been hit by an NCO from 3 Para. Sergeant Chris Phelan
found himself involved:

> You had that prat Smith, the photographer who got twatted,
> yeah, by John Ross, laid him out, and that was horrendous,
> 'cos the RSM thought it was me ... and it was Sammy

Dougherty who went to the RSM and said, 'Look, it wasn't Phelan, it was somebody else, you know,' 'cos I had a bit of a bad name at the time, you know, and er, anybody hit anybody it was Phelan, so he's saying, 'I know it was you . . . you'll be walking the plank.' But he [Smith] deserved that, though, he said, 'You're wearing . . . smocks or frocks, something like that, that's what the women wear . . .' WALLOP! BOOF! . . . Spark out! Yeah, shut up you prat.[31]

While on Ascension, the men were able to witness some of the considerable activity on Wideawake airfield, which was then one of the busiest in the world in terms of aircraft movements. They could watch the take-offs and landings of the RAF Vulcan bombers which were flying south, at the extreme limit of their operational capability, to bomb Port Stanley runway.

Meanwhile, on the island of South Georgia, a Royal Navy Sea King helicopter crippled the Argentinian submarine *Santa Fé*. The island fell back into British hands on 25 April, after an operation to retake it carried out by members of D Squadron of 22 SAS, twenty-five men of 2 SBS and M Company of 42 Commando, otherwise known as 'The Mighty Munch', under Major Guy Sheridan. On 28 April, an air exclusion zone was imposed around the Falklands, on 1 May the Vulcans bombed Stanley, flying the 3500 miles from Ascension Island, and on the second, two frigates and a destroyer shelled Port Stanley military base. On 1 May, the first British servicemen returned ashore to the Falklands, in the shape of sixteen men from G Squadron of 22 SAS, although the honour of being first on land went to Captain Chris Brown, a naval gunfire forward observation officer from 148 (Meiktila) Battery, Royal Artillery.

While 3 Para prepared for war at Ascension, Alexander Haig's mediation mission came to an end. America decided to support the British position, and on 1 May the efforts of Haig were transferred back to the UN, and over to the Peruvian government. This meant that by the end of April Britain had the support not only of the EEC but also of Japan and the United States, the latter having waived possible objections under the terms of the 1823 Monroe Doctrine – by which the US vetoed outside interference within the operational sphere of both the Americas – and decided to supply Britain with

vital satellite intelligence and missile support. While the British
government stated that it was aiming for a diplomatic settlement, if
necessary brought about by the use of minimum force, the decision
of Ronald Reagan's government meant it could now count on
American support. The first Argentinian deaths in the British campaign to recapture the Falklands were only hours away.

On 30 April, Commander Chris Wreford-Brown DSO, of the
Valiant-class submarine HMS *Conqueror*, had found the veteran
Argentinian cruiser *General Belgrano*, escorted by the Type-42
destroyers *Piedra Buena* and *Hipolito Bouchard*. For the next two days
the submarine shadowed the Argentine task group as the British
commander waited for a change in the rules of engagement that
would allow him to attack. This came on 2 May, when it was decided
that any Argentine ship outside the Argentine twelve-mile coastal
limit was subject to attack. Wreford-Brown manoeuvred the *Conqueror* into an ideal attack position, 1400 metres from his target, and
fired a spread of three Mark 8 torpedoes.

The first torpedo struck the bows of the Argentine cruiser, blowing
them off and causing severe, but not crippling, structural damage
to the ship. The second hit about two-thirds of the way down the
vessel, penetrating the armour plating and detonating under a crew
messing area known as 'the Soda Fountain'. Almost immediately,
the *Belgrano* began to flood and the order was given to abandon
ship. In total 321 men were killed, the majority by blast and fire in
the Soda Fountain.

The *Belgrano* was not in the total exclusion zone* when it was
sunk, but in fact that area no longer applied following the changes
to the rules of engagement. It would be foolish to notify an enemy
of one's rules of engagement in a real shooting war (which is what
the Falklands conflict had become), and the subsequent parliamen-
tary and press campaign against the '*Belgrano* cover-up' was naive
in the extreme, when not politically motivated. Nevertheless, the
loss of this major naval unit prompted the pig-headed Argentine
regime into continuing a war that they could not realistically expect
to win.

---

* The British government had announced a 200-mile ring around the Falklands
within which it considered any Argentine ship to be a legitimate target.

The reaction by the men of 3 Para to the news of the *Belgrano*'s sinking was considerably less marked than that when the Type-22 frigate HMS *Sheffield* was sunk a day later by an Argentinian Exocet missile. Morale plummeted that night from an all-time high to a trough of depression. The news also served to signal that the waiting period for the men was over: it now seemed clear that they would be going to war. By the end of the first week of May, the *Canberra* was steaming south through the 'roaring forties', and the time for sunbathing on deck was over. Blue movies were banned, except in the officers' mess, partly in punishment for the theft from P&O's Atlantic restaurant of forty-five salt cellars and 1100 spoons. By the night of the tenth, the ship was 1000 miles north of Tristan da Cunha, zig-zagging through the night to shake off any pursuing enemy submarines. Arctic warfare clothing had been issued to the men, despite the misgivings of some that it made them look like 'hats'. It consisted of a long, quilted smock, padded hat, trousers and gloves. The Paras added it to their normal uniform of DPM camouflage trousers, Para smocks, puttees, and the hated DMS boots. They started to prepare their equipment for the landing which everybody now expected would take place from the second week of May onwards. The weather was colder each day, and the sea rougher, as the *Canberra* sailed along in company with the assault landing-ship HMS *Intrepid*, the aircraft-carrier HMS *Hermes*, a number of frigates and Royal Fleet Auxiliary vessels, and the North Sea ferry MV *Norland*, carrying members of 2 Para and 40 Commando.

Each day on the *Canberra*, the men of 3 Para swapped the rumours which had become their unofficial way of communicating news, and it was only on 14 May, three days away from the Falklands, that they received firm information about when they would go ashore. Lieutenant Colonel Hew Pike passed the orders down to his men through their company and platoon commanders that the battalion was to land on East Falkland, at a beach called Sandy Bay near the tiny settlement of Port San Carlos.

Hew Pike's 'O' Group was a straightforward affair. Intelligence reports suggested that there were 11,000 Argentinian troops on the island, a small number of whom were situated around San Carlos settlement and on the high ground of Fanning Head which overlooked it. 3 Para's strength stood at 671 all ranks, including forty men from 9 (Parachute) Squadron, Royal Engineers. The overall mission of the unit was to secure Port San Carlos settlement, to establish a defensive position and then to carry out a programme of offensive patrolling. B Company was to spearhead the attack on Green Beach and secure the beach-head, before A, C and D Companies came ashore in four landing craft. A Company was to move through B, while C was to occupy the high ground of Windy Gap and Settlement Rocks. The radio codes of 'Indian Hemp', 'Lost Sheep', 'Dry Bone' and 'Silver Fox' meant, respectively, that the battalion was ashore, Port San Carlos was secure, and Settlement Rocks and Windy Gap had been taken. It was a simple plan that depended heavily for its success on the accuracy of intelligence reports that Port San Carlos was undefended. If the battalion was to get ashore unscathed and intact, it had to get off their landing craft, across the shingle and into cover before any enemy present had the opportunity to hit them.

On 18 May, the ship entered the total exclusion zone. The islands were just 280 miles away. GPMGs were mounted on the decks as protection against air attacks. Sergeant Des Fuller from B Company remembered standing at the rail of the *Canberra* on the night of 19–20 May:

> I was talking to an SAS man called Jimmy Davies, whose brother George had served in the Juniors with me. We were standing at the rail of the *Canberra*, and the Sea King helicopter had just gone down with all those twenty blokes from 22 on board.* We were just standing there, looking out at the sea, at all the waves, thinking we really were going to war.[32]

By 20 May, the battalion was preparing to 'cross-deck' to HMS *Intrepid* for the landing at San Carlos. Various scenarios other than

---

* In a tragic accident, a helicopter containing members of D Squadron, 22 SAS, crashed after ingesting an albatross into its engine. Eighteen members of the regiment and two attached personnel were killed, the greatest single loss the SAS had suffered since the Second World War. One of the survivors has recalled that as the helicopter was sinking into the icy waters, dragging him with it by a strap caught round his ankle, he was cut free by an equally trapped comrade who knowingly gave up his own life to save his friend.

an amphibious assault had been mooted for consideration, including such ludicrous ideas as a heliborne assault by a composite unit of SAS men and Paras on Port Stanley, as well as a parachute drop over the islands. Predictably, there was some 'airborne' posturing from the Green-Eyed Boys who complained amongst themselves that they weren't parachuting onto the islands. But as all of them knew, and would secretly have admitted, it would have been absolute insanity for the troops to be landed on the Falklands in any other way than by sea. Chris Phelan recalls:

> We cross-decked from the *Canberra*, and got on the old ship there, the *Intrepid*. That was horrendous . . . It was amazing how these people live, hats off to them, they were sleeping at battle stations so we could be in their bunks. Very frightening, I could never do that, and they locked us in . . . 'Why are you doing this?' 'Just in case we get hit, and this place floods, and the rest doesn't . . .' That was frightening, 'cos it was having, sort of, your bollocks in somebody else's hands.[33]

Preparations had been going on up until the last moment. One of the many tactical problems facing 3 Para was knowing what to do if their reconnaissance parties came across Argentinian sentries on the beach. It was therefore decided to spend time devising the quickest ways of killing sentries silently. Contrary to popular belief, the Parachute Regiment is not now, and wasn't then, composed of men excelling in unarmed combat. They were simply fit, well-trained infantry soldiers who could jump out of aeroplanes and operate with tactical proficiency in the field. The process of obtaining a set of parachute wings, passing P-Company and spending time in an operational battalion did not, much to the regret of some of the men, imbue them with Ninja-like qualities, whatever their letters home or pub exploits might have pretended to the contrary. So WO2 Sammy Dougherty and Sergeant Chris Phelan were looking at ways of 'malleting' the enemy:

> [Major] Collett had got teams of guys, 'cos we had been briefed that there were sentries where we were landing, at San Carlos, it was going to be occupied, and we were going to be brought on by the SBS, flashlights and all this, in the

dark, and at first light we were going to move forward and
take out the sentries. We went downstairs to practise with
the PT buster, Ray Butters, and we made garrottes – like
wire things. But the solution in the end was you're not going
to get that close to put this round his neck, so in the end,
what are you going to do? Right, we're going to use a five-
pound lump hammer. If I've got a five-pound lump hammer,
and I hit him somewhere on the head, he's out. If you get
close enough, and make that last dash . . . SPLOT! . . . He's
gone. But all sorts of ideas were coming out – talk about
budding SAS – crossbows and shit. I mean, where were we
going to get crossbows?[34]

Next, they needed something to practise on. The ever-obliging
P&O staff supplied them with a number of large watermelons from
the galleys, so for a few hours Dougherty, Phelan and some men
from A Company practised creeping up on the large, green fruit and,
with a swing of their hammers, pulping them beyond recognition.[35]

In the real world, the tension between Mike Argue and John
Weeks in B Company had not been resolved during the voyage.
Weeks, a physically tough and intelligent Londoner who had served
in the battalion since the mid-1960s, was of the opinion that his
company commander 'knew fuck-all about tactics',[36] and he took it
upon himself to attempt to give him some instruction. Not unnaturally, this caused even more bad feeling between them.

As the landing approached, Weeks had a conversation with Ian
McKay, the young and enthusiastic sergeant from 4 Platoon, who
confided to his sergeant major that he did not think he would be
coming back from the campaign. There was little Weeks could do
or say. The feeling among the majority of the men, and certainly
the Green-Eyed Boys, was that they wanted to get ashore, off the
boat, and into contact with the Argentinians. The period of time
spent on the *Canberra* was the longest and most uncertain period of
waiting any of them had spent in their lives. Coupled with that,
they felt a deep desire to be back on dry land, and out of the cramped
confines of the ship. The lead-up to war was exacerbated by their
ignorance of what they were going to face once ashore: whether
the enemy would turn and run, whether he would fight, or whether

he would simply surrender. In short, it was the uncertainty and lack of intelligence that got to them.

On the night of the twenty-first, B Company of 3 Para filed into the galley area of HMS *Intrepid*, where Company Sergeant Major John Weeks forced them all forward, sweating and staggering under the weight of their bergens and webbing, as they filed down to embark on the landing craft. Each man was given two hand-grenades by Weeks, and then another two mortar bombs which they were to deposit on the beach once they had landed. The weight the men were carrying was awesome. Each had his own personal weapon, anything up to a thousand rounds of ammunition, hand-grenades, mortar bombs, clothing, food, radio batteries, sleeping-bag, water, rations, medical supplies, entrenching tools, machine-gun tripods, ponchos and anti-tank rounds. Sergeant Des Fuller, attached to B Company, was carrying his SMG with a second maga-zine taped onto the first one for quick reloading, and another fifteen stowed around his body, totalling nearly 500 rounds of 9mm ammu-nition. Lance Corporal Vince Bramley, in charge of one of B Com-pany's SF GPMG teams, was carrying 1100 rounds for his SLR and the team gun, giving him a total weight of some sixty-five pounds of ammunition alone.

From the *Intrepid*, the men were embarked into more landing craft at the back of the ship, and set off through San Carlos Water towards Sandy Bay, while over to their left on Fanning Head, a firefight was in progress as the SBS attacked the Argentinian obser-vation post set up there. The effect was completed by the naval gunfire support which was being called in to support the attack. Chris Phelan:

> We got into the bloody landing craft, and it's dark, and the old hairs were sticking up on the back of the neck. The fear was there, but still not real, 'cos you're still in that time-warp; there's nothing that's actually happened yet, apart from the helicopter going down with the SAS blokes on it. It's coming light, that's the big thing, it's light, and it was daylight, and it was the old white-stick job,* it was too deep,

* A Marine coxswain used a white pole to test the depth of water and the slope of the beach. Phelan famously commented: 'Fuck, he's blind. That's all we need!'

and what they did, they got this big landing craft we were in, and they got a smaller one, and we got on that, and walked along the edge, jumped off into the water, about that deep. FUCKING FREEZING![37]

It was 6 a.m. Falklands time, and 11 a.m. Zulu time* on 21 May. The Green-Eyed Boys were ashore.

---

* Greenwich Mean Time: GMT is used in all military operations to avoid confusion.

CHAPTER FIVE

The Retreat from Stalingrad

When first under fire an' you're wishful to duck
Don't look nor take 'eed at the man that is struck.
Be thankful you're living, and trust to your luck
And march to your front like a soldier.

KIPLING, 'The Young British Soldier'

The landing of 3 Commando Brigade on East Falkland on 20 May 1982 was certainly the most complex and dangerous amphibious operation attempted by Britain's armed forces since the Second World War. For a period of several hours, virtually all of 3 Commando Brigade and many of the naval combat units of the Task Force were squeezed into a comparatively small area of water, at the mercy of Argentine air assets and artillery. Even determined small-arms fire from a well-trained infantry force could have caused innumerable casualties amongst the landing force: enough, perhaps, in these days of media-sensitive politics, to have halted the operation in its tracks. But there was no immediate opposition. A small Argentine force in the area, Equipo de Combate Aguila, under the command of Lieutenant Carlos Esteban, reported the landing and called for air attack, but none was to materialise for several hours, by which time the beach-head was firmly established.

But although there was no opposition to the landings at first, they did not go entirely smoothly. The confined area of Falkland Sound and the limited amount of shipping available meant that the landing force would have to go ashore in two waves, dangerously increasing the exposure of both men and ships to enemy air attack. The first wave, which consisted of Lieutenant Colonel 'H' Jones's 2 Para from the car-ferry *Norland* and 40 Commando RM from the *Fearless*, was

timed to arrive on the beaches at 3.40 a.m. local time, leaving plenty
of darkness for the landing craft to return and pick up the second
wave, including 3 Para, and supposedly allowing for the delays inevitable in such a complicated operation. In fact, the unfamiliarity of
the troops with their task, together with an injury to a member of
2 Para who had fallen whilst climbing into a landing craft, imposed
a much longer delay. According to David Collett of A Company, the
whole landing operation was conducted as if it were an exercise,
with little notion that lives, and even the success of national policy,
were at stake:

> One of the 2 Para guys fell over and broke his leg, or some-
> thing, and that delayed the whole landing . . . When you
> compare that with the D-Day landings where if a guy broke
> his back they just left him there, you know, it was a bit
> 'peacetime-ish'. It actually jeopardised the whole thing . . .
> we actually landed in daylight. There was a real air of
> unreality and it was very worrying because we were stuck
> on board ship in daylight, in the sound, and we should have
> been off. Fortunately [the Argentinians] didn't react, they
> reacted after we had got on to land, but it could have been
> nasty, potentially.[1]

3 Para was fortunate in that it had, according to Collett, 'almost
perfect intelligence' about the Port San Carlos settlement as a result
of Major Southby-Tailyour's yachting research. Additionally, Mrs
Carol Miller, the wife of the settlement manager,* was in England
and had been able to update the Task Force's information with a
reasonable degree of certainty. As Collett and his men carefully
moved into the settlement he was met by the manager, who was
surprised to be greeted by name. 'I said, "Hello, Mr Miller, how are
you?" when he appeared,' remembers Collett. The Falkland Islands
Company official had interesting news for the Paras: there were
Argentine soldiers nearby.

As soon as Lieutenant Esteban had reported that the British were
ashore, he gathered his force of forty-two men together and began

---

* Much of the Falklands is owned by the Falkland Islands Company, effectively
an absentee landlord with an elaborate system of managers and factors in place to
mind its property.

to withdraw to the east, accompanied by 'catcalls and rude signs'[2] from the locals. His intention was, he claimed in his after-action report, to avoid fighting near the civilians, but his action also allowed him to avoid engaging 3 Para, as well as depriving the specially-formed A Company teams of the opportunity to test their lump hammers.

As the Argentinian unit moved out they were able for the first time to engage the British forces, who were by now streaming ashore. David Collett, himself a former helicopter pilot, remembers:

> We went through B Company after landing, and as Miller told us there were Argentinians in the village, we got quite a move on, and started racing towards them. But because of the whole delay the helicopter programme hadn't been changed. So a Sea King with an underslung load, plus two Gazelle helicopters, then flew over us. I was trying – comms were quite difficult – trying to get in touch with battalion headquarters to get them to tell brigade to stop the air plan which was going ahead as normal. And they flew in to San Carlos and fortunately the Sea King pilot was quite switched on, and saw what was going on, and dumped his load and fucked off. But the two Gazelles decided that, having some SNEB rockets,* they'd try and do some damage, and one of them was shot down in San Carlos Water.[3]

The Gazelle had been sprayed with small-arms fire which put the engine out of action almost immediately. The pilot, Sergeant Andy Evans, was hit in the abdomen by a rifle bullet, but despite his wound he managed to put the helicopter down on the water reasonably softly. Evans and his crewman, Sergeant Eddie Candlish, both managed to extricate themselves from the wreck of the helicopter as it sank, but Evans was severely injured. Candlish later described this moment:

> In the next instant Andy bobbed to the surface, conscious but helpless. 'Help me, Eddy. I'm badly hurt, mate.' It

---

* Helicopter-mounted high-explosive rocket system, of moderate effectiveness against armoured and unarmoured vehicles.

seemed like an eternity since we had been shot at but was probably no more than two minutes.

I pulled Andy to me and inflated his lifejacket, at the same time becoming aware of splashes in the water around me. The sudden realisation; we're being shot at . . . [4]

As the two men struggled in the icy water, members of Esteban's detachment opened fire, fortunately without hitting them. International law regards shooting at aircrew escaping from their craft as an offence. Lieutenant Esteban accounted for his men's action by claiming: 'The men who were firing were some distance away and did not hear my order. You must understand that they were only conscripts with forty-five days' service and knew nothing of the Geneva Convention.'[5] This may explain the incident, but does not excuse it.

Collett and his men

were taken to see the pilot [Andy Evans had been rescued from the water by some villagers] who died – we got our medic to work on him but he died – and the aircrewman was a gibbering wreck. They were saying that he'd been shot in the water . . . But it transpired later that it could have been horrendous because that evening or the next morning, we picked out of the water the crewman's flight-plan – his kneepad – and on it, it had the layout of all the ships and all the information you would have needed.[6]

This first helicopter disaster was rapidly followed by another. The second Gazelle was engaged by Esteban's group at very close range and also crashed, killing both crewmen, Lieutenant Ken Francis and Lance Corporal Brett Giffin, immediately. Amazingly, they were shortly afterwards followed by a third Gazelle which was also engaged by the Argentines and was hit by ten rounds; fortunately the pilot managed to get it away.

The loss of the two helicopters – and three of the four men flying them – was a tragic illustration of the failure of some elements of the Task Force to grasp that there really was a war going on, and that basic errors could lead to men dying. The helicopters were shot down because a gamble was taken – that they would be able to defend themselves over ground not yet cleared by the infantry, because the troop landings were held up. In fact a GPMG and a few rockets were clearly insufficient for anything other than covering a rapid withdrawal by a helicopter: the Gazelles certainly lacked the firepower to engage ground troops on anything approaching equal terms.

After their success against the helicopters, Esteban's team departed into the hinterland, moving cross-country in the direction of Douglas settlement, where they arrived four days later, none the worse for their experiences. Neither they, nor the detachment of the unit that had been engaged by the SBS and naval gunfire at Fanning Head, stayed around to direct air attacks onto the landing area.

Following the initial excitement of coming ashore, the next phase for 3 Para was to occupy the positions that had been allocated to them at the Brigade 'O' Group. At that time, British military doctrine demanded that when giving orders for a defensive position, a commander should think two levels of command down, in effect meaning that a brigade commander should be allocating positions to companies, a battalion commander allocating positions to platoons and so on. In consequence, the officers of 3 Para had a very clear picture of where they were to go in the aftermath of the landing. As the Toms began to dig in around the edge of the village, at Windy Gap and on the Settlement Rocks, it seemed, in the words of the brigade commander, 'inconceivable to anyone in 3 Commando Brigade that the Argentines would not mount at least some kind of harassing attack'.[7]

Giles Orpen-Smellie, 3 Para's intelligence officer, was chatting to a reporter who had attached himself to the battalion for the landing. He echoed the brigadier's view: 'Our big fear tonight is infiltration and counter-attack. If we were them, we'd hit us very hard about now.'[8]

But despite their concerns, and in the face of all military common sense, there was no ground response from the Argentines. There was, however, an aggressive aerial riposte from Argentine aircraft based in the islands and on the mainland. Chris Phelan recalls: 'At San Carlos we had the air coming in and that's when I thought, "Fucking hell!" ... looking back to the bay where the ships were docked, it looked like television.'[9]

Tony Mason, still recovering from the icy water at the landing, watched the air attacks in amazement:

> Almost immediately they started the air assaults, and that is something to see: they were incredibly brave. They took off from Commodoro Rivadavia, primarily, which gave them a very short time 'on target' over Ajax Bay or over San Carlos, and they used to come in between Ajax and San Carlos and loop round so they could come in down the valley line. So you felt like you could reach out and touch them, they were that close: you could see the pilot; you could see everything. We shot at them initially but then we said, 'It's a waste of ammunition,' 'cause they were moving so quickly . . .
>
> They were coming down the valley line and they were terribly close, and one of my guys did fire a Milan at one and the CO went *apeshit*, he said: 'What the fuck are you doing?' Mind you, it would have been great if it had hit, he would have been a hero. But the CO just looked at me and said: 'Did you give orders for that?' and I said, 'I might have suggested it, sir, but I certainly didn't give any orders,' and he just looked at me and said, 'Fucking idiot!' But that was Pike's style, he was good, he was a good guy.[10]

Having occupied their position, in a 'horseshoe shape' at the top of the valley above the Port San Carlos settlement, the next task was to secure the general area. The Toms had started to dig into the peaty soil as soon as they arrived, providing themselves with cover from the regular air attacks and stray bullets, shells and anti-aircraft missiles that fell amongst them as they worked. Also required was a patrol programme, with each company taking responsibility for an area to be regularly checked and cleared by small groups, normally of section strength, to ensure that no Argentinians were able to close in to the Paras' positions.

Although finding the manpower for patrolling is a company commander's responsibility, the co-ordination of patrolling is a duty of the battalion's operations staff, and particularly the operations officer, in this case Captain Robertson. Robertson, who was young and inexperienced, did not produce an adequate patrol programme, and neither did he 'deconflict' those patrols that did go out. David

Collett, the A Company commander, was worried by this at the time:

> We never, ever cleared the high ground above us. It was something I was never happy with, not that it affected me, but this area was never cleared and that is, I think, where the OP* was ... This shows the lack of experience on the ops side: we didn't have a battalion patrol programme, it was all done at company level. Poor old Peter Osborne:† I was given a task to send out a patrol and he went out on the patrol with, I think, fifteen guys. It was a clearing patrol because we were told the Argentinians were still in the area. The next morning, he gave me a contact report, seeing enemy movement; and there was a patrol from C Company out as well, doing another 'square', and they also confirmed this report, confirming the grid reference he'd given. But what had happened was he'd actually given his own grid reference – he'd seen these guys but given his own grid reference. It's easy enough to do. But of course, that was confirmed: two sightings of the same patrol, so immediately the guns were brought to bear, and C Company's machine-guns were brought to bear and stonked them [Peter Osborne's patrol] pretty heavily.[11]

The 'blue on blue'‡ contact lasted for sixty-two minutes[12] before C Company commander Martin Osborne realised what was happening and reported it to battalion headquarters. By then, artillery had joined in with the normal platoon weapons and eight men had been wounded, several of them seriously. The incident was halted when Colonel Pike flew up to the site in a Sea King – which then crashed. In fact the pilot had landed too hard, damaging the undercarriage, and nobody was hurt, although another helicopter was required to evacuate the friendly-fire casualties. The entire incident could have been a disaster for 3 Para, and it was fortunate that

---

* Observation post. It is likely that the Argentines maintained observation on the beach-head throughout the conflict.

† Lieutenant Peter Osborne, a platoon commander in A Company.

‡ Friendly forces are marked on military maps in blue. Consequently a 'blue on blue' is when a friendly unit is accidentally attacked by another.

nobody – including the CO and the medical officer on the helicopter – was killed.

As far as the battalion headquarters was concerned, it was recognised that in a real, shooting war, an experienced officer was needed to run the 'Ops Room', and the Support Company OC, Peter Dennison, was drafted in until Robertson had found his feet. Thereafter, company patrolling at least was co-ordinated and deconflicted at battalion level.

Having landed his brigade and established his own headquarters ashore at San Carlos settlement, and in the absence of any response from Argentine land forces, Brigadier Thompson's next requirement was to take the battle to the enemy. The first brigade operation to be mooted was a 'raid' by 'H' Jones's 2 Para against Goose Green, the Falkland Islands' second-largest settlement and now home to an Argentine airbase and military garrison, under the designation 'Task Force Mercedes'.* The advantage of attacking Goose Green was that it was close to the beach-head at San Carlos, and could be reached on foot – the marching distance was about twenty-five kilometres from Sussex Mountain, where Jones's men were established. As the rest of the brigade continued their cautious patrolling around the beach-head, Thompson warned Jones on 23 May that he was to prepare for the Goose Green raid.

Jones's original plan for attacking Goose Green was based on knowledge acquired by D Squadron of 22 SAS, who had launched a diversionary raid on the night of the landings. Having manpacked Milan, GPMGs and Stingers from an HLS (helicopter landing site) to the north of Darwin, the SAS troops launched a 'firepower demonstration' against what they supposed to be the Argentine positions. Accounts of the impact of this raid differ, with British sources – presumably leaked from Sigint – claiming that the Argentines had reported being attacked in battalion strength, whilst Argentinians remember being unimpressed by the incident; in any case, nobody

---

* A raid appears to be a peculiarly Royal Marines – or at least commando – concept, probably based on their World War II experience. In reality, in modern warfare it seems strangely pointless and wasteful in both men and resources, unless there is a compelling reason to conduct such an operation. At Goose Green, this might have been the destruction of the air capability, yet this idea does not feature in any of the published accounts.

was injured on either side and the SAS unit trooped back to where the beach-head was being established. Jones envisaged helicoptering one of his companies forward to seize a position for his artillery support (provided by a battery from 29 Commando Regiment RA) at Camilla Creek House and then bringing the rest of the battalion forward for the raid the following night.

As it happened, the weather deteriorated to the extent that the artillery could not be moved forward, and the attack was called off, causing the impetuous Jones to complain that he had 'waited twenty years for this opportunity, and now some fucking Marine's cancelled it'.[13] Instead, as the container ship *Atlantic Conveyor* approached the islands, Thompson and his staff began work on a plan to move the brigade forward towards Port Stanley using the much-needed helicopter support that was aboard, in the shape of four Chinooks and six Wessexes. During the evening of 25 May, as Thompson and his key staff officers held their regular conference, a message arrived that the *Atlantic Conveyor* had been hit by an Argentine Exocet missile and sunk. Along with the twelve men of the Merchant Navy, Royal Navy and Royal Fleet Auxiliary who died, three Chinooks, all six Wessexes and a naval Lynx helicopter were destroyed. Thompson later recorded:

> I ordered a full staff conference for the following day to include the CO of 22 SAS, the commander of 846 Squadron, Commander Thornewill and Major Minords from Clapp's staff. They were to be tasked with investigating what, if anything, could be done to salvage the wreck of the plan using the existing helicopter and landing-craft assets. As the 'R' Group dispersed somebody said, 'We'll have to bloody well walk.'[14]

In the event, that was precisely what they did.

The loss of the *Atlantic Conveyor* helicopters put Thompson in a difficult position as brigade commander. His plan had been to 'invest' the defences of Stanley using the bulk of his brigade in a series of swift night moves executed by helicopter, but this was no longer feasible. As a result of the sinking, there was only sufficient helicopter capacity to move a company or so each night, with supporting arms, to the area that had been selected. This would inevitably have left any troops thus moved extremely vulnerable to counter-attack by Argentine forces while the remainder of the brigade walked out to join them.* Consequently, Thompson decided that his best option was to wait for the arrival of 5 Infantry Brigade, commanded by Brigadier Tony Wilson, and the divisional headquarters commanded by Major General Jeremy Moore.

In London, amongst Mrs Thatcher's war cabinet and at HQ Cincfleet in Northwood, there was a different set of priorities. The politicians were concerned that the campaign to recapture the islands was losing momentum. Al Haig, the US Secretary of State, was persisting in his efforts to broker a settlement that would have precluded a return to full British sovereignty in the islands, even though the attitude of the US government was one of full support for the British efforts. By the time the *Atlantic Conveyor* was destroyed, the Argentine air offensive against the Task Force had succeeded in damaging or destroying a number of key ships that were supporting and supplying the beach-head, but there was still no offensive action on the ground. On 26 May, Thompson was summoned to the satellite communications (Satcom) terminal at Ajax Bay and given instructions direct from Northwood: he was to get moving without delay.

The obvious solution to the problem of achieving a quick military success was to resurrect the scheme to attack Goose Green and Darwin, which were within an easy night's march of the beach-head. 2 Para, on their Sussex Mountain position, were still the closest major unit to the enemy, and Jones was once again briefed to go. As night fell on the twenty-sixth, Jones led his men off to a lie-up at Camilla Creek House, a short distance from Darwin.

At the same time that Jones was alerted to attack Goose Green, the commanding officers of 45 Commando and 3 Para were also receiving their marching orders. 45 Commando were to make their way to Douglas settlement on foot and 3 Para were to head for Teal Inlet, approximately halfway to Port Stanley. The approach adopted

---

* In fact the Argentine ground forces did not execute any significant counter-moves during the whole campaign: a strong reflection of their almost unbelievable tactical incompetence at company level and above.

by the two battalions for their marches was entirely different. The Marines, veterans of many Arctic winters as part of NATO's defences in northern Norway, opted to 'yomp', carrying all their personal gear with them in bergens. By contrast 3 Para decided that they would 'tab' in 'light order', with weapons and webbing, relying on the tenuous logistic support system to bring their bergens to them at prearranged points. David Collett remembers:

> We saw the Marines going off with their kitchen sink, so we just worked a system of light order and hopefully every two days the bergens would come forward to give us doss-bags. So we just carried our fighting order and slept huddled up.[15]

The two units set off on the morning of 27 May, both adopting long, semi-tactical, snake formations. Des Fuller recalls his reaction when the orders were passed around:

> We looked at the map: sixty miles. No big deal over a few days, but being on the top of the mountains it was rather firmer, and once you got down there every other step was a pothole or a peat bog. God, it was horrendous! The worst thing was that the first night, the bloody OC's signaller went and twisted his stuffin' ankle; course Argue knew I was an ex-signaller and I ended up with the radio. I was really chuffed, I'm sure he [the signaller] faked it![16]

While the main body of the battalion were making their way forward, D Company, the specialist patrolling unit, had been getting to work. According to Lee Fisher:

> We did all the recces around the hills, and that was for a few days. We were told there were still some enemy wandering around so keep an eye out, and we were, like, forward recce for the battalion lines ... It was the strange terrain that threw us, I remember that: looking at nothing for hours, then days. We did an OP on this inlet, to our left, and on the other mount there was another patrol – we'd tabbed down there – and what happened then, there were these sea-eagles, and it was freaky 'cause you didn't see them during the day but at night there was this WHOOOSH! and a big shadow above you, about four foot away, and you

thought, 'What the fuck's that?' And we were sat there one day, looking down at the sea, and we saw the hospital ship coming in. And I turned round and there were these two Skyhawks coming in, and I thought, 'I'll have a pop at these!' And then I thought, 'No, they might come back and they might have bombs!' So I'm sitting there, and it's like they'd seen the *Uganda* over the hill and they both turned and dived, and I thought, 'The bastards! They're not going to take out the hospital ship! That's not allowed!' but then they both turned and went off.[17]

In fact, the tab to Teal Inlet was not the most disciplined event. B Company took the lead, with Mike Argue, the tightly-wound long-distance runner, insisting on his platoon commanders setting a cracking pace. Des Fuller, carrying Argue's radio, recalls:

I think we did point* the whole length of that tab. I think Jon Shaw was doing most of the navigating – you couldn't trust Mark Cox to do it – and maybe Andy Bickerdike did some. He [Shaw] actually led the whole battalion, so Mike Argue was going up to him and we were going up the mountain, down the fucking mountain. I remember we were stopping – it's a totally featureless place during the day and at night it's even worse – and the reference point that Jon Shaw was looking for was a T-junction on a barbed wire fence which, believe it or not, was actually marked on the map. And there was about six or seven of us – the CO came up as well – and the whole battalion was told to go to ground and rest for five minutes, and for the next half hour, I was just like a dog being led by a fucking lead, but going up and down, looking for this barbed-wire fence. It seemed ridiculous at the time, and I don't even know if they ever found it, 'cause I know Mike Argue and I then trundled off back to find the company, and we carried on for another couple of hours and then, to my total amazement we were told to brew up – in the dark! I was fortunate because through doing skiing and climbing I had gaiters with me and

---

* i.e. Acted as the lead unit.

my Helly Hansen fleecy top underneath my smock, so I was
fairly warm and my feet were fairly dry through my gaiters.
And he just said, 'Brew up,' so wherever you looked in this
little fucking valley thing, there were little hexi burners all
over the place, but oh it was great, just to have this heat
coming off onto your face.[18]

In David Collett's opinion:

The move from San Carlos to Teal Inlet was a bit chaotic, to
say the least. It was a bloody great free-for-all. A Company
ended up stopping and going into a house and sleeping for
the night . . . The whole thing was chaotic, it was crazy,
there were casualties going down, people going over . . . It
was a rush to nowhere. When we rejoined the battalion
the next morning, they were in absolute shit order, to be
honest.[19]

Lee Fisher and his patrol supposedly formed part of the battalion's
recce screen:

At times we were patrolling out in front but at other times
we were almost running to keep up. We never actually saw
the enemy, but we saw where they'd been . . . We went up
this hill and they had a tent up, and the strangest things:
they had all this hideous food in tins . . . it just looked hor-
rible, like pasta and stuff, and we thought, 'If they're eating
this, we've won.' But there was actually a little remote-
control electric car as well – and it was just rocks and crag,
there was nowhere flat to run it – and we thought, 'What
the fucking hell's this doing here?' . . . It was a clear day and
you could see for miles, but there was nobody about, just
their kit.

   I remember the night bits most because there's me, 'Trus'*
and a couple of others: our heroes used to be the German
Paras in the war and this was like the retreat from Stalingrad
that we were on; we weren't actually in the Falklands, we
were in the Soviet Union as part of the Sixth Panzer Army,

---

* Lance Corporal Trussler.

with guns on our shoulders and we were having a hell of a
time. It was like, 'Shut up and behave, you two!' Trying to
sing German songs as we marched, 'cause a lot of the time
we were just tabbing, we weren't soldiering, it was just:
'GO!' But me and Trus, we were having a great time in von
Paulus's army with the T-34s on our tail.[20]

As 3 Para stomped through the night towards Teal, their colleagues and rivals in 2 Para began their epic assault on the twin
settlements of Darwin and Goose Green. Although a detailed
account of that battle is outside the scope of this work, nevertheless
an outline of what happened is worth considering.

After lying up for most of 27 May around Camilla Creek House,
Lieutenant Colonel 'H' Jones gave his orders for the attack during
the afternoon. Darwin and Goose Green are both on an isthmus
some five miles long and from one to two miles wide. This links
East Falkland with Lafonia, a boggy peninsula on the south-west of
the island. The isthmus itself has a 'spine' of low rolling hills along
it, many of which are covered by thick gorse, and the whole feature
is roughly oriented on the axis NNE–SSW. As far as 2 Para were
aware, from information culled from Sigint, from their own observation and from a briefing by the 22 SAS troop commander who had
led the diversionary attack on the settlement on the night of the
San Carlos landing, they believed themselves to be facing approximately a battalion of Argentines drawn from the 12th Regiment,
together with some air force personnel.

Jones's complex plan was to attack in 'Six phases: night then day,
silent then noisy, with the general aim of rolling up the enemy from
the north so that the troops in the settlements could be cleared by
daylight, ensuring the maximum safety for the civilians cooped up
in Goose Green.'[21] In support, 2 Para were to be able to call on three
105mm guns of 29 Commando Regiment and naval gunfire support
from HMS *Arrow*, together with limited Harrier close air support.
After he had given his detailed orders to the 'O' Group, many of
whom were apparently taken aback by the sheer mass of detail they
were expected to assimilate, Jones concluded his briefing with a
sentence that has become part of his personal legend: 'All previous
evidence suggests that if the enemy is hit hard he will crumble.'[22]

In fact there was no evidence at this time that the enemy would do anything of the sort: the only ground contacts had been a raid by the SAS against an Argentine airbase at Pebble Island, when the British special forces men were up against a gaggle of air force ground crew, the contacts with Esteban's detachment around Fanning Head and Port San Carlos on the night of the invasion, and one or two brushes with tiny reconnaissance teams. Darwin–Goose Green was to be the first serious ground combat, and it was to demonstrate that the British forces, although clearly superior to their enemy, could not afford to be complacent.

The first problem faced by 2 Para was Jones's plan, which was, quite simply, too complicated. It required company commanders, who in the prevailing conditions had enough difficulty working out their own locations, to keep abreast of the progress of the other companies so that they would know when to trigger particular phases of the operation. More importantly, it relied to a large extent on the enemy being where Jones *hoped* they would be, rather than where he *knew* them to be. In fact, Jones's plan was in tatters soon after the battalion crossed the start line: the company headquarters lost touch with each other and with their platoons almost immediately. As the companies worked their way down the isthmus, confusion prevailed and the battalion eventually became bogged down by stiff Argentine opposition well short of the objectives they had hoped to reach by daybreak.

The action fought by A Company of 2 Para at Darwin Hill, during which 'H' Jones was fatally wounded, has been discussed in great detail elsewhere.[23] It is sufficient to say that Jones died performing an act of enormous courage but one which also, perhaps, demonstrated his flawed judgement. Command was assumed by his 2ic, Major Chris Keeble, who was able to take a wider view of the battle than Jones had appeared to, and managed to reinject some momentum into the Paras' assault. By the time night fell, 2 Para had closed with Goose Green and Keeble was well on his way to persuading the Argentine garrison commander to surrender to avoid further bloodshed. The next morning, after the formality of a short parade, the Goose Green garrison surrendered. To the great surprise of the Paras, in addition to the infantry battalion (Regimiento de Infanteria 12 'General Arenales', minus one company but including a company from Regimiento de Infanteria 25) there were several hundred Argentine air force (FAA – Fuerzas Aereas Argentinos) ground personnel present, and over a thousand prisoners were eventually taken, in addition to the fifty or sixty who died. Eighteen members of 2 Para and two attached personnel died during the assault.

An incident occurred during the battle that was to have serious ramifications on later action in the Falklands, not least for the Argentines. 3 Para had arrived at Teal Inlet on the night of 28–29 May to find that the Argentine patrols who had been there had gone, taking the Falklanders' Land-Rovers with them. During the late morning of the twenty-ninth, as the garrison of Goose Green was being disarmed and searched by the victorious men of 2 Para, the commanding officer and RSM of 3 Para were making the rounds of their battalion, briefing the soldiers on what had happened. Lance Corporal Vince Bramley of Support Company recalls:

> The CO looked grim as he approached the six of us taking a tea-break.
>
> 'Listen in, lads,' said the RSM.
>
> We looked at him, wondering what was coming.
>
> 'During the march, 2 Para attacked Goose Green and Darwin settlements. After a long battle, the regiment liberated the settlement, with the loss of eighteen lives, including their CO, Colonel "H" Jones. Many have been wounded and a casualty list is being drawn up. They captured hundreds of Argies. The war is now a different concept, for the enemy are believed to have shot down members of 2 Para showing a white flag. More information will be given once known.'[24]

What had in fact happened was that a platoon commander from D Company, Lieutenant Jim Barry, had decided to try to persuade a small pocket of Argentine resistance to surrender and, after trying to obtain permission from his company commander – who was otherwise engaged – he went forward, holding his rifle in the air, to talk to the Argentine officer, Lieutenant Gomez Centurión. The Argentines, seeing Barry and his escort, Corporal Sullivan, had come forward supposedly thinking that the Paras wished to surrender to *them*. After a brief exchange between the Argentine officer, who spoke fluent English, and Barry, during which the position became clear, the Argentines gave Barry and Sullivan two minutes to return to their position. But as the two groups parted, a burst of fire from some distance away, probably from 2 Paras' Machine Gun Platoon, struck the Argentine party, wounding several of them. Fearing that they had been tricked, it appears that the Argentines made the highly questionable decision to open fire on Barry and Sullivan – who were clearly not connected with the incoming fire – and killed both. To watching British Paras, it appeared to be a gross act of Argentine treachery.

It was a tragic incident, but not entirely surprising in the 'fog of war'. Jim Barry's decision to attempt to negotiate a local Argentine surrender was naive, and probably reflected the unrealistic view that the Argentines would take any opportunity to surrender. Nevertheless, witnesses to the incident were incensed, and as word spread 2 Para demonstrated a certain reluctance to give quarter to Argentines attempting to surrender.

The full story of the death of Barry and Sullivan took some years to emerge, and it is hardly surprising that it caused enormous anger throughout the Task Force at the time. It contributed towards a widespread mistrust of the Argentines which did not dissipate until well after the final surrender had taken place.

3 Para did manage a small contact with the Argentines just outside Teal Inlet. David Collett recalls:

I spoke to the Marine patrol who had actually recced Teal Inlet, who told me that there were no Argentinians there: in fact there were a couple. And when we got to Teal Inlet, the old dear living there said: 'Ah, I saw your boys the other night,' and they'd been seen wandering about: very professional!

They'd been seen by the locals but I don't think they'd been seen by the Argentinians, and when we got there there was one left, who we caught. We had to negotiate with Mr Barton, the manager, to take this prisoner, he was worried that we'd shoot him. I had to ring up the manager's farm and say, 'Hand him over.' The manager wasn't a very co-operative guy, he didn't like us digging holes in his garden.[25]

Tony Mason also came across Mr Barton:

> We arrived at Teal Inlet and I remember this really obstreper-
> ous fucking plantation manager there. I'd have killed him if
> I'd been the CO . . . I thought, what the hell are we doing
> here? What's all this about? He was stopping us using the
> barns and things like that. We told him to fuck off.[26]

3 Para stayed at Teal for a little more than twenty-four hours
before embarking on the next stage of their march on the orders of
Brigadier Thompson, who made a flying visit to Hew Pike. The next
stage was a further forty-kilometre march (about twenty as the crow
flies) to Estancia House, from where they would be knocking on
the door of Port Stanley. There was not expected to be any Argentine
opposition to the move, but in fact a few stragglers were picked up
by David Collett's A Company, probably members of the group that
had been at Teal Inlet, and some demoralised Argentine Special
Forces gave themselves up after watching a large part of their patrol
being destroyed in a sharp firefight with the Marines' Mountain and
Arctic Warfare Cadre at Top Malo House.

  Conditions had not been easy since the landing, but now they
really began to deteriorate. Tony Mason again:

> After Teal, we're talking cold. That night approach to Estan-
> cia was fucking UNREAL! Oh shit! We got resupplied at Teal
> and the fucking bergens were weighing about 9000 pounds.
> But that fucking approach to Estancia was something else.
> We were lying up a lot of the time and it was COLD! We
> were in belt order with weapons – bergens to follow, which
> is no bad thing. But even belt order is heavy and uncomfort-
> able, and it was wet, and cold, and it chafed: it was miserable!
> Peter Dennison and I always had a joke about Mike Argue:
> we reckoned he couldn't read a map. Peter and I knew what
> blade of grass we were on, plus I carried a laser range-finder
> so I could intersect, resect, putz around and generally give
> you an eight-figure grid reference. But B Company, I mean
> Cox was in B Company and he must have been lethal with
> a map, and Shaw I suspect was lethal as well, though he
> had a brain and probably thought he could do it. But B

Company were fucking all over the place, and I mean, there was a fucking track! It was simple, there was a fucking track![27]

In fact, Mason was being unfair about B Company's navigation, because by now the battalion was being guided by Terry Peck, a forty-four-year-old member of the Falklands Legislative Council whose ardour to get his own back on the Argentinians was, by all accounts, to leave many younger, fitter men trailing in his wake. But others do remember the cold. As they approached Estancia, B Company were forced to lie up whilst the settlement was recced for signs of the enemy. Des Fuller and the other senior NCOs huddled together for warmth:

The 'Patrols' went out to do an OP on it and we just sat there. Myself, John Weeks, John Ross and Pete Gray; and, I must admit, I was close to tears I was so bloody cold. We sat there, we put a poncho round us and just huddled, shivering, and I was so pleased to get the order to move.[28]

John Weeks remembers:

We laid there for about two hours and when we went to move, we were all frozen, stuck to the fucking ground. Seriously, we were solid, stuck to the fucking ground. And we'd all grown moustaches, 'cause we didn't shave ... and the condensation used to freeze under this poncho. I don't know what made me jump up but something made me move, something moved that was out of the ordinary so I was up – and the poncho had frozen to my fucking moustache, so I ripped mine off and I ripped all the others off as well.[29]

'Estancia House' consisted of the house itself, a barn and a few more outbuildings nestling on the edge of the Port Salvador inlet, slightly to the west of the ring of mountains that surrounds Stanley, the capital of the Falklands. It does not, in itself, amount to much, but, crucially, it is less than fifteen miles from Stanley as the crow flies, and it represented the northerly of the two axes by which Stanley was invested. 3 Para was the first large infantry unit to reach this area, and the plan was for the battalion to occupy defensive lie-ups in the hills around the settlement. A little to their south-west,

D Squadron of 22 SAS under Major Cedric Delves had already taken control, without opposition, of the commanding heights of Mount Kent, at 1504 feet the tallest of the peaks surrounding Stanley, where they were joined by a company of 42 Commando and parts of Thompson's tactical headquarters.

Estancia proved to be an excellent location for 3 Para's echelon but the rifle companies and Battalion Tac* needed to push on to defensible locations. David Collett's A Company therefore moved through to Mount Estancia in the early hours of 1 June (followed by Pike's tactical headquarters shortly afterwards), Mike Argue's B Company went on to the southern shoulders of Mount Vernet and Martin Osborne's C Company occupied the main part of Mount Vernet.

By the time 3 Para reached Estancia, it had been established by brigade headquarters that the battalion's objective was to be Mount Longdon, a low feature which overlooked Stanley from the north-west. It would seem that Hew Pike had been briefed about this by Brigadier Thompson either at Teal Inlet during their meeting there or possibly by radio. But having learned what his overall objective was to be, Pike concluded that 3 Para might be able to capitalise on the momentum created by their rapid advance from Port San Carlos. On 3 June, after the battalion had rested for twenty-four hours in their positions around Estancia, he gave orders for them to 'advance to contact' against Longdon. In effect, this meant that the rifle companies would advance until they came upon the enemy positions, which they would then assault and capture as appropriate. The chief drawbacks to this scheme were that the battalion had had no opportunity to conduct detailed reconnaissance of the area, and 3 Commando Brigade had yet to bring up its supporting artillery, meaning that 3 Para would have to rely on their own meagre support weapons. It was a calculated gamble by Pike, about which some in the battalion were distinctly unhappy.

David Collett was nominated as

> lead company at the time. My reaction was nerves! I wasn't
> 100 per cent sure that we had orders to do it, and I went as

* The battalion tactical headquarters. Normally the CO with one or two officers and their signallers.

slowly as I could in the hope that it would be stopped. In the end he said, 'We will do it! Get on with it!' So ... er ... it was like advancing into the valley of death, with no fire support, no anything ... [30]

The incident is also described by a journalist who was present:

The Paras had already been briefed by Brigade that their first task before the advance on the capital would be to secure the imposing peak of Mount Longdon, a hard climb to their north-west [sic]. And, never ones to be slow off the mark, they promptly set out to take it.

Lead units were already over a low hill and out of sight of Estancia House when Brigadier Thompson choppered in with his bodyguard and sternly ordered Colonel Pike to join him in the command post for a serious heart to heart while the friends of Ailsa Heathman [a local resident] let their children play outside.

'What's up then?' asked a confused Tom. 'Go forward, come back, stand still. It's making my bastard head spin.'

'Fucking Marines can't keep up,' one of the officers grunted as he left the CP. 'And when they do, the shits will be given the first chance at Stanley while we piss around in the hills. We're out in front now. We should go and do it now.'

'It's off,' snarled Colonel Pike as he stormed out of the CP with the brigadier. 'As you were.'[31]

This incident has gone down in Green-Eyed legend as the time when the battalion was ordered to stop their advance because the Marines couldn't keep up. It is possible that, if successful, the 'advance to contact' would have unhinged the Argentine defensive system around Port Stanley and brought the fighting on East Falkland to a rapid end. But it could have ended in disaster. One story, probably greatly exaggerated, which was recounted to the authors by Sergeant Major Dougherty, suggested that a senior member of the battalion had ordered one of his subordinates to shoot Hew Pike should he attempt another such assault; the senior man in question would then have led 3 Para back to safety.[32]

The cancellation of the 'advance to contact' ensured the battalion's survival; the battle on Longdon a week later demonstrated that attacking in daylight, without the element of surprise and with no artillery support, would probably not have succeeded. In the meantime, as Major General Moore, the overall land forces commander, manoeuvred his two brigades into position to take Stanley, it was a time for preparation and planning.

In between the British-held mountains Estancia, Vernet and Kent and the Argentine positions on Longdon, Tumbledown, Two Sisters and so on, was an area physically occupied by neither side, yet covered by fire and observation by both the opposing armies: a real no-man's land. Before operations could be launched to dislodge the Argentines from their positions on the hilltops, the British units needed to be patrolling throughout this hazardous area. The reasons were twofold: in the first place, although there were insufficient British troops available to occupy the land, nevertheless it was essential that they dominate it in order to deter the Argentine forces from launching offensive and reconnaissance operations of their own; secondly, with the prospect of a series of major set-piece battles in the offing, it was crucial that all of the British commanders had as full a picture as possible of the enemy they were up against. In fact, the intelligence summaries distributed from both brigade headquarters to the fighting units were notoriously sketchy, reflecting the convoluted chains of command of certain front-line intelligence-collecting units, which prevented their material being widely disseminated (notably 22 SAS, whose detailed reports rarely reached battalion commanders).

One problem which now faced 3 Para in mounting patrols forward of Estancia was deconfliction with the various other reconnaissance units in the area. By the beginning of June, the great mass of the Argentinian occupation force was squeezed into a comparatively small area of East Falkland centred around Stanley and becoming more tightly drawn as the troops of 3 Commando Brigade and 5 Infantry Brigade arrived. David Collett:

> One of the problems with the Falklands was that there were too many guys out front wandering around recce-ing in an area that is normally reserved for battalion patrol units. You

had our own patrol company, you had the SAS, you had the Arctic Warfare Cadre, you had SBS patrolling a bit, you had neighbouring units also doing their bit. The companies had great difficulty doing their own recces. Everyone was trying to get in on the act. They should have said, 'Right, one lot will do it.' You had strategic troops operating alongside tactical troops, which is not the best way of doing it.[33]

Despite these problems, Major Pat Butler's D Company used the time at Estancia to push their patrols well forward into no-man's land and even on to Longdon itself. On the track which leads from Estancia to Stanley is a bridge over the Murrell River overlooked by some low bluffs; here, Matt Selfridge established a patrol base from which, by night, the four-man teams would deploy forward to penetrate and reconnoitre the Argentine position. Lee Fisher, who took part in these patrols, remembers:

We went up Longdon a few times, crawling around in the position. I remember in one place, it was like they'd built a brick wall . . . and 'cause we'd been up there a few times the CO wanted us to take a fighting patrol out there. I remember thinking that he kept saying, 'This is just an armed reconnaissance, I don't want you doing anything,' and I kept thinking, 'Is he saying that because he wants us to overrun the position 'cause he's bored?' . . . It was led by Ian Moore, and there was Sammy 'Dock' and a FOO* party, and we guided them up. And they were like mob-handed and there were a lot of guns in the patrol and bandoliers of ammo slung over shoulders jauntily. It was like a Saturday night downtown – 'Don't come near us!' Hew Pike kept saying, 'Don't do anything outrageous,' almost tongue in cheek, so I thought, 'Oh great, here we go!'[34]

By the time Pike sent the big fighting patrol up, the patrol base had been compromised and withdrawn after a sharp firefight. For Lee Fisher, it was his first direct experience of combat:

* Forward observation officer.

We'd been up Longdon and come back, and we'd come back to Murrell Bridge where there's a river with a proper bridge and this sheer rise, and we used to kip on the top of that because you get a good view, and obviously the bridge is somewhere that bad soldiers would use. So we would keep an eye on it to see if there were any crap soldiers about . . . and one of the blokes is on stag and he just sort of came round and whispered to us, 'There's someone there, we need to lay an ambush.' I remember it was the first time in my army career I ever took my boots off in a night lie-up. My feet were so cold and wet that they were like on fire. Some of the blokes had started going down with trench foot and they were getting casevacced out, and I was thinking, 'There's no fucking way I'm going home with bad feet! In a body-bag with a medal on but not, "Oh, my feet hurt, Sergeant Major!" ' Although I'd had it before in training in Wales and I know it hurts. But I thought, 'I don't care, I'm going to get me boots off, I'm going to get them under me armpits, dry them out and warm them up a bit and put me fresh socks on. I'm going to have one night's sleep with dry and warm feet!' So what happens? Some bastard from the Argentinian recce troop turns up.

We'd met up with Pete Addle's patrol but there was just me and Bill on this little ledge and the others were dotted around. I think it was 'Zip'* came over and shook our doss-bags, and you could see 'em wandering around on their side of the river. You could tell they weren't our blokes, it was like a fighting patrol coming our way as opposed to a foot patrol going their way. I think Pete had been on the radio, and nobody knew of anyone around. I counted eleven of them, just these shadows moving around . . . and the bridge was off to the right, and there was another rise in front of us, and the moment we opened fire, the whole fucking hill lit up! It was like, 'Fuck, there's hundreds of 'em!'

Fisher, who carried a GPMG, began to look for his ammunition:

---

* 'Zip' Hunt, a private in Patrols Company.

We used to carry the ammo in bandoliers – these green plastic carriers – and it was night and I'd run out of rounds for the gun. I was actually walking around, instead of crawling, saying, 'Now where the fuck did I put that bandolier? I'm sure I left it here somewhere,' and I was really mellow because I had Bill Metcalfe next to me, and he was, like, the old sweat and he was saying, 'Yeah, yeah. Just fire a couple of rounds,' he was really casual. So I thought, 'Ah, there it is,' and I picked it up and it was a 66: it was just a green thing on the floor. I thought, 'Oh, I'll fucking have a go with this. BOOOM, yeah!' I don't know if it was the cold but it sort of went *p-o-u-f* and the two blokes behind me thought we were being mortared and they were shouting, 'Prepare to bug out, we're being mortared!' and I thought, 'Now there's a fucking coincidence!'[35]

Fisher and Metcalfe started preparing to quit the position:

I remember catching something out of the corner of my eye, I remember Zip crouching and then running with his rifle down, going like, 'Bug out! Bug out!' So I said to Bill, 'We're going to bug out now,' and he said, 'Yeah, OK,' 'cause he was cool as fuck, Bill. But I think we must have waited too long because there was nobody left on our side: it got very quiet! We bugged out, but the only way off this face was this little opening in the rocks, and once you were through that you were safe. I remember looking at the tracer going through this hole and all round it and thinking, 'Fucking hell, I don't want to go through that!' But there was nowhere else to go. So I said, 'Bill, is there another way round or what?' and he said, 'No, we're going to have to go this way,' so he jumped up first, and he stops in the hole and says, 'Come on, I'll give you a hand with the gun.' I said, 'Fuck off you nutter! Just go! Don't worry about me, just go!' and he says, 'No no, come on,' so I'm passing the gun up, and he gives me a hand up . . . I'd got my boots back on at this point, maybe on the wrong feet, but they were on.

So we got over the other side, and everyone else had gone: the other six had gone. So we thought, 'Fuckin' 'ell, perhaps they're all dead? Well, we'll just bug out and go home then. Just go back to the lines,' so we're walking up and there's this *boo-boo-boomf!* You could hear the tracer and the rounds going over your head and the ones behind you hitting the mud. So I said, 'Fucking hell!' and Bill jumped down and I remember laying there and saying, 'Do you reckon that was a random burst or do you think they've got nightsights?' And he's going, 'No, it's probably just a random burst, just covering the area,' so we got up and it fucking started again and it was all round us, so we lay down and said, 'No, I think they've got nightsights!'[36]

Fisher and Metcalfe managed to 'do a runner' back to another rise:

It's starting to get light now and I gets up there, gets the bipod up and gets the gun out; and I said, 'Right, I'll fucking put a burst down there, find out where they are and fucking sort them out!' and Bill says, 'Naah, no you won't,' and I says, 'Why?' and he says, 'Look, you've got about eight rounds left on your gun and I've only got a few left in me rifle. If we start anything now . . . is this common sense?' I said, 'Ah! OK then Bill.' It was just like that. But then one of our rifle companies put this patrol out – 'cause apparently they reckoned it looked brilliant because all the fire from the Argentines was going up in the air and at night, I think, you tend to fire high anyway – and we met up with them. The tracer was just hitting the top or going over the top and they reckoned it looked brilliant, the tracer just lighting up the sky.[37]

The patrol managed to get out with no casualties, but they were forced to abandon their bergens; when they returned several days later their kit had been removed. The clash at Murrell Bridge – in which it is possible that some Argentines were wounded – was actually against a combined patrol of two of Argentina's top military special forces units: Compania de Commando 601 and Compania de Fuerzas Especiales 601 de Gendarmerie Nacional, both of which were composed entirely of regulars. Lee Fisher and his colleagues acquitted themselves well against at least double their strength of special forces.

For the non-specialists in the rifle companies, the soldiers who would, in the most direct way, fight the battle, the period at Estancia was something of an endurance test. Having been allocated their positions, in simple terms their task was to dig in and secure them whilst the specialists, gunners, mortars, recce and so on, went through their preparations for the battle that they knew was to come. On Mount Vernet, Mark Cox and 5 Platoon set about preparing a position that provided them with cover from fire and observation by the Argentines, and shelter from the tearing wind, rain, sleet and snow. There is an old saying in the army, 'Any fool can be uncomfortable,' and despite the harsh weather the trenches became reasonably snug. As a consequence of this, although the sections were being rotated back to Estancia to warm up and dry out in the farm buildings there, many of the soldiers were reluctant to go. When Mark Cox ordered Corporal 'Scouse' McLaughlin to take his men back, he was surprised to be met by an outright refusal. This quickly grew into a confrontation between the young officer and the experienced junior NCO, as McLaughlin threw what Cox considered to be a childish tantrum. The situation was resolved by Mike Argue, who ordered McLaughlin back to Estancia. The spat between Cox and McLaughlin soon blew over, and Cox recalls later sitting in a trench with the corporal during a particularly fierce shower, singing a duet of 'Always Look on the Bright Side of Life', from the crucifixion scene of *Monty Python's Life of Brian*.[38]

General Moore's original plan to seize the high ground around Stanley envisaged that the assaults would start on the night of 8–9 June, but logistic problems, combined with the move of 5 Infantry Brigade into a position from which they could join in, meant that the operation was rescheduled for the night of the eleventh–twelfth. The loss of the landing ships *Sir Galahad* and *Sir Tristram* in Bluff Cove on 7 June also introduced a delay into the system. Helicopters which would have been moving supplies forward for the assault were diverted to fly the many casualties back for treatment at Ajax Bay, and another twenty-four-hour wait was imposed: the first actions in the battle for Stanley – 3 Para's assault on Mount Longdon and Wireless Ridge, 45 Commando's attack on Two Sisters and

Tumbledown, and 42 Commando's attack on Mount Harriet – would now take place on the night of 11–12 June.

Although the no-man's land between the opposing forces was comparatively narrow, varying between about two and five miles, the precarious supply position of the British dictated that there was no opportunity for a full-scale counter-battery duel between the British and Argentine artillery. Both sides were equipped with 105mm guns as their standard weapon, but the British gun out-ranged the Argentine version (the Italian-made Oto Melara M56 pack howitzer), which could not reach the British gun positions. Argentine 155mm howitzers, which caused problems in the last two days of the fighting, didn't actually arrive in the Falklands until several hours into the battle of Mount Longdon on the night of 11–12 June, though two guns were brought into action almost immediately. Instead of counter-battery work, both sides settled in for a period of harassing fire on positions that, to the British at least, were clearly visible. Even so, the Argentine fire was still dangerous, and there were some casualties. Lee Fisher was resting before beginning a new task:

> Bill had his brew kit on and we were sat around, and we could see Longdon off in the distance, and then these mortar rounds hit the hill and we thought, 'There's nobody up there, is there?' and then eventually they hit the other hill, and then they went halfway between us and the first hit, and then they came half that distance, and I said, 'It looks like bracketing,' and Bill said, 'Yeah,' and I said, 'If they fire again, I reckon they've found us, you know,' and then *boom-boom-boom-boom* WHOOOOSH! Fucking bang! Straight on top of us. And once they found us, they kept on putting rounds down on us, and that was when I got wounded.
>
> I turned round, 'cause I thought Bill Metcalfe had something like a sledgehammer and he'd hit me with it. I said, 'Bill, what the fuck did you do that for?' and he was just laying there, and there was a smoking hole, and in between me and this hole was Bill, who was just laying there drinking the brew he'd made. He was like, been there, seen it, done it: not impressed. I was thinking, 'How did it get me and

miss him, the bastard? It must have been a curved one or something!'[39]

Fisher was wounded and evacuated during the afternoon of 11 June. He and his patrol had just been tasked to lead one of the rifle companies up to the start line for the most dangerous operation any of them had undertaken: the assault on Longdon.

CHAPTER SIX

Snot and Aggression

> If your officer's dead and the sergeants look white,
> Remember it's ruin to run from a fight:
> So take open order, lie down, and sit tight,
> And wait for support like a soldier.
>
> KIPLING, 'The Young British Soldier'

Late in the morning of 9 June, HQ 3 Commando Brigade issued a warning order summoning all commanding officers to an 'O' Group the following day at brigade headquarters. When they assembled at 1630 hrs on the tenth, the COs were given their tasks in the forthcoming operation to seize the high ground to the north-west of Stanley: 42 Commando were to assault Mount Harriet and be prepared to exploit on to Mount William; 45 Commando were to capture Two Sisters and exploit forward on to Mount Tumbledown if possible; 3 Para were to take Mount Longdon and subsequently Wireless Ridge if possible. After drinking some soup and chatting for a while, the commanding officers dispersed to make their appreciations and write their orders.

Mount Longdon, 3 Para's primary objective, is an insignificant geographical feature consisting, in essence, of an east–west-oriented ridge about 1200 metres long and perhaps 200 metres wide. The top and sides of the ridge consist in large measure of enormous rocky slabs that have reared up from the ground, presenting their flat faces to the north and creating channels, gullies and caves that make the whole feature into a natural defensive position. Although many of the slabs and crags look impressive, Longdon itself is not particularly tall, reaching 782 feet at its highest point on the western summit; at the eastern end of the feature is a second, lower summit.

But although Longdon is not big, its isolated position ensures that it dominates a disproportionately large area, particularly to the north-east and south-east, where it overlooks the Moody Brook Barracks abandoned by the Falklands' original Royal Marine garrison in April. While Longdon does occupy a commanding position, it is itself overlooked by Two Sisters to the south-west and Mount Tumbledown directly south, both of which, at approximately 2000 metres, are well within the range of most infantry support weapons.

The Argentine defence of Stanley was organised on the basis that the British would attack from the sea, taking the shortest route to the capital, as they themselves had done during the April invasion. This appreciation suggested that the British landing would take place to the south and east of Stanley, and the main defensive effort was located in this area. Additionally, an outer defensive zone was established in the hills to the west of Stanley to guard against any approach from that direction. In all, the Argentines had deployed six infantry battalions, two artillery regiments and an air defence regiment around Stanley. But the deployment of the Argentine units, their command and control and their concept of operations were almost ridiculously incompetent: by the time 3 Commando Brigade were poised to initiate the battle for Stanley on 11 June, Argentine units in the western outer defence zone had been the subject of reconnaissance, artillery and mortar harassment from British units approaching from the west and south-west for up to ten days. Any half-competent military intelligence analyst should have been able to match up the British units known to be in the Task Force with those employed in the islands and seen that there were no more to come, that the forces investing Stanley from the west represented the British main effort – indeed, the only effort – and that it would be with them that the decisive battle would be fought. But no effort was made to move any Argentine unit, and the only reserve available to the outer defence zone was a single infantry company, largely composed of poorly-trained conscripts. Unless a defender is relying on pure attrition to win a battle, the use of reserves to seize the initiative by mounting a counter-attack is crucial.

The Argentine situation on Mount Longdon was not entirely clear to the British. The intelligence passed to Colonel Pike at Brigadier

Thompson's 'O' Group, according to the battalion log, was that the mountain was occupied by 800 men of the Argentine 7th Infantry Regiment, organised into three companies, but a realistic appraisal of the size of Mount Longdon would show that such a force would be standing virtually shoulder to shoulder. Some remember Colonel Pike quoting a lower figure at his orders on the eleventh. David Collett's notes record that at the battalion 'O' Group the briefing was: 'The Longdon area is held by the 7th Regiment: 800 men in two groups; 2 Companies on Longdon and 1 on Wireless Ridge. South of Moody Brook is 5 Marine Battalion . . .'[1]

Others, Tony Mason for example, recall thinking in terms of 'a company group'.[2] In fact, the briefing at the 'O' Group was fairly accurate, although its forecast of enemy strength was somewhat exaggerated. Regimiento de Infanteria 7 (RI 7) did indeed control Longdon, but there was only one company on the mountain itself – B Company – together with a detachment of engineers from an independent engineer company and five .50-calibre machine-guns from an independent Marine heavy machine-gun company. The other two rifle companies from RI 7, A and C, were both based on Wireless Ridge, whilst the regimental command post was at Moody Brook.

RI 7 was, like the other Argentine infantry units in the Falklands, largely composed of conscripts, in this case from the city and suburbs of Buenos Aires. The Argentine conscription system was organised so that call-up took place in January, and the new draft of conscripts joined their units by February, when they would begin their basic training. Having launched the invasion of the Falklands in April, the Argentine forces were then faced with the necessity of either garrisoning them with men with approximately two months' training or recalling reservists who had been trained the previous year but who had not undertaken military duties for at least four months. RI 7 was able to recall the great majority of its reservists from the previous year, but they were not ideal material. The regiment (in fact a battalion in strength) was commanded by Lieutenant Colonel Ortiz Gimenez, but the Longdon position was under the command of the 2ic of RI 7, Major Carlos Carrizo Salvadores, an officer whose military reputation, such as it was, stemmed from his command of a camp for political detainees during Argentina's 'dirty war' against

Members of the Anti-Tank Platoon at Teal Inlet. Marked with crosses are (*left to right*) Corporal Keith 'Ginge' MacCarthy, Phil West and Peter Hedicker, all of whom were killed during the battle of Longdon.

Support Company members in a sheep shed at Estancia.
Left to right: Company Sergeant Major Thor Caithness, Captain Tony Mason, Colour Sergeant Steve Knights, Sergeant Willy McGachen.

Graham Heaton, John Ross, Stewart McLaughlin and Mark Cox pose at
Estancia with one of the locals.

Milan posts and missiles at Estancia, ready for the move out to Longdon.

Longdon: the route into the 'bowl' at the centre of the Argentine defences.

Argentine prisoners are hustled back through B Company's postion.

OVERLEAF Prisoners lying down at the holding point, sheltering from incoming artillery.

left-wing guerrillas in the 1970s. RI 7 had arrived in the Falklands on 13 April and had been on Longdon and Wireless Ridge ever since, preparing the position for attack from the north and west.

Although the precise strength of the Argentine position was not entirely clear to Colonel Pike, the location of the majority of the Argentine positions was, as the result of extensive close-in patrolling by D Company. Sergeant John Pettinger, one of the senior patrol commanders, had managed to get very close to the Argentine positions on several occasions and had produced a sketch map of where he believed the main trenches to be; this showed a preponderance of enemy around the western summit and a central 'bowl' formed by the craggy rock formations. The Argentine trenches themselves were, by and large, adapted from natural terrain features, and proved difficult to spot during 3 Para's recce phase. Sergeant Des Fuller, who had taken part in one patrol, found that it was

> almost impossible to assess the Argentinian positions because the IWSs* didn't work at all. As well as this, the Argentinians had been in the positions for four or five weeks, and had shoved peat and grass into the cracks in the rocks, which had started growing again. It didn't look like sangars,† it looked like the mountain.[3]

Despite this, Colonel Pike was confident that he had enough information to go on to make his appreciation and formulate a plan. The solution that he went for was quite straightforward.

After setting off from a start line nicknamed 'Free Kick', which was a north–south-running stream about a kilometre from the base of Longdon, the battalion would advance with two companies forward, A Company on the left – or north – and B Company on the right, guided by members of Patrol Company. C Company would hold on the start line to act as battalion reserve. When they reached Longdon, B Company would assault through the known Argentine position on the mountain – the west summit was nicknamed 'Fly Half', the east summit 'Full Back' – whilst A Company would hold on a spur to the north of the main feature, nicknamed 'Wing

---

* Individual weapon sights. An image-intensifiyng nightsight that can be fitted to a rifle or machine-gun.

† Defensive positions constructed above-ground.

Forward', ready to exploit through onto Wireless Ridge with C Company once B Company had taken Longdon. Captain Julian James's Mortar Platoon were to set up a mortar line near the start line whilst mixed GPMG SF/Milan teams from the rest of Support Company would hold on the start line ready to go forward and provide fire support as required. In addition to 3 Para's integral support weapons, Pike had the six 105mm light guns of 79 (Kirkee) Battery of 29 Commando Regiment Royal Artillery in direct support, with further batteries nearby if necessary, together with the computer-controlled precision firepower of HMS *Avenger*'s 4.5-inch gun, guided by a specialist naval gunfire support party.

Pike's decision to attack the position from the west, essentially a frontal assault onto part of the Argentine main defensive position, was made on the basis that:

> Outflanking was not a sound option because of known enemy positions on Wireless Ridge to the east and a minefield to the south. (As things turned out, however, there were also mines on our chosen attack route.) The summit of the feature also dominated the very open ground around it for several thousand metres, adding to the hazards of a flanking approach – even one made during the pitch-black night.[4]

Certainly Pike's options were limited, and even with the benefit of 20-20 hindsight a different approach route is not immediately apparent, but one key element of Pike's plan remains a source of controversy even today amongst veterans of Longdon: he decided to attempt a stealthy approach, without the benefit of a preliminary bombardment of the Argentines.

Surprise is one of the most important principles of offensive operations, and there are many cases throughout history where the advantage of surprise has proved an essential element in victory at both a tactical and a strategic level; but there were reasons for doubting whether Pike's scheme for a stealthy approach up to the Argentine position was a sound one. Although D Company's efforts had been as thorough as they thought possible, nevertheless they did not have the means to do a complete minefield recce, and they could not guarantee that the battalion's approach routes to Longdon

were not mined; similarly, they could not possibly know what sur-
veillance devices were being employed to cover possible approach
routes. The tactical success of 3 Para's reconnaissance patrolling may
well have misled Pike as much as it did the brigade commander,
Julian Thompson:

> The apparent ease with which they repeatedly got right up
> to Argentine defensive positions and either withdrew
> unseen or, if spotted, despatched, or silenced, opposition
> misled me into believing that Mount Longdon would be
> taken quickly by 3 Para. I was far more concerned about
> Mount Harriet, in particular the extensive minefields
> guarding the feature, few of which were marked.[5]

In any case, an artillery bombardment would not necessarily have
compromised an attack, because 29 Commando Regiment had
already been laying down harassing fire on Longdon, amongst other
targets, since 3 June. David Collett was convinced that: 'It wouldn't
have made any difference if we'd been putting fire down because
we were there already, we'd been firing at the position for a week
anyway.'[6] An increase in the intensity of the bombardment would
not necessarily have presaged an infantry attack.

Others were prepared to question this aspect of Pike's plan as
well. Company Sergeant Major John Weeks of B Company attended
the battalion Orders Group with his company commander: 'I asked
at the battalion "O" Group . . . I thought we were going to stonk
the position before we went in, after 2 Para's episode, and I got told
it was a "silent night attack" and that was how it would go on.'[7]

His company commander was also somewhat concerned: Mike
Argue spoke to his fellow company commander David Collett after
the 'O' Group, telling him of his anxiety about attacking without
bombardment, and Collett advised him to press Pike for a change
of plan;[8] evidently this did not happen, and the plan remained the
same.

Following the battalion 'O' Group, the company commanders
dispersed to make their own appreciations of the tasks facing them
and to give their orders to their companies. On the face of it, Mike
Argue's B Company had the most difficult task. Their objective, the
mountain itself, was physically large as a company objective. Even

assuming that the defending Argentine forces failed to offer much resistance, it would be difficult to ensure, with the limited number of men available in B Company plus attachments, that the position was thoroughly 'cleared' of enemy after the fight through. Argue decided to solve this problem – or at least address it – by advancing his platoons 'three up' onto the mountain; in other words, all three platoons would advance in line abreast, and there would be no reserve platoon available to him to reinforce any success he might achieve or to prop up any disasters. His intention was that Andy Bickerdike's 4 Platoon would clear the northern side of the mountain, Mark Cox's 5 Platoon would advance along the central ridge, and Jon Shaw's 6 Platoon would sweep through the southern side of the mountain (this would necessitate a slightly different approach route). The plan was a source of considerable concern to John Weeks and several other members of B Company:

> What the OC seemed to think was because they'd run away across the island everywhere else, they were going to run away now ... I got the impression when the OC gave his orders that he thought it was going to be the fucking same now: 'There'll be a little bit of resistance but they'll fuck off.'[9]

Belief in the supposed cowardice of the Argentines was prevalent throughout the Task Force, although there wasn't a shred of evidence to support the view. Certainly their officers at company level and above were severely deficient in the arts of leadership and tactics, but at Goose Green and elsewhere individual Argentine soldiers, NCOs and officers had fought bravely and competently. All the British experience was actually that the Argentinians could and would stand and fight, and operate weapons systems, from their FN rifles to their Super-Étendards and Exocets, with skill and efficiency; it was the operations of war that they could not handle. The battle of Darwin–Goose Green ended when it did because of a successful psychological ruse pulled off by the British battalion commander, Major Chris Keeble, who persuaded the Argentine commanders to surrender when his own force was in no real state to continue the battle. The 'hype' following this victory made it appear far more decisive than it actually was, and does genuinely seem to have clouded the judgement of other members of the Task Force (there were descriptions at the time of 2 Para triumphing over odds of at least three to one, taking more than 1500 prisoners and killing over 250 Argentines; they had actually fought a single battalion of conscripts and additionally captured several hundred air force ground personnel who were virtual non-combatants. In reality they killed between forty-five and fifty-five enemy and took 'about a thousand' prisoners in total[10]). David Collett has since joked that it was felt that Longdon would be no contest: 'They were native infantry. We were élite troops and couldn't possibly lose: also we had bayonets and they didn't!'[11]

John Weeks and his colleagues were worried that B Company was being split for the assault. Des Fuller, then a spare sergeant in B Company HQ, realised that with 6 Platoon on the south side of the mountain, effectively cut off from the rest of the company by a shoulder of the hill, the ability of the company sub-units to mutually support each other was dramatically reduced.

The orders process continued through the day as junior commanders extracted their tasks and briefed their subordinates. By the afternoon, everybody was in the picture and there was time for individual preparation, some rest, some food, a hot drink. Stewart McLaughlin quietly checked his own personal back-up weapon, an illegal Walther P38 9mm pistol that he had bought from a friend in his Liverpool local, The Magazine. Vince Bramley adjusted his webbing, trying to ensure maximum comfort for the night ahead. Dominic Gray carried on filling magazines: he had managed to acquire eight for his rifle – a total of 160 rounds of ammunition ready to use – but he carried as much in boxes as he could, so that he would be able to refill his magazines after the battle had started. As night fell, 3 Para began the move forward to the start line.

The march from the Estancia positions to the start line, Free Kick, should have been reasonably trouble-free, but circumstances conspired to introduce problems. The fire-support teams of Support Company were meant to be marching parallel to B Company's route, but the two groups bumped into each other. The heavier Support Company equipment – Milan tubes, mortars and so on – was being ferried part of the way by civilians from Estancia and Teal, led by Mrs Trudi Morrison, using their Land-Rovers and tractors to drag wooden pallets over the boggy ground, but after the Support Company men had collected their 'ready use' gear, there was an unfortunate mix-up that led 6 Platoon and half of Mark Cox's 5 Platoon in entirely the wrong direction. John Weeks recalls: 'We had a little fuck-up 'cause we went off on our way and – I think it was the mortars or the anti-tanks – cut off half the company and I had to go off and gather them, which caused a problem.'[12]

The start line was a stream which ran from the south to the north, where it met the Furze Bush Pass, but before A and B Companies – the two assault companies – got there, they had to cross the Murrell River. Assuming the bridge to be mined, sappers of 9 Parachute Squadron Royal Engineers had recced crossing points for the companies. For B Company, they had carefully constructed an improvised bridge. Dominic Gray later recalled: 'We crossed the Murrell River one by one over a bridge of ladders. The ladders had labels on, I remember, reading "Texas Homecare".'[13]

At the start line, marked by Patrol Company with white mine tape, there were a few minutes for rest and reflection. Although they had only marched a couple of kilometres, many of the Toms were already dripping with sweat: the average private soldier's load came to well over a hundred pounds, carried in their webbing and in the pockets of their windproof smocks. Each rifleman in B Company was carrying two 84mm rounds for the Carl Gustav launchers, three individual 66mm rockets, six fragmentation grenades, three phosphorus grenades, 400 rounds of linked 7.62mm ammunition for the GPMGs, as well as their own rifle, bayonet, magazines and bullets, topped off by their newly-issued GRP* parachutists' helmets. But in the few minutes after they stopped, the cold began to bite. John Weeks remembers the weather as being 'fucking horrendous': thirteen or fourteen degrees below zero, with sleet and snow in the wind. Shaking the company out into extended line, he took the opportunity to talk to his men:

> I gave them a pep talk, the facts of fucking life. Now I'm not
> a religious man by any means but I told them, 'If any of you
> fuckin' want to pray, then here's your chance now to really

---

* Glass-reinforced plastic.

fucking talk to the man up there, because you'll need him throughout the night.' Then I told them to fix bayonets and Argue said, 'What do you want to do that for, Sergeant Major?' . . . I spoke to the senior ranks, I told them what I expected of them, I said, 'I don't expect anything less than what I'm going to do, if you don't see me do it, you do it. I'm going to have enough problems supplying you with ammunition and everything else without you causing me problems. Any problems with your platoon commanders, send them down to me and I'll sort the fuckers out.'[14]

The quiet tension of the start line affected people in different ways. Dominic Gray remembers:

It was very quiet. In the dark we passed some of the lads from Support and Patrol Companies; several of them were in tears because it was the Rifle Companies that were going in first. One lad from Patrol Company, Gary Boyd-Smith, kissed me on the cheek. 'Mind how you go, Dom,' he said. He was crying.[15]

Delayed by B Company's mix-up with Support Company, the assault force, A and B Companies and their attached personnel, crossed the start line and began the attack at 0015 hrs Zulu time. In line with Colonel Pike's plan, their advance was silent. John Weeks recalls:

It was open ground, we were just patrolling forward in extended line with two up and one back within each platoon. 4 Platoon on the left, 5 Platoon on the right and Company HQ between those two, one tactical bound behind, maybe fifty metres.[16]

B Company HQ actually made up a strong section in its own right: with Mike Argue were Des Fuller and Private Daly as signallers, Lance Corporal Phil Proberts, the company medic, Captain Willie McCracken, a naval gunfire forward observer from 148 Battery Royal Artillery, together with his signaller, and Sergeant John Pettinger and his patrol acting as guides slightly forward of the main group, in between 4 and 5 Platoons. John Weeks, whose role as company sergeant major was to keep his platoons supplied with ammunition, was a little further back with Private Clarkson-Kearsley, and even further back was Captain Adrian Logan, the company 2ic with his signallers, ready to organise casualty evacuation.

It was about a kilometre from the start line to the base of the mountain, fifteen minutes at the steady patrol pace that the Toms had naturally adopted. As they closed with the looming mountain, the gloom was broken by the moon rising behind the crags directly to their east. With no reaction at all to their presence, B Company were now into the last hundred or so metres from where Pettinger had indicated the Argentine position began. As the open ground with its yellow grass was illuminated by the weak moonlight, Mike Argue gave his platoons the order to close in to the rocks, but almost as he was doing this there was a sharp percussive crack from the left end of the company, followed by the shocked yells of a wounded man. Corporal Brian Milne, commanding the left forward section of 4 Platoon, had stepped onto an anti-personnel mine: it shattered his foot.

With almost stunning incompetence, the Argentine sentries had allowed themselves to fall asleep. 3 Para's approach had been unobserved, but it was clear now that the battle was on. Des Fuller, with Company HQ, was caught out in the open:

> We couldn't actually have been too far from the first enemy, I dunno, perhaps fifty, sixty or seventy metres, something like that. That's how close we managed to get. But of course, laying there, knowing that we were now laying in a fucking minefield didn't make me feel too happy. The thing going through my mind was, 'What do we do now?' It was no good getting our bayonets out and probing for mines . . . I don't know who gave the order to go forwards, I suppose Mike Argue must have done, but we just upped and ran like fuck for the nearest bit of cover.[17]

The first Argentines, the sleeping sentries in all probability, now began to lay down ragged defensive fire. Mark Cox, just behind the leading sections of 5 Platoon, remembers his immediate reaction to the explosion and the enemy fire: 'After Brian Milne stepped on the mine, I looked at this peat bank and knew that I could quite happily spend the next eight hours lying there and come out unscathed.'[18]

He didn't stop. Dominic Gray, also in 5 Platoon, now realised: 'It was time to fucking rock and roll . . .'[19]

Although it was a member of 4 Platoon, Brian Milne, who had initiated the firefight by treading on a mine, it was Mark Cox's 5 Platoon who were the first into the battle. The lead sections actually found themselves *in* an Argentine platoon position close to Fly Half, the western summit of Longdon. When the Paras reached the position – a little huddle of American pup-tents was all that was visible – they momentarily hesitated: they were so conditioned by their experience on the ranges and in Ulster that they were scared to open fire without a direct order from an officer or NCO. But after a few moments one of them broke the deadlock and began pumping bullets into the tents. In a matter of moments, terrified Argentine conscripts began to return their fire from bunkers and trenches previously concealed by the darkness, and the fight was on. It would seem that this was the platoon of Lieutenant Juan Baldini, but whoever commanded it, it was in a chaotic state, with many of its members still asleep in their tents and trenches. Baldini himself appears to have been killed as he scrambled out of bed; his body was subsequently found lying half out of a bunker with his pistol in his hand but no boots on.

Meanwhile Jon Shaw's 6 Platoon had made rapid progress. After crossing the start line they had approached the mountain without difficulty, guided by Corporal Jerry Phillips of Patrols Company, and were about to start making their way up when they heard the mine explode. Corporal Jimmy Morham, a member of Support Company who was leading a fire-support team attached to 6 Platoon, remembers:

> We all knew what the sound indicated, and could not understand why the enemy did not open fire on the platoon which had set off the mine. We continued to move higher up the feature and, as we did so, Corporal Cooper [a Support Company mortar fire controller attached to 6 Platoon] received a radio message from the company commander's MFC to the effect that a soldier had indeed stepped on a mine. Seconds later, our own artillery started coming overhead,

aimed at targets outside Port Stanley – and not on Mount Longdon.[20]

6 Platoon made rapid progress up the hill, passing a series of empty sangars, bunkers and tents, some of which they grenaded as they went through. The positions included one of the .50 heavy machine-guns, manned by the supposedly élite Argentine Marines who were asleep with the rest of the defenders. Near the top of Fly Half, the platoon paused momentarily before Corporal John Steggles took his section over the central ridge to take out a mortar position that was located there. As Steggles's section went over the top, the other two, commanded by Corporal Trev Wilson and Lance Corporal 'Doc' Murdoch, shook out to begin their sweep along the north side of Longdon. Although 5 Platoon were now heavily engaged below them and to the north, Jon Shaw's men had still had no contact with the enemy.

As the 6 Platoon sections moved they suddenly began to receive heavy fire from all directions, and several members of Steggles's section went down wounded. In fact they were being fired on by a bunker containing seven Argentines that they had bypassed in the dark, and from the Argentine positions further along the ridge that had yet to receive the attention of any artillery fire. As the firefight continued, Private Mark Dodsworth, the platoon medic, was called forward to deal with the most serious casualties, Lance Corporal David Scott and Private Tony Greenwood, who had been attached to Steggles's section from Company HQ to make up the numbers. Corporal Morham had an 84mm launcher with his fire-support team:

> . . . we were called forward, as the 84mm was needed urgently. We sprinted over the top and headed towards the nearest voice. Although the moon shone intermittently through the cracks in the clouds, we could see only three to four lads from the top section; we headed for them. This group comprised a lad firing a GPMG, a rifleman and the medic – who was bending over the body of Lance Corporal Scott. The entire area was under intense fire. People were shouting target indications to the 84mm team – none of them too clear. We had taken cover around the area of

the body, with myself behind it. The medic said that Lance Corporal Scott was dead and that his magazines and grenades were being removed for the use of other soldiers.[21]

Lying nearby, and also dead, was Private Tony Greenwood.

As Morham and his friends watched, the intensity of the Argentine fire began to increase, identifiable by the green flashes of the Argentine tracer ammunition (British tracer was red).

As 6 Platoon suffered their first casualties, Mark Cox was bringing 5 Platoon up towards the top of the western summit. Although they had attracted a great deal of fire, most of it had been ineffectively aimed above their heads, and nobody from the platoon had been wounded. The principal obstacle to their advance was an Argentine GPMG in a bunker near the summit, and Cox ordered a GPMG team forward to suppress it. As this was happening, Corporal McLaughlin was readying his section to advance but, just before he gave the order, another member of 5 Platoon, Private Hindmarsh, was hit. Seeing him lying out in the open, McLaughlin fired a '66' towards the Argentines, called for covering fire and ran twenty or thirty metres in full view of the enemy to retrieve Hindmarsh and drag him back into cover. Meanwhile Private Grinham, McLaughlin's 2ic, led the section further up the hill towards the machine-gun.

Returning to his section after dealing with Hindmarsh, McLaughlin turned his attention back to the Argentine gun. Supported by McLaughlin's GPMG fire, Corporal 'Beetle' Bailey's section managed to bring 66 and 84mm fire into the bunker, and promptly silenced it. This allowed 5 Platoon to reach the top of Fly Half and to observe, for the first time, the full extent of the Argentine position which stretched along the ridge to the east.

The three platoons of RI 7's B Company were arranged along the ridge of Longdon with their principal arcs of fire to the north and west. Baldini's 1st Platoon, which the Paras had partially overrun in the first half hour of fighting as they took the first summit, held a position that should have allowed them to observe and dominate 3 Para's approach to the mountain. Apart from their normal platoon weapons, they were co-located with two of the .50 machine-guns, one of which was still firing when 5 Platoon reached the ridge, and an 81mm mortar that had been taken out by John Steggles's section

from 6 Platoon (the crew were still blundering around in the dark
and didn't have a chance to fire it). In addition to this they had
a personnel-locating radar system, but this had, by chance, been
switched off before 3 Para began their approach march and had not
detected anything.

B Company's situation when 5 Platoon reached the top of Fly
Half looked reasonably promising. Although 6 Platoon had taken
casualties, their situation was not, at this stage, out of control, and
casualties in 4 and 5 Platoons were minimal so far. As 5 Platoon
gained the top of the feature, Andy Bickerdike's 4 Platoon were
working their way round the northern side of Fly Half in dead
ground to the Argentine positions further along the ridge. Taking a
wider view, A Company, who had crossed the start line simultaneously with B Company, had yet to encounter any opposition as
they advanced towards the Wing Forward feature.

Although B Company had made good progress to the top of Fly
Half, seemingly justifying the decision to attack without a preliminary bombardment, they began to suffer a series of reverses soon
afterwards and the momentum of their assault significantly faltered.
Corporal Morham, with 6 Platoon, was in cover looking eastwards
along the ridge, and had just heard that his platoon sergeant, Pete
Gray, had been shot in the hand whilst throwing a grenade:

> Lance Corporal Murdoch's section came sweeping across
> our front from the right and was engaged by the enemy at
> close quarters. In the space of a few seconds, most of the
> section was wounded. 'Doc' Murdoch was directly in front
> of me; whilst I could not see him, I could hear him quite
> clearly. A yell, followed by 'I'm hit! I'm hit!' and moans of
> pain. We shouted out to his section, and received a reply
> from Private Barrett – who had been shot in the backside.
> He was flapping a bit, as anyone who had been shot would
> have been, and it took me a few minutes to make him under-
> stand that he was going to be OK. All this was shouted back
> and forth over the noise of battle. He said that he could both
> see and hear Doc, and that the latter had been shot in the
> head. There was no possibility of him being able to reach
> Doc because of the intensity of the fire. He did not know

where the remainder of the section was, although he could
see Private 'Mushrooms' Bateman – who had also been
wounded. In fact, there was someone else with him but to
this day I have been unable to identify him.

Our main priority became to reach Doc whilst he was still
alive. Throughout all this, we could hear him moaning and
talking to himself; it made us all the more determined to
reach him. The only problem was that the moment anyone
raised his head for longer than it took to take an aimed
shot, he was shot at himself. It became obvious that the
enemy were using nightsights – and extremely good ones
at that.

At about this time, the first friendly NGS [naval gunfire
support] fire was being put down on Mount Longdon. Most
of it was very close, and my main fear was that it would hit
the men of Doc's section. I was surprised by the lack of
smoke and illuminating rounds – both of which would have
affected the operation of the enemy night-fighting aids, and
helped us in closing with the enemy positions and recovering
our wounded. However, the use of these rounds was virtually non-existent.

Private Stew Laing, my 84mm No. 1, and I could no longer
bear listening to Doc; we agreed to try and rush forward to
him. I decided to dump my webbing to ensure that it would
not slow me down. Just as I was lying on my back and
slipping off the straps, someone shouted out, 'I'll cover you,
Geordie!' and Stew was off. Shots rang out, together with a
sharp intake of breath – Stew had been hit three times in
the chest.[22]

Murdoch had been shot in the head: he survived long enough to
attempt to treat his own injuries – he was found with an unwrapped
field dressing in his hand. Laing was killed instantly as a result of
his efforts to help his friend.

As 6 Platoon's situation worsened, Graham Heaton's section in 5
Platoon were achieving a notable success. Advancing over the top
of Fly Half they had come under fire from the surviving .50 at the
western end of Longdon, and the section deployed to neutralise it,

initially sheltering in the Argentine latrine area (many Paras found themselves, at the end of the battle, covered in human excrement as a result of taking shelter in the Argentine 'shit-pit': it formed part of the most sheltered route onto the mountain and most went through it). Their first efforts were with 66mm rocket launchers, but the two tubes they tried both misfired,* and instead Lance Corporal Lenny Carver and Private 'Gaz' Juliff gave covering fire as Dominic Gray and Ben Gough grenaded the position and charged in with bayonets, killing the occupants. Gray and Gough then turned their attention to a second bunker containing three riflemen. Both small men, the two Paras found themselves unobserved beneath the lip of the bunker as the Argentines continued to fire out of it. Following the drill, they got grenades out of their pockets and prepared to attack.

A problem that a number of the Paras faced during the battle came from the safety pins on their L2 fragmentation grenades. The pin consists of a stout wire ring around which is bent a split pin which passes through the detonator assembly of the grenade, holding the striker lever in place. For safety reasons, the end of the split pin is splayed outwards to prevent it from slipping from the grenade. Prior to battle, it should be standard practice to squeeze the ends of the split pin together with pliers so that it can be easily withdrawn. But live grenades are expensive, and therefore comparatively rare in training,† and few of the Toms had thought to prepare their grenades for throwing before the battle. Crouching a few yards from the Argentine bunker, Gray and Gough had to stand on the grenades and heave to get the pins out.

After posting the grenades into the bunker, Gray and Gough again charged in with their bayonets to the fore: 'As [the grenades] went off, we were round on top of them, and jumped into the bunker, bayoneting three of them. I leapt in and they were that fucking surprised: "Welcome!" I shouted, as I stuck the first cunt.' According to Gray, the best way to bayonet somebody was: 'Through the eye,

---

* The '66' is a disposable sealed unit. If it doesn't work, there is nothing for the soldier to do but throw it away.

† In six and a half years in the regular army, and three and a half years in the TA, Adrian Weale threw a total of six live hand-grenades in training. An infantry soldier would throw more, but not enormously so.

then turn and pull it out. It went straight into the brain like that, although often you just shoved it in wherever you could.'[23]

At around this time, as 5 Platoon continued to work their way along the ridge summit of Fly Half, one of the most controversial incidents of the battle is alleged to have taken place. Two Paras were sheltering amongst a cluster of large boulders and crags when they became aware of movements nearby. As they watched, four Argentine soldiers crawled gingerly past, apparently without realising the Paras were watching them. As the first of the Argentines drew level, one of the Paras shot him in the head, at a range of a few feet, killing him instantly. The others immediately surrendered. Different versions exist of what happened next: the following has never before been published:

> So we started laying into these cunts, and one of them takes an American passport out of the side pocket of his trousers, and I'm saying to him, 'What are you, you cunt, some fucking Yank or what?' and then I start filling him in again. Then [X*] says, 'What are we going to do with these cunts?' so I turn to [X], he goes off behind the rock and talks to [Y], who talks to somebody else [Z]. Then [X] comes back over and says, '[Z] says get rid of them.' So me and [X], we lined them up against this rock, and then stood back, and then just started firing . . . he put a belt of fifty into them, and I helped finish them off. Then we had to shift the bodies around because it looked a bit suspicious.[24]

Were there Americans – perhaps mercenaries – on Longdon? The answer is almost certainly not. It has been consistently denied by both Argentine and American authorities, and no Argentine veterans have, so far, publicly recalled meeting any Americans before or during the battle. Despite this, the claim that there were Americans present – which was first made at the 3 Para Regimental Aid Post during the battle[25] – has persisted.

The most likely explanation, if we accept that some such incident occurred (and the narrator of the above account is insistent that it did), is that the 'American' speaker had either received all or part

---

* Names deleted for legal reasons.

of his education in the United States, or was of US extraction. Despite subsequent hype, there were no members of Argentine Special Forces present (it is possible that Argentine SF had received secret training in the US), and the deaths of Argentine regular officers and NCOs, who might have been in the army long enough to have benefited from training in America, are all accounted for. The likelihood is that the soldiers who died were conscripts who thought that pretending to be American might save their lives: they reckoned without the Green-Eyed Boys.

Jon Shaw's 6 Platoon was still not out of trouble on the south of Fly Half. As 5 Platoon moved forwards, 6 Platoon found themselves on the receiving end of some of the fire aimed at the 5 Platoon sections, in addition to the firepower of the Argentines they were still trying to deal with. Apart from the unsuppressed Argentine positions further to the east, many of the bunkers close to them were still occupied and needed to be flushed out. It was a slow process; Corporal Morham describes how he and his No. 2, Private Charlie Hardwick, went through a laborious and dangerous procedure of target indication with rifle and grenades for Morham to fire the 84 into a nearby bunker, only for the rocket not to explode. Almost immediately after this:

> a group of three or four people appeared on our right, heading towards the enemy. We yelled at them to get down and that the only men in front of us were either dead or wounded. It was the CO and his party moving forward to assess the situation.[26]

At about this time, after assessing his situation, Jon Shaw radioed to Mike Argue for permission to 'go firm' (adopt a defensive posture) in order to deal with his platoon's casualties. Accepting the reality of the situation – 6 Platoon had suffered five dead: Lance Corporals Murdoch and Scott, and Privates Laing, Greenwood and Dodsworth (the medic), as well as eight wounded, including the platoon sergeant – Argue agreed, with the proviso that they should be in a position to support 4 and 5 Platoons as required.[27] In fact, the casualties they had already suffered effectively ruled out any further move forward by Shaw's platoon.

By now Andy Bickerdike's 4 Platoon were working their way

forwards of Fly Half on the northern side of the mountain, below 5 platoon. Up until now they had, by and large, been in dead ground to the Argentine positions east of Fly Half, but the terrain they had to cross was considerably more open than the ground being fought over by the other two platoons. As they came forward, they now came into the arcs of a series of bunkers, including a .50, sited around the crater-like bowl in the middle of the ridge. It did not take long for the Argentines to notice them.

The Argentine platoon in the centre of the position, 3 Platoon under Lieutenant Nairotti, had attached to them two of the .50 machine-guns and an American 105mm recoilless rifle (RCL), as well as a normal complement of GPMGs and rifles. As Bickerdike's platoon came into their arcs, they switched fire with devastating effect, hitting several members of the platoon, including Private Neil Grose, whose eighteenth birthday it was, Private Dave Kempster, Private Logan, Private Parry, Private Mick Cullen, Bickerdike's radio operator, who was shot in the mouth, and Bickerdike himself, who was hit in the thigh. Heavy fire from the area around the .50 kept the remainder pinned down in position. With Andy Bickerdike down and incapacitated, Ian McKay, his platoon sergeant, took over command of the platoon. As they had advanced, the right forward section of 4 Platoon had become mingled with the left forward section of 5 Platoon, both of which were now pinned down. McKay, recognising that the area around the Argentine .50 was one of the keystones of the defence of the centre of the ridge, now pulled together a composite group including men from his own platoon and Corporal 'Beetle' Bailey's section from 5 Platoon, and led them forward to assault the position. Corporal Bailey later described what happened:

Ian and I had a talk and decided the aim was to get across to the next cover, which was thirty to thirty-five metres away. There were some Argentinian positions there but we didn't know the exact location. He shouted out to the other corporals to give covering fire, three machine-guns altogether, then we – Sergeant McKay, myself and three private soldiers to the left of us – set off. As we were moving across the open ground, two of the privates were killed by rifle or machine-gun fire almost at once; the other private got across and into cover. We grenaded the first position and went past it without stopping, just firing into it, and that's when I got shot from one of the other positions which was about ten feet away. I think it was a rifle. I got hit in the hip and went down. Sergeant McKay was still going when I last saw him, he was just going on, running towards the remaining positions in the group.

I was lying on my back and I listened to men calling out to each other. They were trying to find out what was happening, but when they called out to Sergeant McKay there was no reply. I got shot again soon after that, by bullets in the neck and thigh.[28]

Sergeant Des Fuller was still operating a radio for Mike Argue:

Then the word came over that Bickerdike was down, that 'Sunray 21' was down and that 'Sunray Minor' – Ian McKay – had gone off and was missing. And that's when Mike Argue told me to go. I can't remember his exact bloody words but they were so fucking stupid . . . they were to the effect that I should meet up with Ian and discuss who was the senior and who would be the platoon commander and who would be the platoon sergeant. This was as I walked past, and I didn't want to get into an argument or anything like that but I would have been quite happy for Ian to take over – he was the platoon sergeant, so it would have been the logical thing for him to take over and me to take over as platoon sergeant. But as I walked past John [Weeks], he just very bluntly said, 'Des, you're fucking in charge.' That was it. So then I went wandering off up the fucking mountain on my own. I hadn't a clue where to go.

So there I was, wandering up and down the mountain, looking for them . . . the only one I knew there was [Corporal] 'Ned' Kelly so I started shouting for Ned and listening for voices. I was a bit worried about making too much noise and giving the enemy my position, but eventually I got to the end of 4 Platoon and Ned came and met me. He briefed me very quickly that Bickerdike was down and Ian McKay had gone and I said, 'Well, let's go and speak to Bickerdyke and see what he can tell me.' He was just laying there in a lot of pain, shot through the thigh and couldn't tell me too much, and there was a Tom with him, and I just said to the Tom, 'Stay with him,' and got Ned and said, 'Fill me in more,' and he told me that Ian McKay had gone off on a recce or whatever with Beetle Bailey's section and two of the guys who were actually stopgap guys, mess stewards or something. But apparently he was now between the enemy and us and he'd been shouting to the guys, and we were trying to find out where the enemy were 'cause there was no movement, they were not shooting at us at that time, apart from the sniper who was some distance away . . . and I just asked Ned to go and get all the section commanders together. Des Landers was the only one there, but he said, 'Scouse McLaughlin's up on the high ground just on the right side of us.' He was with his section, he'd kept his section totally together. I didn't know where John Ross was, I didn't know where Cox was, and so I called Scouse down; he didn't know either. So I made a plan to carry on going forward, it was as simple as that really. We actually couldn't see where the enemy were, the guys were saying: 'They're out in front,' 'They're over there,' 'They're there,' but it was pitch black. So I told Scouse to go back and give us covering fire; I told him what I wanted him to do; that we would continue to go forward until such time as we came upon them or they opened up on us; and Scouse was to give us covering fire all the way through.

From the time we started moving, he started firing into the likely positions – that was the idea – and it was coming over our heads. Of course, as soon as we actually broke out into the open, then they started firing at us, and the only thing to do now, now that we were actually in the open, was to push on forward.

I'm not sure quite how far we'd gone when Ned went down but I saw him hit – Ned was just in front – and I sort of ran past him and patted him on the leg and said – it was a stupid thing to say – 'Stay there Ned, I'll come back for you.' He wasn't going anywhere.

Basically, once Ned had gone, I'd lost all my experienced guys, my section commanders, so I was running up left and right, pushing the guys into the sangars. The guys were top, excellent, superb. They had a job to do: they knew what they had to do; they'd been trained to be able to operate on their own, not necessarily with a guy screaming and shouting at them. Mine was just encouragement, I wasn't telling guys, 'Take those two out!' 'cause I couldn't see what they were doing, or where they were. It was just, 'Keep going forward! Keep going forward!'[29]

It was now over two hours since B Company had crossed the start line, and their early momentum had all but evaporated as the firefight became a vicious attrition battle. Although events since Brian Milne trod on the mine take only a short while to describe, the reality of the fighting on Longdon was that each bunker could take fifteen or twenty minutes to assault, and more if they were particularly fiercely defended. In between the lung-tearing dashes from cover to cover, the Green-Eyed Boys lay or crouched behind rocks, steeling themselves for the next move forward, ensuring that their weapons were ready and trying to ease the discomfort they felt from their cold, sodden clothing and battered feet.

Although McLaughlin's section on top of the ridge were still providing covering fire, Des Fuller's group from 4 Platoon now

hit a really bad patch. They must have stayed low, hoping we'd go away, and didn't want to give their position away, but again, another huge barrage of fire came down . . . I actually didn't see any of my Toms go down but then I went further and one of the section gunners – GPMG guy – he'd actually been shot in the finger, he'd been shot in the trigger guard or the pistol grip of his gimpy. One of the guys there was trying to give him morphine, and what he'd done was, as opposed to pushing the needle in and breaking the seal, he'd managed to pull the bloody thing out: fuck knows why. I spent five or six seconds in the pitch black trying to find the bloody hole to put this pin back in so this poor bugger could have his morphine.

Then I went forward again and that's when we came up to the sangar with about three or four of our Toms there and one of them said, 'This is Ian McKay,' and . . . well I assumed we'd taken the position, there was no more firing and we started shouting 'All clear! All clear!' I told the guys to get in and go firm.[30]

At the forward edge of B Company's assault, Fuller was now plotting his next move:

I was laying there and I'd called for Scouse McLaughlin to come down to me, 'cause we were firm and I wanted to do another 'step' forward, and I wanted Scouse to go ahead of us. There was a little ridge at the top and Scouse had seen people scurrying about, or his section had seen them running, and he was still firing at them. That's why it took a bit of shouting to get Scouse down. And then that fucking prick [Lieutenant] Cox suddenly appeared next to me: he must have heard me shouting and recognised that that was where the command was coming from. He had no rifle, no webbing* and he was saying, 'What's going on? What's going on?' just as though it was a field training exercise. He'd just appeared from . . . I don't know where.

But within a couple of seconds, Scouse came down and laid next to me, and I said, 'Look, I want you to bring your guys and come through me and go up to the top there and get a firm footing on the top there, and we'll cover you from this side.' Not knowing if there was going to be anyone there, or whatever. And that was it, Scouse had got his orders, and he was gone. A couple of minutes later the guys actually came walking through like a full section, and they were gone. And I'd told them to take this prick [Cox] with him.

I was still on the radio, trying to convince Mike Argue

---

* A myth has grown up amongst the Green-Eyed Boys that Lt Cox lost his rifle: in fact this wasn't the case.

that I needed support for the wounded – I don't think he believed me – and I know I started effing and blinding: a good, trained, professional signaller was not supposed to do that![31]

Fuller's group had not reached the .50 sangar which was still active, but they were in a 'sound position which could be held if necessary'.[32] Corporal McLaughlin now began to move his section forward to see if they could get close enough to the machine-gun to silence it. As they approached along the ridge, they were temporarily halted by a group of Argentines who rolled grenades down the rocks towards them, fortunately without causing casualties. Having deterred the grenade rollers from continuing, McLaughlin himself managed to crawl to within grenade-throwing range of the .50, but, despite several efforts with grenades and 66's, he was unable to silence it; nevertheless he was able to move his section into a position to bring effective fire down on the enemy sangar which partially suppressed it.

One of McLaughlin's section, Private Tony Kempster, remembers his corporal's demeanour at this time:

I was trying to dig myself into the rocks. We were under very, very heavy fire. I knew that if I so much as farted I was a goner. Suddenly, ahead of us, there was Scouse, standing up on a rock, tracer everywhere, shouting: 'Come on lads, I'm fucking bulletproof, follow me!' And we did. We followed him. On that mountain he was an inspiration to us all. He found his hour.[33]

From his new position in the Argentine sangars, Des Fuller was now able to get a sitrep back to Mike Argue, who had remained with his company headquarters group in cover amongst the rocks on Fly Half. A rumour has since grown up amongst the Green-Eyed Boys that Argue, by limiting his exposure to direct enemy fire during the battle, in some way showed cowardice; the reality is that this was simply not the case. There are certainly situations when it is necessary for a commander to lead from the front, but on Longdon this would not have been wise. The combat was almost 'technical' in quality, requiring individuals and small groups to observe and assess each individual enemy position before destroying it; had the company commander become involved in this he would not have been able to exercise effective command – indeed any command – over his company. Nevertheless, it is clear that Argue was unable to assert very much control over events, and this undoubtedly led to greatly increased friction between himself and his forceful company sergeant major, John Weeks.

By the time Des Fuller had got his group in cover in the Argentine sangars it was quite clear that the original concept of operations had failed: B Company were not going to be able to sweep through as their orders had envisaged, and any opportunity to clear Wireless Ridge as well was clearly evaporating. In his company headquarters, Mike Argue recognised that it was time for a rethink. One of the first priorities was to recover the many wounded who were still lying in forward positions, but there was also a requirement to suppress the Argentine positions in the central and eastern parts of the ridge that were preventing his surviving soldiers from closing with them. Up until this point, some three to four hours into the firefight, the majority of the artillery support that B Company had been receiving was being fired on targets registered before the battle, and it was not being adjusted with any great precision, although the British guns were well surveyed and capable of pinpoint accuracy. In addition, Captain Willie McCracken, the naval gunfire observer, had been bringing fire in from HMS *Avenger*, but although very accurate, this lacked the volume of firepower that an artillery battery is capable of generating. This meant that much of the artillery fire which was arriving was not necessarily landing where it would do most good (it should be said that McCracken managed to bring the NGS in to within fifty metres of the Paras' forward positions).

As Mike Argue was conducting his reappraisal, A Company, in their forward position to the north of Longdon, were also receiving sporadic fire. Their first casualty had been Corporal Steve Hope, apparently shot through the head by a sniper as the company approached their objective. But they only received occasional attention from the Argentines on the mountain who were, of course, preoccupied with B Company. Even so, as the battle wore on the volume of fire coming down on A Company slowly began to increase, and included mortar and artillery rounds.

A Company's response to the fire they received was necessarily muted by the fact that B Company were still on the ridge and were not clearly visible to their comrades down below. The Australian Second Lieutenant Ian Moore was in command of A Company's left forward platoon (1 Platoon), and had established them in a good position sheltered by a peat bank. From this location they were able to identify the positions of several enemy snipers using their IWS nightsights (the Argentines were given away by the infra-red light emerging from their night-vision equipment), and these were engaged by rifle and GPMG fire from 1 and later 2 Platoons. As this was taking place, Private Jenkins of 2 Platoon was hit in the head and killed by fire coming down from the mountain. Although A Company were confident that they could suppress at least some of the sniper fire that was holding up Mike Argue's men, their own fire began to fall amongst B Company's forward elements (Dave Kempster, already lying wounded by an Argentine bullet, was hit by A Company's fire as well), and they were ordered to stop. Lieutenant John Lee, an artillery forward observer from 79 Battery, was given similar instructions.

With further forward movement by B Company now stalled, John Weeks was sent ahead to organise the casualty evacuation. With him went his right-hand man, the storeman Private Clarkson-Kearsley, and as many others as could be spared. Des Fuller headed back with Lance Corporal Phillips, to guide Weeks to his position:

> So I went off with Phillips to go and find these guys. I don't know how far we'd gone but we had two grenades thrown at us . . . one went off, I don't know, two or three metres away – it appeared to be that close – but it had no effect on us at all. I didn't feel any shrapnel or any blast or whatever . . . but eventually I bumped into John with the remainder of his guys and we actually came down and we started to extract the wounded: with the wounded out of my way, we could carry on. Although we were slightly depleted, we had Scouse's section to bolster us.
>
> We had some of the guys down there and we were organising getting the wounded out. Ned wouldn't be carried out, he walked out, but every time someone got up, the sniper

was there, zapping off from a great distance. I went to pick Andy Bickerdike up and carry him out and managed to get him on my shoulder and take about two paces and all he did was scream in my ear. So I put him down, saying, 'This guy's going to have a stretcher,' and John just pushed past, grabbed him, threw him on his shoulder and let him scream.[34]

The burly sergeant major hurried back towards the cover of Fly Half, where he could leave Bickerdike in the care of the medics. The young lieutenant was still in great pain, and Weeks remembers: 'He shat on me. Crapped all down the back of my smock!'

The evacuation of B Company's early casualties coincided with a lull in the fighting during which, according to Mark Cox:

Momentum was suspended and a quiet settled on the hill apart from shouting and the occasional 'crack' of sniper bullets (or, less glamorously, occasional rifle fire, although I do believe there were snipers with effective sights looking down on us). I looked around to help some of the wounded get back to cover as well as to check out the location of the OC and everyone else.[35]

Cox made his way back to Fly Half, following the line of wounded soldiers, where he found Hew Pike, Giles Orpen-Smellie, the intelligence officer, and Jon Shaw. He gave Pike a situation report and headed back to his platoon 'feeling that I had been too long away from my guys'. Finding his platoon at the eastern edge of the 'bowl', he settled down to directing a GPMG at enemy muzzle flashes. It was obvious now that the position was going to take considerably longer to clear than Pike had originally envisaged. He recalls:

It was clear to me that I must now use A Company, now closer than C, to take the fight through to Full Back and to maintain the pressure of the attack. I reported all this to the brigadier, as I crouched next to three bayoneted enemy corpses, telling him of our situation, but leaving him in no doubt that we would succeed in the end. There were, however, moments when I wondered, almost desperately, what more we had to do to force the Argentinians to give up the fight: positions thought to be suppressed burst into life again with fire as heavy as ever. There was only one thing to do, of course – to battle on until the will of the enemy was broken.[36]

None of the official accounts, including the published version of the battalion log, makes any reference to the next orders that Pike gave. David Collett recalls: 'I was told then to turn right and "take the hill". You know, just go up . . . B Company were to go firm and I was to assault up the hill, which I politely refused to do.'[37]

In the heat of battle, it is possible that Pike's customary cool judgement was momentarily off-balance. An assault straight up the hill from A Company's position on Wing Forward would have taken them into the primary arcs of the Argentine position, and it is probable that casualties would have been severe. An alternative option was required.

Meanwhile, at the very furthest forward point of the Paras' assault, Corporal Stewart McLaughlin was taking the opportunity afforded by a lull in the fighting and the good cover in his current location to empty his bowels. Having eased off his webbing and dropped his trousers, he was squatting quietly in a crevice amongst the rocks when an Argentine emerged from a hidden bunker nearby. Without pausing, McLaughlin drew out his P38 pistol and clinically shot him.

Instead of a suicidal attack into the teeth of the Argentine defensive position, it was now decided that A Company would snake their way back to the western end of the ridge and resume B Company's assault along the same axis. With 2 Platoon leading, A Company now retraced their steps back to the western foot of the mountain.

Back on the ridge, the majority of 4 and 5 Platoon's casualties had now been extracted by Company Sergeant Major Weeks and his assistants. It had been a difficult and dangerous task, made worse by the ever-present hazards of snipers and stray Argentines left behind or hiding amongst the jumbled rocks and well-concealed bunkers. At one stage earlier in the battle, as the company headquarters group was moving forward, John Weeks remembers: 'I jumped into a fucking trench and, lo and behold, there was something moving in the bottom . . . that wasn't fucking English! I nearly shot my foot off as I gave it to him with my SMG.'[38]

A little later, Weeks and Clarkson-Kearsley were leading the company HQ group forwards again when they came across a body lying under a blanket:

> You don't find that in battle, a body just like that, under a blanket, I mean, who do you think put it there? The man is obviously injured but he's not dead, and inquisitiveness will fucking get you! Because you pull that blanket and he's either got a weapon or he's got a fucking grenade, and I said to Clarkson-Kearsley, 'That man's got a fucking grenade there!' Told them to hold it, said, 'We got a problem up here, I need a couple of guys.' And I got an Engineer corporal, Clarkson-Kearsley and myself, and Argue is coming up and I said, 'It's quite safe to come up but we've got a fucking problem and we're going to sort it out.'
>
> I was saying, 'Right, we'll pull the blanket off, and if he's got something in his hand he'll fucking get it.' I said to Clarkson-Kearsley, 'You pull it from the top,' so he did, and the guy from 9 Squadron had his head covered. So we pulled, and yeah, the guy was still alive, he had a phosphorus grenade in his hand with the pin pulled. I had twenty-nine rounds in the magazine of my SMG . . . He got the lot . . . He let go and it all went inwards, the phosphorus. But fucking Argue comes up and he said, 'What the fucking hell have you done? That's murder!' And I tried to educate him then: if he'd flicked that phosphorus – there was about eight or ten of us – that grenade would have taken out the entire HQ and FOO party.[39]

Clarkson-Kearsley had an eventful night as Weeks's assistant, but he could not have had a better mentor than the experienced and volatile sergeant major. Weeks recalls the start of the casualty evacuation, when he briefed Clarkson-Kearsley on what was going to happen:

> I said, 'Me and you, son, have got to go forwards and get these casualties,' and Clarkson-Kearsley said to me, 'Do we

have to, boss?' I said, 'Yes we do, we have to go and get them. You and me, and we'll get a few other people on the way, we're going to have to get the casualties out.' And he said, 'But where are we going to go? How are we going to get there, boss?' I said, 'Well they're that way and we're going to go that way.' He said, 'But we don't know what's there,' and I said, 'Well, we'll fucking find out then, won't we?' We were getting sniped at all the way and I was carrying Scrivens and he got hit again. And 'cause I had him over me shoulder, he got hit and not me, and he died. I was trying to turn him over 'cause he had a lung wound, and you turn them on the opposite side to keep them alive, and he was trying to fight it . . . he was getting drowned anyway and there was nothing I could do . . . and I remember Clarkson-Kearsley saying to me, 'It could have been you, boss,' and I said, 'Yes, but if it had been me, it would have been me, there's nothing you can do about it, son.'[40]

Hew Pike's 'R' Group, which had joined Mike Argue at the summit of Longdon, included, apart from Pike's signaller and his bodyguard team (provided by CSM Ernie Rustill's patrol from D Company), the BC of 79 Battery, Major John Patrick, and his presence provided an opportunity for Argue to lay some heavy precision artillery-fire down on the Argentine positions. At much the same time, the fire-support team commanded by Captain Tony Mason arrived at Fly Half, with its mixed grouping of Milan and gimpy in the SF role, also on a mission to suppress Argentine activity. Firing at targets spotted by CSM Thor Caithness of Support Company, the support teams combined with the artillery gave Argue the opportunity to withdraw Des Fuller and Stewart McLaughlin's groups and to reorganise his company. Jimmy Morham was able to observe the preparations for this phase of the action:

Major Dennison and Sergeant Major Caithness arrived just below the lip of the feature to the rear and right of Platoon HQ, and set up a night observation device [NOD]. The GPMGs of the Drums Platoon were pulled back to this position and set up in a rough line along the lip in order to engage the targets that everyone was engaging *en masse*. The aim was for the OC and CSM to 'fire in' each gun in turn and get it on target by observing the strike through NOD. Once completed, the guns were to engage and saturate the target. Once again, the bad state of the weapons let them down, and it was not unusual to hear the command 'Fire!' followed by a dull, hollow '*clunk!*' However, one GPMG (fired by Lance Corporal Bramley) did perform well, and did not stop once.[41]

Now, with properly directed fire support, it was time for B Company to make one last major effort. Mark Cox was tasked by Mike Argue to lead an outflanking attack along a sheep track on the north side of Longdon. Cox took command of a 'platoon' that included members of 4 Platoon, 5 Platoon and the Support Company teams that had joined the B Company assault. Reunited with his platoon sergeant, Cox was leading this disparate group, now organised into three sections, back along the sheep track that they had withdrawn along when he spotted a group of enemy directly in front of him, and only a few yards away. He and Private Kevin Connery were moving in single file on the track, Cox with his rifle at the 'high port' and thus not easily aimable. A small group of enemy fired at them from 'point-blank range',[42] and then ducked back into cover. Cox and his men couldn't return the fire, which had wounded Private Reagan and Lance Corporal Carver, and killed Private John Crow, because they couldn't see where the Argentines had gone. Cox asked Company HQ, who were following up behind, to give a target indication, and consequently Willie McCracken, the NGFO, fired a 66 into the Argentine position. But this was still insufficient for Cox and his men, who were unable to observe the point of impact, so the young lieutenant ordered his rear section to throw grenades, knowing that he and his men would be in the danger area from the shrapnel. One grenade thrown from behind landed short, bounced on a rock, and exploded harmlessly five yards away. Cox then pulled the splayed pin out of a hand-grenade, with the same immense difficulty that Gough and Gray had earlier experienced, and 'posted' it over the rock behind which the Argentines appeared to be sheltering.

After the grenade exploded, Cox and Connery ran through to the

Argentine bunker, to discover three Argentinians lying wounded and semi-comatose. One of them was muttering prayers and whimpering. Cox tried to pick him up; in his excited state he was saying to Connery, 'Let's see what would happen if we took back wounded enemy,' but he became concerned the wounded Argentinian might stab him. He dropped him back down, wondering what to do, and Connery, a decisive and instinctive soldier, took the initiative: 'What about covering me, then?' he shouted at Cox, who immediately dropped into a watchful crouch. Connery looked about them, assessing whether they were likely to receive any support. 'We can't leave live enemy in front of us,' he shouted, and, using an Argentinian FAL that he had picked up after his own GPMG had packed up, he fired a burst that finished off all three.[43] In the circumstances it was a harsh but justified act.

Cox's successful outflanking move appeared to indicate that it might be possible to continue the advance, and his composite group carried on edging their way forward, passing the position where Ian McKay had died and which Des Fuller had earlier managed to seize. But as they reached the area they were opened up on from both flanks, and three more members of 5 Platoon were injured. One of these was Dominic Gray, who had fought with outstanding courage and tenacity all night, and who now had the most extraordinarily fortunate escape. As he looked about for cover, a bullet struck the side of his helmet full-on, penetrated the bullet-resistant material but, instead of going straight through his head, was diverted by his skull into the lining, around which it ran before exiting the other side. Gray was knocked flat by the impact but, finding that his wound was more or less superficial, he picked himself up and rejoined his section; a little while later he was ordered to get treatment by John Weeks.

B Company could go no further. It was now 0725 hrs Zulu, three hours before dawn and almost exactly seven hours since Brian Milne had stepped onto the landmine that signalled the start of the firefight. B Company had lost more than half of its strength wounded and dead. David Collett had already arrived at Fly Half to recce his route through and be briefed by Mike Argue and Hew Pike on the difficulties facing him. The remnants of 4 and 5 Platoons were being pulled back to the rocks where the surviving NCOs, Fuller, Ross and

McLaughlin, were trying to instil some order into the shocked and exhausted Toms. At this point Mark Cox returned from his final foray forward, visibly shaken and upset. He gave an order to his platoon – he no longer remembers what – but was immediately contradicted by Corporal McLaughlin. 'I can shout just as loud as you can, Corporal McLaughlin!' he yelled, but he was embarrassed because his voice began to crack up. Standing there, he was gently pulled to one side by Corporal Gary 'Louis' Sturge, who had just arrived leading the main body of A Company. 'Come on now, sir, we don't want to see our young officers not keeping it together,' Sturge quietly told him.[44] David Collett, who also witnessed the scene, decided not to allow any contact between his men and B Company: he did not want their resolve weakened. For Chris Phelan the sight of B Company was shocking:

> Now we were in the thick of it, and there's bodies every-where. Now it's real! We were up behind them when Johnny Weeks was still going round the bottom of the hill, bringing back bodies: he had Bickerdike on his shoulders, he had ammunition . . . amazing. And he was steadying them down.[45]

After surveying the position, Collett decided that he would con-tinue the advance along the same axis, but this time it would be done his way. His first priority was to establish a firm firebase on the top of the ridge. Chris Phelan again:

> Collett got hold of Adrian Freer and said, 'Get all your machine-guns up on that ridge.' He said, 'I want a heavy firebase there,' so that's when I went with [Private] Bojko . . . brilliant bloke . . . he'll probably be dead now, drunk himself stupid . . . he was a smelly little oik . . . but what a guy! He got up there, he got his GPMG up and he opened the bipod legs – I think Freer was with Sammy Dougherty then . . . they were on the left – and I was in a groove with Bojko, full of fucking water! But he was like he was on the 200-metre firing point on the range and I said, 'Put the fucking bipod down!' and he said, 'No, I can't fire it like that.'[46]

From their final assault position, the route that A Company were to take looked daunting:

> It was that bloody great black hole . . . it was like the gateway to hell . . . it was unreal . . . it was a big doorway and then there's the bowl and it just went in to nothingness . . . and that's where the sniper had us pinned down, and there's the .50 cal . . . horrendous.[47]

Collett did not want to emulate B Company's assault:

> I'd brought my company up through what we found out later was a minefield, and because it was such a narrow ridge and we weren't sure what was on the southern side of it, I decided just to assault one side, the northern side, because I knew that was where the main force was and we were out of sight of Tumbledown. We stripped off all our gear down to smocks and weapons and ammunition, because I felt there was too much weight being carried in the assault. I put Adrian Freer with his gun team up on the top, firing down the middle, and we then crawled them down across the ridgeline. I'd told them, 'You assault at the crawl rather than the run and gradually clear the position.' So I sent, first of all, a section, and that was old 'Sturgey', and gradually the platoon went across. And once they were forward, I then sent 1 Platoon down the right-hand side and they did the same . . . B Company had been across and come back so we were taking on new ground. Old Willie McCracken was up there with us, dropping the rounds down . . . he was very good.[48]

Collett's slow and methodical approach paid off. Although Corporal Sturge's section had to use all of their grenades and 66's, and all of Corporal Lawrie Bland's section's 66's (Bland's section followed Sturge) as they methodically and carefully cleared the Argentine trenches, nevertheless, only one man in the *entire company* was wounded during the A Company assault: Private Coady received a fragment of one of his own grenades in the hand.

Collett remembers:

We put a lot of fire down and I'm sure their spirit had been broken, but you couldn't really see what was happening and there was fire coming in from Tumbledown at that stage, from their RCLs.[49]

In fact the RCLs were to cause the last fatalities of the battle, although they were fired from Wireless Ridge. The fire-support teams were still operating on top of the ridge in support of A Company when a 106mm round streaked the length of the mountain and scored a direct hit on Corporal 'Ginge' MacCarthy's Milan team, instantly killing Private Peter Hedicker and seriously wounding Mac-Carthy, Private Phil West, Private Sinclair and Lance Corporal Cripps of the Royal Signals. Tony Mason was close by:

The 106 recoilless went straight between us. Peter [Dennison] and I are lucky to be alive. It exploded a little way back, landed behind us, and it was terrifying. I think about it, have nightmares about it now. It just cut MacCarthy in half ... Jimmy Morham tried to save him, gave him mouth to mouth ... [Lance Corporal Pat] Harley came up and said, 'Sir, we've got a real problem,' so I went back down and left the guys firing at will, MacCarthy was in a bad way, West was completely dead – he had a few tiny marks on his chest – it was just sheer shock, and Hedicker ... he was literally blown to pieces. We found half his head the next day ... he just took the full brunt of it. We tried to save Ginge, and do all we could, and I remember the smell of morphine and blood, and the smell of a battlefield really hits you: it's morphine and blood and cordite.[50]

A Company were still winkling out the Argentines from their bunkers when an Argentine Strela missile found its mark, this time a bunker being used for shelter by members of B Company. The most seriously wounded was Stewart McLaughlin. A splinter had torn through the muscles of his back to expose his ribs, spine and internal organs, and Grant Grinham, his 2ic, lost a leg. Despite this, the iron-hard Liverpudlian remained on his feet as his platoon commander and members of his section delicately removed his webbing to treat him. Mark Cox recalls:

There was a massive explosion, I don't know if it was an artillery round or a rocket. We had seen rockets placed around Longdon. I was flat on my face . . . I got up quickly and saw my back and the back of my trouser leg was covered in blood and bits. I believe I had been protected from the blast by McLaughlin's body. McLaughlin was on the ground near me. There was a large palm-sized pink hole in his back. He was wearing a kind of SAS-issue webbing. The hole seemed about an inch deep. Grinham was shouting 'The bastards took my leg!', and he was halfway out of the bunker he had just been inside. If he'd stayed he would have most likely been alright, but his leg caught the full blast and all the flesh had gone. His boot continued to swing underneath a clean knee joint. We pulled him the rest of the way out of the bunker. I found his morphine and administered it in his right thigh. His leg disturbs me now when I think of it, we had no clue how to handle it . . . I hurried off to find the medic . . . I yelled his name and he responded from the other side of a large rock. I said I was coming over and there was another large explosion. When I found him he was lying back freshly dead on a rock. His eyes were half open . . . his helmet fell off with part of his head. I grabbed his medic bag and sprinted back to Grinham. We put as many field dressings on Grinham's leg as made it look like a normal leg again. It seemed to feel best that way. While stretcher-bearers were being called we looked at McLaughlin. He was flat on his face on the ground yelling 'I'm going to suck!' [i.e., that he had a punctured lung]. I told him no, he wasn't, that he was OK, and he was going to be OK. He said 'What could an officer know?'. I felt for his morphine but it wasn't there. We'd all been told not to use our morphine on anyone else, it was for us. The only new source was from a dead body. We put a dressing on McLaughlin. Grinham had gone already, limping away with the stretcher bearer who had come up the mountain while we were under attack. Higgs, another stretcher bearer, appeared and McLaughlin was got to his feet. I'm sure he would have been fine at that point.

They both hobbled off, Higgs supporting McLaughlin under his arms . . .

I and another soldier got inside the bunker that Grinham had just vacated and listened in fear to the scream of incoming artillery rounds. The other soldier started to pray but I asked him not to. Something about Major Argue's original request that we find some way of protecting ourselves against artillery fire made me want to continue to find a solution, but the praying felt like giving up.[51]

The anti-tank weapons being fired from Argentine positions on Tumbledown and Wireless Ridge combined with a renewed onslaught from Argentine artillery positions around Stanley. Major Peter Dennison had begun to manoeuvre his fire-support teams into positions from which they could assist any exploitation by A Company forward onto Wireless Ridge. Sergeant John Pettinger, B Company's guide in the earlier phases of the attack, was tasked to lead several groups, including Vince Bramley's team, into the new positions. Bramley has described how:

After we had gone about four or five steps a hand dropped out of the rocks, grabbing at my ankle and denims. The shock of it made us jump. Instantly, Sergeant P[ettinger] was back with me. Still holding my denims was a wounded Argie. His eyes were staring at me; pleading perhaps, full of sorrow? Sergeant P shouted, 'Step back, Brammers.'

I tried to step back, but the wounded soldier tightened his grip on me. I leaned back as Sergeant P pointed his weapon and fired two bullets into the man's head.[52]

The man shot was almost certainly Corporal Oscar Carrizo, a regular soldier who, incredibly, survived the incident, and has subsequently described how he was 'executed' by two British soldiers. In reality, in that situation, Pettinger had no choice but to act as he did: the Argentine could have been armed, or even booby-trapped, and there is no question but that it was a legitimate act of war. After Pettinger and Bramley had recovered their composure, they continued towards their destination.

CHAPTER SEVEN

¡Arriba Los Manos!

There was no clear moment when the battle ended: dawn began to break around 8 a.m., as David Collett's A Company were clearing the last of the Argentine positions at the eastern end of the ridge. Collett recalls:

> We'd cleared through to the [Argentine] company commander's bunker by first light and *at* first light we cleared the rest of the position out . . . Pike was trying to make me go faster but I wasn't prepared to . . . my feeling was, having seen the carnage back there, I didn't think it was worth it. It could be done quite easily and we weren't going to go any further.[1]

Major Collett decided to settle himself into Major Carrizo Salvadores's command bunker, the most strongly built defensive position on the mountain, where he discovered, to his surprise, a stock of about 2000 cigarettes under his counterpart's bed. He handed the cigarettes out to the smokers in the company and gave the Argentine officer's pistol – a .45 automatic that he found hanging on a nail – to Corporal Sturge.[2]

As Collett's men finished their task, B Company were attempting to reorganise at the other end of the ridge. Company Sergeant Major John Weeks was criss-crossing the western end of the mountain, encouraging his shocked and exhausted Toms, helping the wounded, supervising the removal of prisoners and centralising the British dead. Mark Cox, 5 Platoon's commander, was making his way through the Argentine position in the bowl when he came across the body of a dead Para: 'I turned him over with my boot, the toe of it, and recognised him . . . a typical overweight, short-arsed sergeant.'[3]

In fact it was Ian McKay.

As Cox headed back, the fire-support teams from Support Company were settling themselves in to the Argentine positions around him. In the meantime, Chris Phelan, A Company's spare sergeant, had stayed with Sammy Dougherty giving supporting fire to the rifle sections as they took the final bunkers: 'Then it's daylight, I suppose, is the next thing I can remember . . . we're exhausted . . . the fear is gone, I suppose, I mean you get used to seeing dead bodies now . . . there's blood and shit everywhere . . . lots of Argentinian dead bodies around . . .'[4]

David Collett, the company commander whose assault had cleared the centre and east end of the mountain at a cost of only one man slightly wounded, was now able to take stock of the position:

> At first light we firmed up and then we saw the extent of where we were . . . we never exploited forwards because come dawn we realised what a position we were in. We could see Stanley below us, but they could see us, literally, and they knew the position and they were throwing in a lot of flak . . . I then decided I wanted to find out what the fuck was going on, because we hadn't got a clue, so I went back on my own, which was probably stupid, and I left the guys getting their heads down – I didn't take a signaller because we'd lost Hope – to try and find Pike and find out what the hell was going on. We were getting no sense at that time.[5]

Even so, Argentine mortars were still firing on the hill, along with 105mm and 155mm artillery from the gun-line on Port Stanley racecourse. Any movement in the open was extremely hazardous, but there were vital tasks still to carry out that made it inevitable. Chris Phelan was on the northern side of the mountain:

> We then started searching bunkers, me and Sammy [Dougherty] . . . so off we went together, a couple of dead Argies here, dead Argies there . . . and while we're in there looking for documentation that can help . . . we then came under fire . . . We were out in the open, basically . . . There was shit flying everywhere – small arms fire, machine-guns probably – and the old crack and thump overhead, this was

a long way away, 800 metres probably, which is why they were missing . . . and we turned and ran back to the mountain. And he says now that that was the first time I beat him in a hundred metres dash – and I did.[6]

Shells were now coming over with increasing regularity, spotted by Argentine artillery observers on Mount Tumbledown to the south and Wireless Ridge to the east, and Sammy Dougherty, Chris Phelan and A Company's 2ic Adrian Freer huddled into a coffin-shaped bunker together. From outside their shelter it was now possible, in full daylight, to see Port Stanley away to their east: the ultimate goal of the British land forces. Phelan remembers:

It was then that a guy from 2 Platoon, A Company – a guy called Bull* – got it, a direct hit with a shell, but it was the incoming and outgoing – I can now tell what it sounds like . . . I can distinguish the two 'cause we had both . . . That was a hairy time when we just sat there and took the bombardment.[7]

One 'stonk' came particularly close:

It was absolutely horrendous, that was nerve-shaking – shit – that was naked fear if you like . . . We were wedged in – I was closest to the door being the junior – and the furthest in was Captain Freer – no, it was Sammy Dougherty, the authority of a sergeant major I suppose! – and we had this brew . . . We'd saved this packet of drinking chocolate, me and Sammy, 'cause we knew that we might not be getting a resupply . . . and we had ten minutes clear and we thought, 'It's usually half an hour before they come again,' so we said, 'Yeah, let's have it now.' So I got this drinking chocolate out and got the hexi on with the cup on top, and we're like, 'Yeah, this is great!' and we heard the old boom, boom, boom and we thought, 'Oh fucking hell!' and Sammy says, 'Don't worry, it's outgoing,' and then – WHOOOOSH! BOOM! – fucking hell! And he says, 'Get your helmet off!' and he took my helmet off my fucking head and put it

---

* Private Gerald Bull: he was eighteen years old.

over the drinking chocolate to stop the shit going in it!
He said, 'You fucking spill that, I'll never speak to you
again!'[8]

When the bombardment had slackened off slightly, B Company
also went through the process of collecting the dead, wounded and
prisoners on their section of the hill. CSM Weeks had asked Sergeant
Des Fuller to help him collect the company's dead, but Fuller
couldn't face the thought of confronting the body of Ian McKay:

> After first light came, John [Weeks] and the guys were going
> to go down to the actual battle area and go and gather our
> dead and wounded and all that sort of stuff. And I said,
> 'John, I'm fucking not going down there today. I don't want
> to go and see Ian,' so he said, 'All right, I'll go down there.
> You do round here.'[9]

Major Argue also told Fuller to try to obtain intelligence from the
prisoners.

Meanwhile, Weeks was beginning the task of centralising and
documenting B Company's dead:

> You can't order anybody to do that, it's the fucking worst
> job I've ever done. You can't order people to do that, to go
> through bodies – stiffs – of people you fucking know who're
> badly injured, dead I mean but some of the injuries were
> horrendous: they had half their heads missing and all sorts.
> And then to go through their fucking kit, itemise it: it's a
> fucking job, right enough!

Weeks went with his friend and predecessor as B Company's
sergeant major, the tough Ulsterman Sammy Dougherty, to collect
McKay's body:

> Me and Sammy went forward to lift Ian McKay up. We both
> knew Ian very well: we were in fucking bits but you can't
> show it . . . You should have seen the state of him, you knew
> what he fucking took . . . bullet-wise and everything else,
> horrendous, he was hit all over the place . . . he was riddled.[10]

McKay's body had been, in the opinion of Dougherty, the post-humous recipient of SF fire from 3 Para's machine-guns, and shrapnel hits from mortars and artillery. Nearby was the corpse of seventeen-year-old Jason Burt, who had followed his platoon sergeant into the enemy trenches. Also riddled with bullets, he had fallen with his bayonet stuck into the turf, propping him dead in a kneeling position; Sergeant Colbeck of Support Company, a budding amateur photographer, wanted to take his picture in this position, but he was shooed away by Burt's friends.[11]

Others found the task just as appalling as Weeks. Tony Mason of the anti-tanks remembers:

> The sheer carnage the next day . . . there were a lot of dead bodies and, you see, Crow underneath a poncho . . . I knew it was Crow, I could tell by the way he tied his puttees . . . and taking the dog-tags off young Laing, who was shot – you take the dog-tags off but because the body's so frozen, the skin comes off . . . it was pretty vile, pretty unpleasant. And as I say, you had this smell, this combination of blood, morphine and cordite.[12]

Another fatality was 'Scouse' McLaughlin, who was killed by a mortar round as he walked with Lance Corporal Higgs of Patrol Company to the regimental aid post (RAP). McLaughlin had taken his first wound calmly, even though it had torn a huge flap of flesh out of his back, but the second hit virtually decapitated him. Lieutenant Cox, his platoon commander, came across the two bodies and, recognising McLaughlin's by the personalised webbing equipment that was still attached, he decided to check whether McLaughlin was carrying any useful food, in particular a sachet of compo porridge. Instead he made a horrifying discovery: one of McLaughlin's ammunition pouches contained a number of human ears.* Aghast, Cox retreated to where the company was sheltering from the sporadic shellfire below the western summit.

---

* A figure of twelve sets of ears has been mentioned by several interviewees (but none actually saw them). Neither Cox nor CSM Weeks, who came across the ears independently of each other, counted them. Twelve sets is a highly unlikely figure, bearing in mind the total Argentine dead of twenty-nine all-ranks.

The next man to discover McLaughlin's grisly trophies was John Weeks:

> I had to do the documentation, and obviously you check everything, see what's in there, for the next of kin and that – and the next of kin didn't really want the ears . . . and I didn't think any more about 'em, I just left the equipment and sent it down to the RAP.[13]

McLaughlin's comrades argue strongly that although his behaviour was 'unacceptable',[14] nevertheless the dead Argentinians had no further need of their ears. In fact, there is strong evidence that at least one Argentine was still alive when he was mutilated. Vince Bramley remembers:

> Some lads from B Company were pushing a few prisoners to join the three or four already on the ground. One prisoner held his head in both hands. As he was thrown to the ground he released his hands to break his fall, and I saw that his ear was missing. A gunshot wound was also visible on his left knee. It had been bandaged, but the bandage was loose and trailed from the wound. Blood ran down from his ear and from his leg. He hit the ground and started to cry like the others.[15]

Des Fuller saw something similar:

> They [two Paratroopers] tossed this guy off the end of the sangar and he rolled down . . . and he hit the boulder and he fucking sat up! He scared the shit out of these two Toms . . . and he started going '¡Frío! ¡Frío!', which is Spanish for cold . . . and the guys started teasing him – offering him a hard-tack biscuit and pulling it away . . . He'd been hit twice on the side of his head and there was a big flapping gap at the back of his head, and his ears were gone . . . I said, 'Go and grab a medic,' and I don't know who the Tom was who was teasing him with the hard-tack biscuit, but he got a good kick in the thigh.[16]

As 3 Para continued to comb the position, the Argentines' bombardment of the mountain became increasingly fierce. Defensive positions with artillery cover are normally allocated a number of 'defensive fire tasks', or DFs. These are pre-determined, 'registered' and numbered targets, usually representing areas where attacking troops are thought likely to concentrate during an assault. Artillery spotters calculate ranges and bearings, and have this information ready in case of attack. When the time comes, it is much easier for the defenders to call for, for example, 'DF Two-Nine' than it would be to adjust fire onto an individual grid reference. In addition to the DFs surrounding the attackers' approach route, there are often others sited extremely close to, or even on, the defensive position itself. In British Army parlance this is known as the 'Final Protective Fire', or FPF, and is a genuine last resort for defending troops; even so, it is not as suicidal as it might sound. Artillery fire is usually only truly effective against unprotected targets, and a properly dug fire trench with overhead protection should give the occupants security against anything other than a direct hit. Although the Argentines had surrendered Mount Longdon itself to 3 Para, the registered DFs were still eminently usable, as the British had largely remained on the mountain. Tony Mason recalls:

> I remember being pinned down under artillery fire . . . We were pinned down for about an hour . . . This fucking fire . . . we cannot move . . . I looked at my map and realised that we were right in the centre of the position, and it's got to be a DF and – Wow! – you certainly learn the difference between a 105 and a 155 – but quickly! I thought I was going to die . . . but all of a sudden Sergeant Pettinger came up and showed us a track down the side and took us back, and that's when the dreaded incident with Louis occurred.[17]

As Captain Mason was making his way back to Support Company HQ, several of his subordinates were settling down there to make a brew. Vince Bramley remembers giving Mason a gore-covered Argentine bayonet that he'd found just before he sat down with Denzil Connick, Tony Peers and a few other members of the mixed Support Company teams that had accompanied the rifle companies through the Argentine position. Just as they settled, a disturbance arose.

On the north side of Longdon, the 'reverse slope' out of sight of

Tumbledown, teams from A Company were still combing through the Argentine bunkers and burying Argentine dead in an open pit. One group, led by Corporal Sturge, recovered a wounded Argentine who had been shot earlier by CSM Alec Munro as he attempted to run from the position in the last moments of A Company's assault. Although Sturge had led his section with bravery and skill during the A Company assault – to the extent that he was subsequently recommended for a decoration – he was a man who was widely disliked: a 'loony' according to David Collett, his company commander, and a 'pariah' in the view of Tony Mason of Support Company. The Argentine had been wounded in the foot or lower leg but, according to Private Stuart Dover, he was conscious and aware of what was happening around him. Corporal Sturge called to Alec Munro, and asked: 'What shall I do with this one?' Munro's response was ambiguous: 'Put him with the others.'[18]

Sturge dragged the Argentine to a rocky outcrop and produced the Argentine officer's pistol that Major Collett had given him earlier. The terrified prisoner suddenly realised what was about to happen. Shouting with fright, he produced a crucifix that he was wearing on a chain round his neck and held it out as if to show Sturge that he too was a Christian.[19]

The shouting alerted Tony Mason, who was sharing a brew of tea with his company commander and company sergeant major higher up the ridge:

> Dennison, myself and Caithness were sitting there, shooting the breeze and having a cup of tea or something like that . . . whatever, just saying: 'Now what are we going to do now, this is the deployment etc. etc. etc., how are we going to make this happen . . .' I just heard some shouting . . . then I heard a shot . . . and I saw a guy get shot in the head, obviously, over an open grave . . . I think about there somewhere [indicates on photograph] . . . and ah . . . Peter [Major Dennison] said: 'Fuck, get down there,' I ran down there and . . . Sturge was shaking visibly . . . right on the edge . . . and I thought he was going to shoot me.[20]

Mason was amazed by what he had just witnessed, and he tried to elicit a reason: 'I said, quote: ''What the fuck did you do that for?'' . . . and his reaction was, his answer was: ''He was a sniper, he was a sniper . . .'' he was totally irrational . . . He'd actually flipped I think.'[21]

Thor Caithness arrived, brandishing his rifle at Sturge: 'Caithness told him to drop the weapon actually . . . Thor had his weapon right in his shoulder . . . I was carrying my rifle at the trail.'[22]

As they craned to see what had happened, the other ranks were swiftly moved out of sight of the incident while the Support Company hierarchy set about dealing with it. Major Dennison sent Bramley to look for documents and other items of potential intelligence interest in the Argentinian bunkers. Bramley did not finally discover what had happened until he was on the *Norland* on the way home.[23] Sturge was hustled back to the A Company position, probably by Caithness, as Major Dennison reported the incident to battalion HQ.

Caithness remembers:

> He [Dennison] left and went down to the battalion headquarters very angry . . . Being in the job I've been in for a long time, I was rather unemotional about it but the boss wasn't, he was very angry. I mean, I thought it was a bit out of order but, you know, war's war. I could live with it, but if anyone was to ask me in a court of law, I'd just tell the truth and say, 'Well, that's justice.'[24]

What subsequently happened to Sturge is not clear. In some versions of the story he was arrested, removed from Longdon and held for subsequent 'summary dealing' by his commanding officer, Hew Pike, whilst in other versions – most notably that of his company commander, David Collett – nothing at all was done about him until after the battalion had reached Stanley. Certainly Collett had the opportunity to speak to him after the incident had taken place:

> He said to me, 'I was given the order on the radio to shoot the prisoners.' . . . I said 'Fuck off!' and at the time it meant very little . . . Stories have built up round what happened afterwards – not so much what he did but what happened afterwards . . . The story that Pike and 'the Gang' – the head-quarters – were putting out was that he was taken off the

hill. Now I never remember him being taken off the hill . . .
And this is the story that's gone to the police: that he was
actually removed from the hill . . . which I don't think he
was, I don't remember him being removed from the hill,
and he was one of my guys.[25]

Artillery fire from the Argentine gun-line, which had been comparatively sporadic until now, began to intensify as the 7th Regiment's commander realised that the position had been completely
lost to the Paras. All of the 3 Para wounded and the great majority
of the dead had now been moved back to the RAP, and were waiting
for onward passage to the field hospital at Ajax Bay and the hospital
ship *Uganda* for the worst cases; a count of the dead revealed that
seventeen Britons had been killed during the night. The RAP itself,
commanded by the medical officer Captain Burgess but in reality
run by Colour Sergeant Brian Faulkner, a forceful Yorkshireman,
had been a site of great deeds. Since Corporal Brian Milne had
stepped on the mine during the approach to the Argentine position,
a stream of seriously wounded men, both British and Argentine, had
threatened to overwhelm the hard-pressed system, ranging from
Captain Adrian Logan of B Company, with a small gash on his wrist,
to 'Mushrooms' Bateman, with a 7.62mm bullet through his throat.
Amazingly, they had managed to cope: Faulkner had even found
the time to lead casualty collection parties himself, carrying
wounded men back for treatment out of the immediate battle area.

One notable absentee from the RAP was a senior NCO whose
tasks would normally have required him to remain close by throughout the battle and its aftermath. In fact, the NCO was a victim of
battleshock, a psychological condition apt to strike at moments of
extreme tension and fear, and which can, in extreme cases, induce
'fugue', in which victims retreat into themselves, and even psycho-
somatic paralysis of limbs and speech, blindness and deafness.
Battleshock is usually the result of the accumulation of nervous
tension in a single susceptible individual rather than a reaction to
one specific incident, and it is likely that the soldier had been in a
state of mounting anxiety for some time before the battle. In any
event, he had not been seen by anybody since the attack had started
but, in the chaos of the night, few had realised that he wasn't there.

In the light of day, as the flow of casualties from the mountain slackened off to a trickle, the soldier reappeared and the realisation grew amongst his comrades that he had panicked, taken a load of blankets from an incoming medevac chopper, and built himself a nest amongst the nearby crags in which to hide, curled up asleep in foetal security. It has since been claimed that during the course of the row that followed this discovery, another NCO took it upon himself to empty a captured Argentine pistol in the direction of the battleshocked NCO in an attempt to 'execute' him for cowardice. In any event, it was soon realised that although the soldier was not, of course, a physical casualty, he was a psychiatric victim of the war, suffering from a condition just as real as if he had been, for example, shot; and when tempers had cooled he was properly evacuated with the wounded.

Two further incidents occurred at the RAP in the morning after the battle, one of which, although in some respects comic, had potentially tragic consequences. After he had found the two Paras taunting the earless wounded Argentine, Des Fuller continued with his task of searching and centralising the enemy dead. A feature of Longdon and the other battles of the Falklands was that Argentine conscript soldiers, who were poorly trained and incompetently commanded by officers with only the weakest understanding of the principles of leadership, often sought the illusory security of sleep and warmth in their blankets and sleeping bags. There is plenty of anecdotal evidence, from Goose Green, Tumbledown and the other major set-piece infantry engagements of the war, of conscripts taken prisoner while asleep in their trenches. A result of this on Longdon was that for several hours after the battle had finished, individual Argentines emerged from trenches to be made captive: a group of these were handed over to Des Fuller to escort back to the RSM's POW collection point:

> I was told to take all the prisoners down . . . to find Lawrie Ashbridge the RSM . . . I came over this crest and looked down, and I went to ground straight away and told all these other guys to get down as well because seventy, eighty metres away . . . there were these seven or eight guys and they were all in green so they were Argentine – we'd been

told to keep our helmets on and we were in cammo so that we could distinguish ourselves – and I shouted to them: 'Argentinos, do you surrender? Argentinos, do you surrender?' . . . I actually stood up and shouted at them, and there was this big rock or boulder, and I was edging round that and they just took a bomb-burst* and I let go with half a magazine into the general area, and fortunately I never hit anyone 'cause it was a fucking Para burial party, with the Padre, Tom Smith the cameraman and some other guys.

But the situation then escalated:

At that stage I saw, on the right-hand side, all these fucking heads pop up from this rock feature, and all hell let loose . . . and [Private] Southall and I were under this bloody boulder and all the Argies were just laid out in the open. Not one got hit: they must have been firing at us for ten minutes . . . This was 9 Squadron engineers, battalion head-quarters, the RAP . . . firing at us, thinking we were Argies . . . and young Southall and I were in there, and we were scr-e-a-ming: 'We're 3 Para! We're 3 Para!' 'cause I could hear English-speaking voices: I actually heard Brian Faulkner giving fire-control orders! In the end it was the old fucking beret out . . . and throw the beret over the rock, and then we started hearing, 'Cease fire! Cease fire! Stop firing, they're ours!' But it still took me two or three minutes before I dared put my fucking head out.[27]

Once the confusion had died down, Fuller took the opportunity to rest a while at the RAP; it was only then that he began to realise the scale of the casualties during the battle:

I really felt it then because I could see our . . . I think there were four or five body bags laid out, and the helicopters were coming in, taking away the wounded . . . and you started hearing now, who's there, you know, from 6 Platoon . . . A Company . . . Support Company . . . very, very good friends. 'Ginge' MacCarthy, Scotty from 9 Squadron, Doc

---

* Military slang: they ran off in all directions.

Murdoch, Dodsworth . . . it was sort of building up . . . but when I initially got there, there were five or six bags there . . . Nobody had seen Scouse McLaughlin at the time . . . So I sat there, had a cup of tea and chatted to Brian . . . But I actually had to leave because I could feel the tears welling up in my eyes because every minute, or two or three minutes, when I looked over there was another body bag. You know, they say the Toms were bloody good, but the fucking cooks were good as well: those guys were up and down the mountain with the artillery going, still bringing the bodies back and the wounded back.[28]

Some time after Fuller had left the RAP, the battalion padre, Derek Heaver, came across McLaughlin's webbing amongst a pile of dead men's kit. He too found the ears. In the words of John Weeks: 'He went *apeshit!*'[29]

It was at around this period that a quick-thinking NCO from Patrols Company spotted that one of the wounded Argentines, who was being treated for serious leg injuries, had produced a weapon. In an instant, as the medics worked on the Argentinian's lower half, the NCO shot him in the upper body, killing him immediately.

The evening of 12 June came, and with it another problem. The transport system was so stretched by the task of bringing ammunition forward and taking casualties and dead bodies back that it had not proved possible to bring 3 Para's rucksacks on to the position. This meant another icy night for soldiers who mostly hadn't now slept for at least thirty-six hours, with only the protection they could gain from the Argentine trenches and any blankets or sleeping bags that were left lying around. There was an eerie feeling of anticipation on the mountain as 3 Para waited for the counter-attack they assumed was inevitable. Lance Corporal Bramley summed up the heightened emotions and anxieties:

No one moved that night. The battalion stayed put in their little corners, sleeping or guarding, waiting for the counter-attack. On my shift I spent more time looking behind me than facing the vast empty space across my arc. Behind me was the very edge of where the battalion had surprised an attack the night before. Surely the enemy had more

The battle is over, and the Paras take shelter on the north side of Longdon. *Clockwise from left*: Mick Matthews (who was subsequently murdered by the IRA), Clive Taylor, Steve Gaines, Johnny Cook.

In the foreground, members of Support Company rest, brew tea and prepare snacks. In the background, members of A Company and prisoners are centralising the Argentine dead. Moments later, one of the prisoners in the group was shot dead.

ABOVE LEFT Members of
A Company pose in the burial
pit with Argentine dead.

ABOVE An Argentine body still
smouldering hours after being
phosphorus grenaded.

LEFT The burial pit.

BELOW Mount Longdon: view
from the north-west.

3 Para's temporary mass grave at Teal Inlet.

HRH the Prince of Wales, colonel in chief of the Parachute Regiment, and General Sir Anthony Farrar-Hockley, colonel commandant, greet Lieutenant Colonel Hew Pike at RAF Brize Norton as the battalion returns to Britain.

Hew Pike, awarded the DSO, and Mrs Marika McKay, widow of VC winner Ian McKay, with other members of 3 Para who won awards in the Falklands honours.

Rifle and helmet on Longdon mark the spot where Ian McKay died.

opportunity to attack from Tumbledown than from the open area in front of me? It didn't make sense to me to guard a suicidal route but I could only follow orders and the intelligence reports.

Even after changing positions and crawling into my sleeping bag I couldn't sleep. The Argentinian blankets smelt, and the bag stank like shit. The whole night was a blank, waiting for daylight. The only noises to keep us awake were those of war. The odd shell would crash on to the hill in the night and the ground would shake suddenly with the explosion. Then silence would abruptly return.[30]

Captain Mason had similar concerns:

We were thinking about what further operations would be, but at this stage it was to hold the position. We had no sleeping equipment, obviously, so I found an old Argentinian blanket and rolled up in it – and it STANK![31]

For Brigadier Thompson, 3 Commando Brigade's operations on the night of 11–12 June had been an outstanding success. Along with Longdon, his units had taken both Mount Harriet and the Two Sisters. Now it was his turn to wait

for 5 Infantry Brigade to capture Mount Tumbledown and Mount William before mounting the next full brigade attack in its turn. However, there was one operation which I aimed to carry out at the same time as 5 Brigade's attack. This was to capture Wireless Ridge as a preliminary to launching my brigade round the southern side of Port Stanley from a start line on the north-east shoulder of Mount Tumbledown, to take the Argentines on Sapper Hill and other positions south of Port Stanley in the flank and rear. The operation to capture Wireless Ridge had to be timed to coincide with 5 Brigade's assault on Tumbledown. The latter overlooked Wireless Ridge and, if still held by the enemy, would have made any battalion position there untenable.[32]

3 Para had already been warned off that they would be supporting 2 Para, their sister battalion, who were back under the command of 3 Commando Brigade for the operation. The Mortar Platoon would

join 2 Para's mortar line, whilst the fire-support teams from the previous night would wait 'on task' on the flank of Wireless Ridge, ready to bring their firepower to bear if needed.

It had snowed during the night, but the morning brought with it glorious, springlike sunshine, and the light dusting of snow which covered the valley between Longdon and Tumbledown soon melted away. Daylight brought with it a renewal of the barrage from the Argentine gun-line at Stanley, and a particularly fierce bombardment set in about an hour after first light, pinning the men of 3 Para in their commandeered Argentine trenches and bunkers as shrapnel, earth and rock splinters swept across the face of the mountain. Vince Bramley remembers: 'We sat in silence, grinning at the shells as they landed near us, as if to reassure ourselves that if one went we all did. Everyone had gone to ground; no one moved out in the open.'[33]

After more than an hour of intense fire, the shelling eased off and the 3 Para teams who had been earmarked for the Wireless Ridge attack were able to begin their preparations. Tony Mason was ordered to reconnoitre fire positions for Support Company:

> Peter [Major Dennison] said, 'You'd better go and have a look at the position for tonight,' so I moved out that afternoon . . . to [the A Company location], and Matt Selfridge was there under fire from some silly little Argentinian position, so I said, 'Matthew, stop fucking around,' and we brought some mortar fire onto them, two rounds fire for effect and smoke, bang! . . . Then we move off and recce the position, and remember, we've been under artillery fire for two days at this stage . . . and I'm probably the furthest forward troop in the British Army . . . I spot the gun-line in Port Stanley – it's on the racecourse – but they move them, they're self-propelled guns, they move them around . . . I go straight into Golf whatever his call-sign was: 'This is India Seven-Zero, fire mission, over.' He wouldn't give me a fire mission, and Nine* says, 'Look, come back to my position and come back through my position and I'll tell you why.'

---

* The callsign of battalion HQ in 1982.

So all we had to do was mark the positions and 'lase'* the ranges and do what we had to do for 2 Para that night.[34]

With the task complete, Mason returned with his team commanders to the Support Company location. Mason had marked his map with the enemy positions and ranges, and while he discussed the forthcoming operations with his company commander and his platoon sergeant, he sent his signaller, Denzil Connick, to show the map to Lieutenant Colonel Pike. Connick had a secondary mission as well: a rumour had spread that a resupply of cigarettes had arrived at battalion main HQ, and Connick had promised to see if he could get hold of some. As he was making his way back across the mountain he bumped into two mates, Corporal Alex Shaw and Private Craig Jones, both of whom were Royal Electrical and Mechanical Engineers weapons technicians attached to the battalion. As they paused for a quick chat they were surprised by the scream of an incoming shell. All three dived for cover but the shell actually landed between them, killing Shaw instantly, fatally wounding Jones and blowing Connick's left leg off. Vince Bramley was one of the first on the scene, and he tried to help Jones: 'He looked at me and a slight smile came across his face, his eyes laughed at me, bright and wild. His grin spread, then all expression faded. He faded away.'[35]

Craig Jones and Alex Shaw were the last 3 Para fatalities of the campaign.

During the afternoon of 13 June, Brigadier Thompson held his last major Brigade 'O' Group of the campaign. His mission statement was simple: he told his commanding officers that the brigade's task was 'to capture Port Stanley'. Covered by fire from the Scots Guards on Mount Tumbledown, 3 Para's task would be to advance to the eastern edge of the town and take control of the Esro building. Following this, the other battalions of the brigade, 42 and 45 Commandos and 1 Welsh Guards, would encircle and cut off the town to the south, hopefully enforcing a decision to surrender by the Argentines. The first phase of 3 Para's operation would require C Company, which had been held in reserve during the Longdon battle, to seize Moody Brook Barracks, the former home of the

* i.e. Use his laser rangefinder.

Royal Marines garrison, which was about three kilometres from the position they were now holding. Major Martin 'Fatty' Osborne, the company commander, was warned to begin preparations for an operation on the afternoon of the fourteenth.

In mid-afternoon of the thirteenth, the forward companies of 3 Para got a resupply of rations, water and ammunition as the final preparations were made to support 2 Para's assault on Wireless Ridge. Most took the opportunity to cook themselves huge quantities of food to help stave off the numbing effects of cold, fatigue and hunger. As the light began to fade, Major Dennison held his final briefing for the support teams, and at 2000 hrs they moved out, laden down with vast quantities of belted machine-gun ammunition (as much as 3000 rounds per man), heading for a low ridge on the north side of Wireless Ridge from where they would be able to engage the Argentine defences during the early phases of the attack. Apart from the mortars, firing with the 2 Para mortar line, 3 Para had deployed five Milan posts and five sustained-fire GPMGs, a significant addition to 2 Para's firepower. The lessons of Longdon had been learned; the attacks on both Wireless Ridge and Tumbledown were to be massively supported by artillery and naval gunfire in addition to the battalions' own integral assets. There was no question of 2 Para, after their blooding at Goose Green, attempting a silent attack.

When Tony Mason saw the CO after his recce:

> He actually told me that we didn't have enough ammunition to support the attack tonight and neutralise that gun position . . . which is a pretty salutary story, but then 2 Para put on that fireworks display that night, which frankly could have been done with half the support, and the Scots Guards had all the support in the world . . . I watched Tumbledown that night and they rippled the position from east to west and back; the north side of the hill and the south side; you could see the frigates firing out at sea, and I remember thinking, 'Fuck it's cold and thank fuck this will soon be over!'[36]

The support teams had a grandstand view of both Wireless Ridge and Tumbledown that night, but they weren't actually called on to provide fire. After nine hours lying out on the freezing ground they were called back to Longdon to begin preparations for the battle for Stanley.

During the early morning of 14 June, 3 Para once again went through the orders routine – preparation for battle – this time for C Company's attack on Moody Brook. Tony Mason recalls:

> I was in the process of giving orders to put in a firebase to hit Moody Brook Barracks and then push down the hill, and that was rapidly countermanded and we just basically upped sticks with what we'd got and pushed straight into Port Stanley . . . We hit Ross Road and walked straight in down Ross Road. It looked like surrender, and that was the best feeling I've ever had. It was incredible . . . we'd fought a war and won . . . yeah![37]

Chris Phelan:

> We're going down into Stanley and we're going to attack . . . We'd had a quick set of orders, I can't remember the specifics, but we were going to go in and attack Stanley, let's go . . . But on the way down there was a message: they'd surrendered. So there was a big cheer and all that, and we were then trying to keep the blokes in trim, you know, 'Don't relax, keep steady, they're still there,' and all the rest of it, and then we're on into Stanley.[38]

Des Fuller:

> We were told they'd fucking surrendered, so helmets off, berets on, and we were off like fucking jackrabbits down the mountain just to beat the Marines in – which we did! Although in the papers they were putting the Union Jack up, having taken it down from when 2 Para put it up the first time. Going in to Stanley it was like something out of a bloody movie; there was bodies laid on the floor, there was Argie wounded just lying there, there were weapons laid all over the place, there were broken-down trucks. It actually looked like something that you'd see in a war movie.[39]

The fighting was over, although the surrender did not in fact come into effect until much later in the day. Now for the Green-Eyed

Boys, for 2 Para and for the crap-hats, there was a chance to wind down and an opportunity to try to rebuild the sub-units, like 3 Para's B Company, which had been devastated during the fighting. Chris Phelan was 'cross-decked' from A Company to take over as platoon sergeant of Ian McKay's 4 Platoon: 'They were in a hell of a state ... The company was wiped out basically, non-effective, and they were in shock, a lot of them ... One of them had a nervous break-down on the way back – but that was 'cause of Duffy,* not the fighting.'[40]

On the hospital ship *Uganda*, 3 Para's wounded were also going through the recovery process, but were not being helped by the fact that one of the Royal Marine bandsmen who were aboard insisted on practising his trumpet through the night. As a hospital ship, all weapons were banned on board the *Uganda*, and many had been thrown over the side in order to preserve the vessel's neutrality, but one Para had accidentally smuggled a grenade aboard in his voluminous combat gear. When he discovered his error, he disposed of the offending weapon by hiding it in the air-conditioning trunking where, he reasoned, it would remain undisturbed. In fact the vibra-tion of the engines and the motion of the sea caused the grenade to rattle and clatter around in the pipes above the heads of the wounded Paras in their dormitory as it worked its way slowly through the system.

In response to the Marine trumpeter, it was decided that

> they were going to throw the grenade into his room if they could get it out of the piping, 'cause he was playing his trumpet while the blokes were trying to sleep. It was like, 'What is this, band practice? If you don't stop, you're going to get a grenade in your room!'[41]

Cut off from the rest of the battalion, the *Uganda* was a mass of rumours: the story of the 'American mercenaries' first grew up amongst the wounded at the RAP, but some equally melodramatic tales were developed on the hospital ship. One wounded Para recalls that: 'When we heard that Steve Hope had died, the sigh of relief

---

* Private Duffy was a celebrated figure in the Parachute Regiment; he served his full twenty-two years without being promoted.

went right round the ship: no more getting your chinky nicked or being filled in in the scoff queue.'[42]

This slightly callous reaction was embellished to the point that it was suggested that the unpopular NCO had been 'fragged' by his own side, and a culprit was named. In reality, he died at the hands of one of the several skilful Argentine snipers operating on Longdon during the battle. During the campaign Hope, who believed that he would not return from the islands, had behaved with uncharacteristic restraint and professionalism, much more to the liking of those who had to work with him.

Apart from supervising the clear-up of Port Stanley, using Argentine POW labour, the last formal duty for 3 Para during the campaign was the provision of escorts for the mass of Argentine prisoners as they were returned home on the *Canberra*. It is distinctly unusual for POWs to be returned so quickly, particularly when, as was the case in the Falklands, there had been no formal cessation of hostilities as a whole, but simply a surrender of the Argentines' garrison on the islands. Nevertheless, there were eminently sensible reasons to get rid of them as quickly as possible: the total number of Argentine prisoners to be fed, watered, housed and cared for after their surrender was 12,978,[43] a huge additional drain on resources. C Company of 3 Para, together with Royal Marines units, acted as the guard force during the *Canberra's* journey to a private dock at Puerto Madryn in Chubut province in the south of Argentina. C Company's new task also gave its commander, Martin Osborne, the opportunity to renew his acquaintance with a certain member of the *Canberra's* crew, who remained aboard for the voyage. If it did nothing else, this raised his morale after the rigours of the campaign.

3 Para finally left the Falklands at 1115 hrs Zulu on 25 June 1982. Of the battalion of 671 men that had left Tidworth a little more than two months before, twenty-three were dead and nearly fifty were wounded. It had been a ferocious baptism of fire for the Green-Eyed Boys. Now they were faced with the slow boat back to Ascension, the North Sea ferry *Norland*, on which, reunited with their friends and rivals from 2 Para, they would have a chance to unwind and attempt to put their experiences into some form of perspective.

There was also 'Airborne Forces Day' to celebrate on the first weekend of July, when, in normal times, members of the Parachute

Regiment would congregate in Aldershot, drink beer, reminisce about the good old days and do the things that Paratroopers like to do. It goes to show that you can't keep good men down: on Airborne Forces Day 1982, the rioting on the *Norland* went on into the small hours.

CHAPTER EIGHT

The Aftermath

> When you're lying out wounded on Afghanistan's plains,
> An' the women come out to cut up what remains,
> Jest roll up yer rifle an' blow out yer brains,
> An' go to yer God like a soldier.
>
> KIPLING, 'The Young British Soldier'

6 June 1991 was the forty-seventh anniversary of the D-Day landings. At war memorials across Britain, the men who had liberated
Nazi-occupied France gathered to remember their colleagues who
had been killed during the landings on Juno, Gold and Sword
beaches; who had served in the air with the RAF; or at sea with the
Royal Navy. A fourth group of men assembled at various locations
throughout the country, as they always do on 6 June, to commemor-
ate their arrival in France by glider and parachute. On the night of
5 June 1944, and in the early hours of the sixth, the first men to
arrive in occupied Europe had been soldiers of the 6th Airborne
Division.

6 June 1991 marked another occasion for the Parachute Regiment, but one which veterans of the regiment may prefer to forget.
As the commemorations took place, that day also saw the publication by Bloomsbury, a relatively new independent publisher with
a small military list, of *Excursion to Hell* by Vincent Bramley, a first-
hand memoir of his part in the Falklands campaign of 1982, particularly the battle for Mount Longdon.

A vivid and excellent soldier's-eye view of the conflict, Bramley's
book was well reviewed and accepted as a modest contribution to
contemporary war literature. Bloomsbury managed to sell an extract

from the book to the *Today* newspaper, and *Excursion to Hell* swiftly joined the bestseller list at Campaign Books in Aldershot, where the more literary-minded inhabitants of the garrison can obtain a wide selection of military reading. Some measure of approval also came from the Parachute Regiment itself: a copy of the book was displayed at the Airborne Forces Museum which is located underneath the regimental headquarters offices in Aldershot. In any case, Bramley had been careful to circulate a copy of the manuscript to RHQ prior to publication.

A second copy of the manuscript was sent to Hew Pike, now a major general, who Bloomsbury hoped would provide a foreword. Pike read the book but declined to write a foreword: he later told a journalist that 'There were a couple of passages I did not like.'[1]

The specific sections of the book to which Pike apparently objected were Bramley's eye-witness description of the Sturge shooting, and an account of the 'American mercenaries' incident, as described to Bramley afterwards by one of the supposed participants.

The tabloid serialisation of the book created a few ripples of controversy, but these faded swiftly, leaving Bramley, by now a self-employed builder in Aldershot, to enjoy the modest profits from his writing. It wasn't until *Excursion to Hell* was published as a paperback in the summer of 1992 that serious attention was paid by politicians and the media to the incidents Bramley had described. On 16 August 1992, the *Independent on Sunday* ran a front-page story about the allegations by journalist Don McIntyre. In the days that followed, press and political interest grew until, on 19 August, the Serious and International Crimes Section at New Scotland Yard, under Detective Superintendent Alec Edwards, was briefed to begin an investigation into Bramley's claims. To the horror of most members of the Parachute Regiment – including Bramley himself – and a large, vocal section of the media, it appeared possible that the police enquiries might lead to the trial of members of the regiment for 'war crimes'.

In fact there was nothing particularly new in Bramley's account of what had taken place during and after the battle for Mount Longdon. The first published version of the 'American mercenaries' story appeared in the *Observer* newspaper in the autumn of 1982, in a garbled version recounted by Private Logan, who had fought, and been wounded, on Longdon as a member of 4 Platoon; whilst variations on the Sturge shooting were common currency throughout the army from soon after the end of the war.* Quite reasonably, though, most military professionals were sceptical: the idea that mercenaries might have been present during the battle of Longdon has always seemed plain silly to them, as has the notion that British soldiers might get away with shooting prisoners.

The Metropolitan Police inquiry lasted for eighteen months, and during the course of it the police team interviewed more than 400 witnesses in Britain and abroad, taking 470 separate statements. At one stage Thor Caithness, now a captain but still with 3 Para, was taken back to Mount Longdon to point out the site where he had arrested Corporal Sturge; there the policemen dug up the burial pit, supposedly in the hope of finding loose ears left behind when the Argentinian dead were removed for reburial after the war.

As the inquiry continued, another battle was fought out in the British media between newspapers that were for and against the inquiry. In essence, those opposed to it – spearheaded by the *Daily Mail* – argued that no public interest was served by conducting an expensive investigation into isolated incidents that had happened in exceptional circumstances more than a decade before; those in favour – led by *Today* and the *Independent* – believed that honour and justice demanded a resolution of the allegations.

The early 1990s had not been a good period for 3 Para, certainly insofar as their public image was concerned. Although the majority of the Green-Eyed Boys had left the army within a few years of the Falklands campaign, 3 Para's ability to cause controversy had not been curtailed. On 30 September 1990, a 3 Para patrol had fired on a stolen car as it sped through a checkpoint in West Belfast, killing two of its occupants, one of whom was a teenage girl, Karen Reilly. Although the soldiers claimed that the car had been driven at them, thus justifying their decision to open fire, a policeman who was present claimed that he saw the Paras fake an injury to one of their number after the car had crashed. In any case, the car was driven by 'joyriders', not terrorists, and it is unlikely that they set

---

* Bizarrely enough, these stories, together with the taking of ears as trophies, appeared in a collection of 'urban myths' published in the late 1980s.

out with the intention to kill soldiers that night. In 1993, in a controversial murder trial, Private Lee Clegg was convicted of murdering Karen Reilly, and imprisoned for life. From a common-sense point of view, Clegg's conviction was deeply flawed: to believe, as the judge appeared to, that it is possible for any person to have sufficiently cool judgement to fire three legitimate shots and one murderous one in the space of a four-round burst is to inhabit the realm of James Bond fantasy. Nevertheless, although Clegg has since been released and returned to the army, the conviction still stands and the damage to the Parachute Regiment's reputation is done.

More harm was perpetrated during the early summer of 1992 by a further series of incidents in Northern Ireland. On 11 May 1992, a member of the battalion lost both legs in an IRA bomb attack in Cappagh, County Tyrone; later the same day, apparently in revenge, members of the battalion led by a young officer fought with customers in two bars in the town of Coalisland, breaking up furniture with batons, and punching and kicking customers and staff. Although the officer and soldiers were subjected to serious disciplinary measures almost immediately, tension in the town remained high and, a week later, a patrol from a 'hat' unit, the King's Own Scottish Borderers, were set upon by a crowd of youths who stole a rifle and a machine-gun from them. A 3 Para patrol called in to assist the KOSB was also attacked, but responded by firing at and wounding three of its assailants (there is no suggestion that this shooting was not justified). In the week that followed, the brigade commander responsible for 3 Para, Brigadier Tom Longland, was relieved of his command, whilst serious consideration was given to removing the battalion from Ulster altogether. Thus it was that when the Longdon inquiry was announced in September 1992, and wild rumours of atrocities were circulating amongst fantasists and conspiracy theorists, many members of the public were prepared to give them some credence.

On 13 July 1994, Barbara Mills QC, the Director of Public Prosecutions, finally announced that no charges were to be brought following the inquiry, on the grounds that 'the evidence is not such as to afford a realistic prospect of conviction of any person for a criminal offence'.[2] In the end, the inquiry had focused on allegations of murder, incitement to murder, looting, assault and maltreatment of the dead. The only individuals to be interviewed under caution were Hew Pike, Louis Sturge, Alec Munro and John Pettinger. Pike was by then commandant of the Royal Military Academy at Sandhurst; the others had left the army. For those four, and for several others, the period of the inquiry had been long and anxious. Now they had an opportunity to get back to their normal lives.

The British military tradition is long, glorious and, for the most part, honourable; it encompasses a range of actions and campaigns that most armies can only envy. 3 Para's epic assault on Mount Longdon is undoubtedly another heroic chapter in that tradition. This does not, however, mean that we should not attempt to draw lessons from what occurred. There is a natural and entirely understandable tendency to portray military campaigns in the best possible light (usually from the victor's point of view, of course). To do otherwise, when they have often cost human life on a large scale and involved untold suffering, horror and tragedy, would be callous and inhuman. On the grand scale, it is entirely possible to write military history that is fair and even-handed, and which treats the claims of both sides in an objective manner, but since the Second World War the majority of conflicts in which Britain has found itself involved have been small, almost intimate, affairs. In these cases, criticism of any aspect of military conduct is usually very directly personal, and it seems to be almost bad taste to criticise men who have fought, and risked their lives, on our behalf.

Nevertheless, once the dust of war has settled, there is a pressing need to analyse objectively what took place in any conflict, and this is something that the British, a naturally deferential and polite people, do not do well. A good example can be found in the continuing controversy over Field Marshal Douglas Haig's command of the British Expeditionary Force in the First World War. An objective analysis can really only lead one to the conclusion that Haig lacked the creativity, imagination and, indeed, the basic intelligence to exercise supreme command in any theatre of war. Yet there are still those who champion his cause, in the face of all the evidence. General Claude Auchinleck in the Second World War is a similar, although less extreme, case: in many ways a great man, he was unable to rise to the task of supreme command in North Africa, and under his leadership the powerful Eighth Army was pushed back almost to the gates of Cairo by the numerically inferior but superbly-led Afrika Korps under Rommel.

The economic crisis at the end of the Second World War forced Britain to begin the long and painful process of relinquishing her Empire, and with that came a profound change in the national self-image: we have had to accept that Britannia no longer rules quite so many of the waves as once she did. As the Empire disappeared, the armed forces grew in public esteem; as Britain's economy limped along like a sick dog and her sportsmen and women were thrashed from Trent Bridge to Tokyo, 'the professionals' have been consistently, sometimes spectacularly, successful. France, Britain's closest neighbour, suffered agonies through military defeat in Indo-China and political collapse in Algeria but, because of the professionalism and skill of her forces, Britain managed to avoid similar fates in Malaya, Kenya and many other imperial possessions, and to leave them with a certain grace. But this pride in the achievements of the British military has also led to a reluctance to criticise them – even when their mistakes have been obvious – and this is not necessarily a healthy state of affairs.

Any large organisation which refuses to admit its mistakes is creating a rod for its own back. It fosters a climate which forces personnel who have made errors – as they inevitably will – to cover them up in order to protect their careers and maintain their professional status, and this more often than not compounds the situation. The disastrous Vietnam War, fought by the supposedly 'zero-defect US Army',[3] produced many examples of outright dishonesty by the American military, and there is now a distinct and disturbing tendency towards this form of behaviour throughout the British political establishment, and the armed forces as well.

The essentially feudal nature of the military hierarchy exacerbates the tendency for its members to refuse to acknowledge errors: the enormous authority that accrues to individual officers – particularly unit commanders, who are even vested with quasi-judicial functions – means that they are rarely, if ever, questioned by their subordinates. A recent commanding officer of 22 SAS has been quoted as saying that 'The CO's word is law.'[4] At the most basic level, military officers are taught that to lead effectively they must exhibit confidence at all times in front of their subordinates, and many take this as a licence for arrogance.

In practical terms, what has happened in the last twenty years is that criticism of British military operations is acceptable if it relates to the performance of equipment, for example, but generally not when it refers to personnel and military units. With regard to the Falklands War, probably as much ink and paper has been expended on the dismal, leaky DMS boot that was in service with the British Army at the time (a new combat boot was on its way, but wasn't issued to troops until a year or two after the war) as has been used to analyse the comparatively poor performance of the 1st Battalion of the Welsh Guards, who were demonstrably not properly prepared for the rigours of soldiering in the islands. A recent study of the battle of Goose Green, based largely on interviews with key participants, by a former Parachute Regiment officer, which dared to suggest that Lieutenant Colonel 'H' Jones had produced an overcomplicated and unworkable plan for the battle,[5] was roundly attacked by journalists not for being inaccurate, but on the basis that it traduced the memory of a great man. This would not be such a cause for worry if there were lively and vigorous internal debate within the army, but there isn't: only a small minority of service personnel are genuinely prepared to rock the boat. In general, the army sticks with the authorised version, mistakes are repeated, and their perpetrators rise to positions of great authority. Hindsight can be a dangerous weapon, allowing the comparatively ignorant a licence for arrogant pontification, but used judiciously it is a genuinely helpful tool.

So, what, if anything, went wrong in the Falklands War? After all, the British won in fairly short order against a numerically superior enemy with comparable equipment and much shorter lines of communication. The answer is that in the land campaign at least, there were two persistent errors which led to British soldiers dying, and which could have had serious consequences for the whole operation.

The first of these stemmed from the difficulty that many, perhaps a majority, of the British personnel had in simply coming to terms with the fact that they were in a real shooting war, in which it was quite possible for large numbers of men to be killed in a very short period of time. There are numerous examples of the way that this 'exercise-attitude' affected the operation, but it was most starkly illustrated by the Bluff Cove tragedy which left forty-eight men dead and many more injured because military officers on board the landing ship *Sir Galahad* failed to heed urgent warnings that they should disembark their men. Much less costly in the event was the delay in landing 3 Commando Brigade at San Carlos on D-Day itself, although this was potentially a far more serious error. The operation was held up for nearly an hour whilst a member of 2 Para was treated for injuries he had received in a fall as he was embarking on his landing craft. The result was that two battalions of troops landed in broad daylight when a strategically competent enemy would have been launching massive attacks on the invasion force. It has to be a rule of military operations that injury to one or two men cannot be allowed to hold up a large-scale operation when the stakes are high: Bentham's maxim, 'The greatest good for the greatest number,' must apply.

At a more basic level, the tab across East Falkland undertaken by 3 Para, and the Marines' yomp – now an essential part of the Falklands legend – were hardly necessary operations. Both of them inflicted casualties on units which, having arrived exhausted, cold and hungry at their destinations, then had to wait around for ten days as preparations were painstakingly made for their attacks on the hills. A fast march followed by a quick attack would undoubtedly have impressed the directing staff on a brigade exercise, and might just have unhinged an unprepared defence; in reality a fast march followed by a ten-day wait while stores were brought up and recces made was pointless.

In the case of 3 Para, there were a number of examples of this essentially unrealistic outlook. After the immediate post-mobilisation period, when the battalion had had to fight through reels of red tape to get properly prepared and equipped for action, serious problems remained. An example of this was the way in which foreign exchange personnel were dealt with. Major Buck Kernan, the American commanding C Company, had to be replaced at extremely short notice; Ray Romses, a Canadian captain with B Company, also had to leave. By having personnel in key command appointments who, in the event of war, might not be able to accompany the men they have become accustomed to leading and training, the army is certainly reducing its potential fighting power.

Hew Pike's proposed 'advance to contact' on 3 June demonstrated a certain unreality. Although there could have been clear military benefits to such an operation, the high risks it entailed arguably outweighed them. With hindsight, it is fortunate that it was stopped. One of Pike's company commanders recalls:

> A lot of the time it was like being on exercise without umpires . . . [Pike] wasn't trying to get anybody killed, it's just that that's what we do on exercise: if you don't want to bring your artillery up, or it can't get up in time, you call on notional artillery – and [if you can do that in training,] you then tend to do it for real.[6]

The second serious flaw in the approach of the entire Task Force was an underestimation of Argentine military capability. Throughout the literature on the Falklands conflict, references are made by British personnel to their expectation that the Argentine defence on any given position or area would cave in 'as they had done before'. A graphic example of this was 'H' Jones's prediction at the end of his 'O' Group before the Darwin–Goose Green battle that Argentine resistance would 'crumble' if attacked with sufficient ferocity. As has already been pointed out, at the time of this statement there had been no substantial ground combat between British and Argentine forces from which this inference could possibly be drawn. The battle proved, if anything, just the opposite: despite fierce attacks by a better-trained and more cohesive enemy, the Argentine conscripts stood their ground and fought hard. A myth has grown up to the effect that 2 Para defeated an enemy of at least twice their strength at Goose Green. In a sense this is true: the total Argentine garrison numbered about 1200. But the fighting strength of 'Task Force Mercedes' was actually about the same as 2 Para, and few, if any, of the hundreds of Argentine Air Force personnel present fired a shot.

A similar myth persists amongst veterans of the Longdon fighting. In an article published in 1984, Hew Pike wrote:

> The force holding Mount Longdon was not expected to provide the bitter resistance that it did; but British expectations that only one Argentinian company held the position were

mistaken. The infantry company from the 7th Infantry Regiment was in fact supported by Special Forces Unit 601 and by Argentinian Marines, while elements of another company of the 7th Infantry arrived during the battle.[7]

The description of the battle in the Parachute Regiment journal *Pegasus* claims that the position was held by '7 Regiment complete [that is, all three rifle companies and the support weapons company], reinforced by specialist elements and snipers from 601 Company and the Marines'.[8]

In reality, the British expectation at the time was that Longdon was held by two companies who also had several medium machine-guns (.50s) in support:[9] this was an *over*estimate. As we have seen, Longdon was held by RI 7's B Company, with a detachment of engineers (of about platoon strength) and five or six Marine HMG* teams. There were no Special Forces personnel present on either side.

After the battle, it is believed that twenty-nine Argentine bodies were found, and about fifty soldiers were taken prisoner by 3 Para. The remainder fled to Wireless Ridge. Yet a number of British interviewees quoted figures of between 400 and 700 as their estimate of the number of Argentines present during the battle, even though, in the confusion of the fighting in the gloom and shadow of Longdon, few Paras caught more than an occasional glimpse of their enemy.

What happened, of course, was that the expected Argentine collapse failed to materialise, and it was therefore assumed by British participants that the defenders were more numerous than they really were. The supposed presence of large numbers of Marines and Special Forces is emphasised because it is assumed that they were responsible for the fierce and resolute defence of the position. This is, once again, inaccurate. In much the same way that the British soldiers who took the position were ordinary Toms, so those that defended it were ordinary Argentine conscripts (Argentine Marines are also conscripted). There was certainly a feeling that the Argentines were 'very much a third-world army'[10] before the war

---

* Heavy machine-guns: .50 Brownings.

started; it didn't take long for the British soldiers to discover that an Argentine was just as capable of operating his weapon as a Briton.

It is normal doctrine in the British Army in conventional war that a deliberate assault on a prepared enemy position requires physical superiority of at least three to one. Thus a battalion would attack a company position, a company a platoon position, and so on. In situations where this superiority cannot be achieved, other factors must be strongly in favour of the attacker in order to compensate for the manpower deficiency. These might include overwhelming artillery or air support, or a similar perceived superiority. Such factors were absent when the Green-Eyed Boys stormed Longdon.

The plan with which 3 Para went into battle envisaged that B Company alone would be able to sweep through the Argentine company position spread along the summit of Longdon, and that A Company, followed by C Company if necessary, would do the same on Wireless Ridge. As we have seen, this was, in military terms, a somewhat unconventional plan: a one-to-one fight, an infantry company pitched against an infantry company, even though this company, as Hew Pike has written, 'was not expected to provide the bitter resistance that it did'.[11] Pike appears to have hoped that a silent approach and the advantage of surprise would overcome his lack of numbers. To some extent he was proved right. B Company did, after all, get very close to their initial objective, the western summit of Longdon, without alerting the defenders, and although this was largely the result of an unlikely amount of good fortune, luck has always been a significant factor at the tactical level.

But having had the good fortune – and skill – to reach their objective unobserved, the apparent lack of flexibility in the fireplan then became an obstacle to B Company's success.* According to his own account of the battle, published in *Pegasus*, Mike Argue in command of B Company had artillery support on call 'at his command' on pre-registered targets at the eastern end of Longdon, and he began to call on this from soon after Corporal Milne had stepped on the mine. But Argue and his FOO were unable to reach a position from which observed fire could be brought down on the Argentine

---

* Precise details of the fireplan were not available to the authors, primarily because of Lieutenant General Pike's unwillingness to co-operate with them.

positions in the centre of the ridge until well into the battle. Argue states that 'adjustment of our own artillery fire on to the enemy positions began in earnest' only *after* the arrival of Hew Pike at his OP position, and that, similarly, it was only around this time that the battalion's mortars could be brought into action, having arrived at their baseplate position at the rifle companies' start line.[12] This took place after 4 and 6 Platoons had both been virtually wiped out and the casualties evacuated by John Weeks. After this bombardment, Mark Cox was able to lead his *ad hoc* platoon much further into the Argentine position than any part of B Company had penetrated before, which does suggest that if an effective bombardment had taken place much earlier – after contact had been made at Fly Half – then a less depleted B Company might have been able to make even greater gains, perhaps with fewer men killed. This reflects a serious weakness in the overall plan.

The most controversial aspect of the story of the Green-Eyed Boys remains the so-called 'war crimes'. Although rumours have circulated within the army for some years about the nature and extent of the incidents which took place during and after the battle of Mount Longdon, there is unequivocal evidence of only two cases: the mutilation of corpses – and probably living wounded as well – and the shooting of a wounded prisoner after the battle had finished.

Corporal Stewart McLaughlin's command and leadership during the battle of Longdon represented an outstanding feat for a soldier who had not been in battle before. He led his section with enormous skill and determination, keeping them together as a fighting unit and picking up strays from other sections whose leaders were wounded or otherwise out of action. For his feats during B Company's bitter struggle amongst the rocks on the spine of Longdon, McLaughlin undoubtedly deserved the very highest recognition, but when the Falklands honours list was published he received nothing. The reason lay in the small and grotesque collection of trophies found in his webbing after his death. Mark Cox, McLaughlin's platoon commander, recalls a conversation he had with Mike Argue during which Argue mentioned his determination to recommend McLaughlin for a posthumous decoration. Cox felt strongly that McLaughlin couldn't be decorated after having been found to have cut the ears from corpses, and with the rumoured intervention of other members of the battalion, this was the view that prevailed.[13] Inasmuch as McLaughlin was dead, there was no immediate disciplinary problem to be handled. Nevertheless, the fact that, although clearly one of the outstanding figures of the battle, McLaughlin received no recognition has been a perennial source of bitterness amongst his friends and comrades ever since.

Why had McLaughlin performed this grim ritual? His father subsequently suggested that it had been discussed by McLaughlin and members of his section as they tabbed towards Teal and Estancia. It was a way of establishing psychological dominance that the Argentines, a largely Latin nation, would understand: just as bullfighters cut the ears from their victims, so would the Paras.[14] Another possible source of the idea is to be found in the Vietnam War classic *Dispatches*, which enjoyed a great vogue in the British military in the late 1970s. In the book the author, journalist Michael Herr, describes being offered a small bag containing severed Vietnamese ears by an American soldier. But whatever the motivation, it was an undeniably vile act.

The second incident, in which Corporal Sturge shot a wounded POW, presented a far greater problem, not least because Sturge was still around afterwards to be called to account. The battalion log and the several 'official' accounts of the battle contain no record of the incident or its aftermath, but the 'authorised version' of events in the wake of the shooting – apparently accepted by the police inquiry – is that Corporal Sturge was arrested and charged, isolated from his company and subsequently summarily tried by the commanding officer in Port Stanley. In effect this means that Sturge went through a legal process equivalent to court-martial and carrying the same force in law: a commanding officer can legitimately impose fines, sentences of detention, reprimands and other punishments; he can also dismiss charges entirely. The outcome of Pike's 'summary dealing' is not clear, but Sturge was subsequently sent home on a separate ship from the rest of the battalion. He was then posted to the depot at Aldershot and afterwards to 1 Para, where he was given the nickname 'Line 'em up Louis'.[15] He left the army as a colour sergeant in 1994.

The supposed 'trial' in Port Stanley is, however, disputed. David Collett, who commanded Sturge's company and would normally be present at any summary dealings, has no recollection of any such event, and does not believe that it took place, suggesting that it was invented for the benefit of the Metropolitan Police inquiry.[16] What is however abundantly clear is that every effort was made to suppress the story, and that these efforts were, by and large, successful. Although rumours of the incident could often be heard in military bars and messes, there was no published version until Vincent Bramley's book appeared in 1991, in which he described the shooting and the reaction of the Support Company hierarchy who witnessed it, but did not name Sturge.

What is not in doubt is that soldiers are not entitled to shoot prisoners under the circumstances in which Sturge carried out his act. There is no evidence that the prisoner made any effort to resist or escape, nor has it been suggested – except by Sturge himself, who claimed the Argentine was a sniper when he was disarmed by Mason and Caithness[17] – that he had been involved in anything previously that might have raised the corporal's ire. Neither can it truly be said that the incident took place 'in the heat of battle', unlike the unprovable allegation of the shooting of the 'American mercenaries'. The final excuse, that it was the result of a misunderstood order, is also invalid: the Nuremberg tribunals amongst many other courts have shown that soldiers are under a legal obligation to disobey unlawful orders of this kind.

Despite these facts, the Sturge shooting, while in itself appalling, was an act of a sort that has taken place in war since time immemorial. The military historian and journalist Max Hastings, who accompanied the Task Force to the Falklands, has written that:

> in every conflict in history inexcusable episodes have taken place in the heat of battle. In writing about the Second World War, I would go so far as to say that most units that took part had some experience of isolated episodes of appalling behaviour to prisoners, but it was very rare indeed for any such cases ever to be subjected to disciplinary proceedings.[18]

Perhaps the difference is in the nature of the war. The Second World War was a titanic struggle for national survival for most of the parties involved, whereas the Falklands conflict was on a far less dramatic scale. It is, perhaps, all the more horrifying that a soldier in the army of a humane liberal democracy should shoot a prisoner during a war fought, by the British at least, on a matter of principle.

Whatever the reasons for the shooting, it is necessary to recognise that, in war, we must adopt a different perspective on such incidents. In an ideal world, soldiers would be able to switch off the emotions of battle when the fighting ends, but we must recognise that in the real world that simply does not happen. Soldiers who have been legitimately killing their enemy one minute may have difficulty in recognising when to stop, and it would be an unusually self-righteous person who confused such an act with premeditated murder. Sturge's action should have been treated as a serious disciplinary matter – as some claim it was – within the fundamentally military context in which it happened. The Metropolitan Police inquiry into the shooting was inappropriate but, in the circumstances in which the story emerged, unavoidable. Justice, to be effective, must be seen to be done, and by allowing details of the incident to remain unreported, albeit for entirely honourable reasons, those involved have done the Parachute Regiment a great disservice.

So, what of the Green-Eyed culture of 3 Para? Whatever the rights and wrongs of the tactical and command decisions taken at company and battalion level, the battle of Mount Longdon was won to a considerable extent by the persistence and determination of a relatively small group of soldiers who continued to slug it out for dominance against a well-entrenched enemy. In reports and reminiscences of the battle, the same names crop up again and again: McKay, McLaughlin, Weeks, Fuller, Gough, Gray, Pettinger. They represent a litany of uncompromising professionalism and focused aggression. The importance of clear-cut command, co-ordination and control in a battle like Longdon should not be underestimated, but it is evident that after B Company's attack had run up against the brick wall of Argentine opposition in the centre of the ridge, there was precious little clear thinking about the means to regain the initiative until the arrival of David Collett's A Company. In the several hours before Collett got his men into position to continue the assault, the fighting was essentially being controlled by Des Fuller, Stewart McLaughlin and Jon Shaw: all well down the chain of command. In turn, they were supported by the Green-Eyed Boys, young men who were finally realising the opportunity to live up to the recklessly aggressive poses they had adopted as peacetime soldiers.

The Green-Eyed culture lives on in the army, as one would expect, because the army continues to recruit the same kind of soldier from the same kind of background. Only the name has changed: the self-proclaimed Green-Eyed Boys had left the army by the mid-1980s, their places taken by younger men with the same aggressive motivation, arrogance and wild *joie de vivre*. The Falklands conflict proved, for many who were present, that while young people may change with the times, they aren't getting softer. What it also showed was that the Green-Eyed behaviour that can be so trying in a peacetime scenario can be a positive boon in a shooting war. Although the worst extremes of such behaviour – McLaughlin's trophy-hunting, the Sturge shooting and the 'American mercenaries' killing – can be appalling, it is significant to note that the principal participants in each incident were considered for gallantry or distinguished service decorations. The positive side of it was the extraordinary courage shown by the vast majority of the young men of 3 Para.

There were negative aspects to 3 Para's campaign in the Falkland Islands, and it is easy, with the benefit of hindsight, to harp on them. But, if nothing else, Mount Longdon proved that when the chips are down, the 'Maroon Machine' will deliver. If you want a five-day-week army of milksops and mother's boys, there are plenty to choose from around the world. Only a fool goes to war without knowing that he has an edge over his enemy, and if you want to fight a war and know that you are going to win, you send for the Green-Eyed Boys.

NOTES

Notes

Chapter 1: The Maroon Machine

1 Winston Churchill, *The Second World War*, Vol. 3, p.682.
2 Max Arthur, *Men of the Red Beret*, p.5.
3 Ibid.
4 Isaiah 22:13.
5 G.G. Norton, *The Red Devils*, p.16.
6 Ibid., p.17.
7 Letter to Adrian Weale from John Warburton, Friends of OM, September 1994.
8 The character 'Rimmer' in the BBC television comedy series *Red Dwarf* is a classic recent example.
9 Dominic Gray, interview with Christian Jennings.
10 Personal experience. Adrian Weale was the Recruit Training Officer at the Intelligence Corps Depot in 1987 when training policies began to be relaxed.
11 Dave Robson, interview with Christian Jennings.

Chapter 2: Airborne Infantry

1 David Collett, interview with authors.
2 Des Fuller, interview with Christian Jennings.
3 Dave Robson, interview with Christian Jennings.
4 A.F.N. Clarke, *Contact* (Secker & Warburg, 1983).
5 Chris Phelan, interview with authors.
6 John Weeks, interview with authors.
7 Lee Fisher, interview with authors.
8 Ernie Rustill, interview with authors.
9 Ibid.
10 Ibid.
11 Des Fuller, interview with Christian Jennings.
12 Ibid.
13 Chris Phelan, interview with authors.
14 Dave Robson, interview with Christian Jennings.
15 Lee Fisher, interview with authors.
16 Rucksacks only went on general issue to the infantry at the end of the 1980s, by which time most soldiers had bought their own.
17 Chris Phelan, interview with authors.
18 Jim O'Connell, interview with Christian Jennings.
19 Sammy Dougherty, interview with authors.
20 Dominic Gray, interview with Christian Jennings.
21 Ibid.
22 Yvonne Weeks, interview with authors.
23 Conversation with Christian Jennings.
24 Lee Fisher, interview with authors.
25 Personal experience.
26 Name withheld for security reasons. Interview with Adrian Weale.
27 Mark Cox, interview with authors.
28 'Mac' McKenzie, interview with Christian Jennings.
29 Private information.
30 John Weeks, interview with authors.
31 Lee Fisher, interview with authors.
32 Ibid.
33 Private information.
34 David Collett, interview with authors.

35 Lieutenant Colonel the Hon. A.C.P. Campbell, interview with Adrian Weale.
36 Dominic Gray, interview with Christian Jennings.
37 Mark Cox, interview with authors.

Chapter 3: Rumours of War

1 Martin Middlebrook, *Fight for the Malvinas*, p.10.
2 Ibid.
3 Ibid., p.1.
4 Martin Middlebrook, *Task Force*, p.44.
5 Martin Middlebrook, *Fight for the Malvinas*, p.31.
6 Julian Thompson, *No Picnic*, p.1.
7 Tony Mason, interview with authors.
8 Lee Fisher, interview with authors.
9 Chris Phelan, interview with authors.
10 3 Para Battalion Log, hereafter referred to as 'battalion log'.
11 Lee Fisher, interview with authors.
12 Tony Mason, interview with authors.
13 Ibid.
14 Des Fuller, interview with Christian Jennings 29/10/94.
15 Vincent Bramley, *Excursion to Hell*, p.4.
16 Des Fuller, interview with Christian Jennings 29/10/94.
17 Battalion log.
18 Vincent Bramley, *Excursion to Hell*, p.5.
19 Brian Faulkner, interview with authors.
20 David Collett, interview with authors.
21 Vincent Bramley, *Excursion to Hell*, p.5.
22 Tony Mason, interview with authors.

Chapter 4: Going Down South

1 Battalion log.
2 Ibid.

3 Lee Fisher, interview with authors.
4 Des Fuller, interview with Christian Jennings.
5 Battalion log.
6 Ibid.
7 Vincent Bramley, *Excursion to Hell*, p.10.
8 Chris Phelan, interview with authors.
9 Battalion log.
10 Lee Fisher, interview with authors.
11 Vincent Bramley, *Excursion to Hell*, p.11.
12 Chris Phelan, interview with authors.
13 Dominic Gray, Kevin Connery, interviews with authors.
14 Dominic Gray, interview with Christian Jennings.
15 Tony Kempster, Grant Grinham, interview with Luke Jennings, *Independent on Sunday*, 16 May 1993.
16 Battalion log.
17 Vincent Bramley, *Excursion to Hell*, p.15.
18 Battalion log.
19 Mark Cox, interview with authors.
20 Lee Fisher, interview with authors.
21 Vincent Bramley, *Excursion to Hell*, p.19.
22 Private Jago, interview with Christian Jennings.
23 Battalion log; interview with Dominic Gray, Tony Kempster.
24 Robert Fox, *Eyewitness Falklands*, pp.44–5.
25 David Collett, interview with authors.
26 Vincent Bramley, *Excursion to Hell*, p.18.
27 Kevin Connery, interview with Christian Jennings.
28 Chris Phelan, interview with authors.
29 Battalion log.
30 Lee Fisher, interview with authors.
31 Chris Phelan, interview with authors.
32 Des Fuller, interview with Christian Jennings.

33 Chris Phelan, interview with authors.
34 Ibid.
35 Sammy Dougherty, interview with authors.
36 John Weeks, interview with authors.
37 Chris Phelan, interview with authors.

Chapter 5: The Retreat from Stalingrad

1 David Collett, interview with authors.
2 Martin Middlebrook, *Fight for the Malvinas*, p.147.
3 David Collett, interview with authors.
4 'Operation Corporate': 3 Commando Brigade Air Squadron', *AAC Journal*.
5 Martin Middlebrook, *Fight for the Malvinas*, p.147.
6 David Collett, interview with authors.
7 Julian Thompson, *No Picnic*, p.65.
8 Robert McGowan and Jeremy Hands, *Don't Cry for Me Sergeant Major*, p.112.
9 Chris Phelan, interview with authors.
10 Tony Mason, interview with authors.
11 David Collett, interview with authors.
12 Battalion log.
13 Major General John Frost, *2 Para Falklands*, p.58.
14 Julian Thompson, *No Picnic*, p.78.
15 David Collett, interview with authors.
16 Des Fuller, interview with Christian Jennings.
17 Lee Fisher, interview with authors.
18 Des Fuller, interview with Christian Jennings.
19 David Collett, interview with authors.
20 Lee Fisher, interview with authors.
21 John Frost, *2 Para Falklands*, p.56.
22 Ibid., p.58.
23 Spencer Fitz-Gibbon's *Not Mentioned in Despatches* is the outstanding critique of Jones's command at Goose Green.
24 Vincent Bramley, *Excursion to Hell*, p.68.
25 David Collett, interview with authors.
26 Tony Mason, interview with authors.
27 Ibid.
28 Des Fuller, interview with Christian Jennings.
29 John Weeks, interview with authors.
30 David Collett, interview with authors.
31 Robert McGowan and Jeremy Hands, *Don't Cry for Me Sergeant Major*, p.198.
32 Sammy Dougherty, interview with authors.
33 David Collett, interview with authors.
34 Lee Fisher, interview with authors.
35 Ibid.
36 Ibid.
37 Ibid.
38 Mark Cox, interview with authors.
39 Lee Fisher, interview with authors.

Chapter 6: Snot and Aggression

1 David Collett, interview with authors.
2 Tony Mason, interview with authors.
3 Des Fuller, interview with Christian Jennings.
4 Colonel H.W.R. Pike DSO MBE, 'With Fixed Bayonets', *Élite Magazine*, 1984.
5 Julian Thompson, *No Picnic*, p.130.
6 David Collett, interview with authors.
7 John Weeks, interview with authors.
8 David Collett, interview with authors.

9 John Weeks, interview with authors.

10 2 Para Post Operational Intelligence Report, dated 30 July 1982.

11 David Collett, interview with authors.

12 John Weeks, interview with authors.

13 Dominic Gray, interview with Luke Jennings.

14 John Weeks, interview with authors.

15 Dominic Gray, interview with Christian Jennings.

16 John Weeks, interview with authors.

17 Des Fuller, interview with Christian Jennings.

18 Mark Cox, interview with authors.

19 Dominic Gray, interview with Luke Jennings.

20 Corporal J.S. Morham, 'An Account of the Battle for Mount Longdon' (unpublished report).

21 Ibid.

22 Ibid.

23 Dominic Gray, interview with Christian Jennings.

24 Interview with Christian Jennings.

25 Lee Fisher, interview with authors.

26 Corporal J.S. Morham, 'An Account of the Battle for Mount Longdon'.

27 Battalion log.

28 Corporal Ian Bailey, quoted in Martin Middlebrook, *Task Force*, p.334.

29 Des Fuller, interview with Christian Jennings.

30 Ibid.

31 Ibid.

32 Battalion log.

33 Tony Kempster, interview with Luke Jennings.

34 Des Fuller, interview with Christian Jennings.

35 Mark Cox, letter to Adrian Weale.

36 Hew Pike, 'With Fixed Bayonets', op. cit.

37 David Collett, interview with authors.

38 John Weeks, interview with authors.

39 Ibid.

40 Ibid.

41 J.S. Morham, *An Account of the Battle for Mount Longdon*. In fairness to the men of the Drums Platoon, they had been prevented from 'balancing' their GPMGs before the battle by the quartermaster in order to save ammunition, and thus it is not entirely surprising that they had a good number of stoppages.

42 *Pegasus*, October 1982.

43 Mark Cox, interview with authors.

44 Ibid.

45 Chris Phelan, interview with authors.

46 Ibid.

47 Ibid.

48 David Collett, interview with authors.

49 Ibid.

50 Tony Mason, interview with authors.

51 Mark Cox, letter to Adrian Weale.

52 Vincent Bramley, *Excursion to Hell*, p.119.

Chapter 7: ¡Arriba Los Manos!

1 David Collett, interview with authors.

2 Ibid.

3 Mark Cox, interview with authors.

4 Chris Phelan, interview with authors.

5 David Collett, interview with authors.

6 Chris Phelan, interview with authors.

7 Ibid.

8 Ibid.

9 Des Fuller, interview with Christian Jennings.

10 John Weeks, interview with authors.

11 Private information.

12 Tony Mason, interview with authors.
13 John Weeks, interview with authors.
14 Des Fuller, interview with Christian Jennings.
15 Vincent Bramley, *Excursion to Hell*, p.120.
16 Des Fuller, interview with Christian Jennings.
17 Tony Mason, interview with authors.
18 Stuart Dover, interview with Adrian Weale, 1987. An alternative version, from David Collett, a non-eyewitness, is that Munro said: 'Get rid of the prisoners.'
19 Ibid.
20 Tony Mason, interview with authors.
21 Ibid.
22 Ibid.
23 Vince Bramley, interview with Adrian Weale.
24 Thor Caithness, interview with Christian Jennings.
25 David Collett, interview with authors.
26 This entire incident was described by Brian Faulkner during an interview with the authors in 1995.
27 Des Fuller, interview with Christian Jennings.
28 Ibid.
29 John Weeks, interview with authors.
30 Vincent Bramley, *Excursion to Hell*, p.152.
31 Tony Mason, interview with authors.
32 Julian Thompson, *No Picnic*, p.170.
33 Vincent Bramley, *Excursion to Hell*, p.153.
34 Tony Mason, interview with authors.
35 Vincent Bramley, *Excursion to Hell*, p.155.
36 Tony Mason, interview with authors.

37 Ibid.
38 Chris Phelan, interview with authors.
39 Des Fuller, interview with Christian Jennings.
40 Chris Phelan, interview with authors.
41 Lee Fisher, interview with authors.
42 Dominic Gray, interview with authors.
43 Martin Middlebrook, *Task Force*, p.385.

Chapter 8: The Aftermath

1 *Today*, 12 November 1993.
2 *The Times*, 14 July 1994.
3 Colonel David Hackworth, *About Face, passim*.
4 In Spencer Fitz-Gibbon, *Not Mentioned in Despatches*, p.54.
5 Ibid.
6 David Collett, interview with authors.
7 Hew Pike, 'With Fixed Bayonets', op. cit.
8 *Pegasus*, October 1982.
9 David Collett, interview with authors; also Robert Fox, *Eyewitness Falklands*, p.243, quoting Hew Pike.
10 David Collett, interview with authors.
11 Hew Pike, 'With Fixed Bayonets', op. cit.
12 *Pegasus*, October 1982, p.51.
13 Mark Cox, interview with authors.
14 Edmund McLaughlin, interview with Christian Jennings.
15 Alastair McQueen, interview with Adrian Weale.
16 David Collett, interview with authors.
17 Tony Mason, interview with authors.
18 Max Hastings, letter to Adrian Weale, September 1995.

Glossary

44 pattern A type of canvas webbing equipment specially designed for jungle warfare and introduced in the British Army in 1944.

58 pattern The general-issue webbing equipment in use by British forces during the Falklands conflict.

66 A light, portable, American-made, hand-held anti-tank rocket of 66mm nominal calibre and a maximum range of 200 metres. When fired accurately (no mean achievement), the 66 was found to have an impressive effect on static positions.

9mm The ammunition calibre used by British forces in pistols and sub-machine-guns. '9mm' is also the generic term in the army for the Browning Hi-Power pistol issued to some personnel.

Adjutant An officer, normally of the rank of captain, who acts as the commanding officer's right-hand man in peace and war, with special responsibility for personnel and discipline. In 3 Para in 1982 the post was held by Captain Kevin McGimpsey.

Advance to contact A form of operation in which a unit, or sub-unit, travels along a set route until it meets an enemy position which it then engages. Normally used when the precise location of the enemy is unclear.

Bandolier A green plastic pouch issued to hold belts of 7.62mm machine-gun ammunition. An unpopular and fiddly item, the majority of soldiers prefer to carry belted ammunition slung around their bodies.

Basha An improvised shelter, normally constructed from the rainproof nylon poncho issued to all soldiers.

Battalion A military unit typically composed of between 500 and 1000 soldiers commanded by a lieutenant colonel.

Belt-kit Webbing equipment adapted to be worn without a shoulder harness or yoke. In the British Army it suggests membership of a Special Forces or specialist patrol unit.

Bergen	The generic term in the British Army for any military-type rucksack.
Brigade	A military formation comprising two, or more, battalions.
Brigadier	A one-star general of the British Army or Royal Marines.
C-130	A four-engined turboprop-driven aircraft used as a general transport and paratroop drop aircraft.
Captain	Junior officer in the British Army, typically employed on the battalion staff or as a company second-in-command.
Chinook	Large twin-rotor transport helicopter which can transport up to half a company of infantry.
Clansman	A reliable, hard-wearing, battlefield communications system introduced into British service at the time of the Falklands War.
CO	Commanding officer. Normally a lieutenant colonel, a CO in the British Army commands a unit of battalion size or its equivalent.
Combats	Generic army term for the heavy-duty camouflaged clothing worn in the field.
Company	A sub-unit of an infantry battalion, normally comprising about 100 men commanded by a major. Equivalent-sized units of other arms are squadrons, batteries etc.
Compo	Generic term for field rations issued by the British Army. In 1982, these came in two forms: GS (General Service) rations provided a tinned main meal, but the most prevalent in the Falklands were 'Arctic' rations, which were dehydrated on the assumption that plenty of water would be available for cooking. In fact, although the Falklands climate is harsh, there was little safe water to be found and there were constant shortages for the soldiers. In addition to the main meals, both types of compo provide a similar selection of snacks, chocolate, biscuits, tea and coffee, and lavatory paper; this latter is known as 'John Wayne' because it is 'rough, tough, and takes no shit from nobody'.
Corporal	A junior non-commissioned officer, often to be found commanding a section of eight or ten men.
CQMS	Company quartermaster sergeant. Appointment normally filled by a colour sergeant (E5). The CQMS is responsible for channelling stores from

the quartermasters' department to his company, and for controlling their issue.

Crap-hat (or 'hat'). Any soldier who does not wear the maroon beret of airborne forces. According to Lee Fisher of 3 Para: 'We had blokes [*who*] used to slag off the SAS for being hats.'

Crow A newly-joined, inexperienced soldier.

CSM Company sergeant major. A warrant officer class 2 who acts as right-hand man to a company commander. In battle, the CSM's task is to organise ammunition resupply for his fighting soldiers.

D-Day The specific day on which an operation takes place.

DF A specific location onto which pre-arranged artillery fire can be brought.

Division A military formation comprising two, or more, brigades, and commanded by a major general.

DMS 'Direct Moulded Sole'. Cheaply made rubber-soled ankle boots issued by the British Army from the 1960s to the mid-1980s. They were supposedly waterproofed by the addition of cloth puttees, but in reality these made little difference. By the end of the Falklands campaign, considerable numbers of soldiers were suffering from agonising trench foot as the result of wearing these dreadful boots.

Dog-tags Metal discs worn by all soldiers in combat as a means of identifying their bodies afterwards. They bear the owner's name, number, religion and blood group.

Doss-bag Military slang for sleeping-bag.

DPM Disruptive pattern material. British-pattern camouflaged cloth.

Endex 'End of exercise'. Used on completion of virtually every task.

Exocet Effective French-built anti-ship missile used to devastating effect by Argentine Navy.

FAL Belgian-made 7.62mm automatic rifle used by Argentine forces.

FAP Final assault position. Sheltered location where attacking troops can 'shake out' into the formation they will assault in. In the Longdon assault, this was the start line 'Free Kick'.

Field dressing Sterile pad with attached bandages issued to soldiers for emergency first-aid in the field.

Fleece   Civilian-made thermal jackets worn by many
                      soldiers underneath combat clothing in the
                      Falklands.

FN   Fabrique National. Belgian arms manufacturer,
                      responsible for the design and/or manufacture of
                      the majority of the small arms used by both sides
                      in the Falklands.

FOO   Forward observation officer. Artillery officer,
                      normally a lieutenant or captain, who
                      accompanies infantry troops and brings in aimed
                      artillery fire onto targets at their request or on
                      his own initiative.

FPF   Final protective fire. A high-priority DF used as
                      a last resort very close to a friendly position if it
                      appears likely to be overrun.

G1   The military staff branch dealing with personnel.

G2   The military staff branch dealing with
                      intelligence and security.

G3   The military staff branch dealing with operations
                      and training.

G4   The military staff branch dealing with logistics.

Gazelle   A light reconnaissance helicopter.

GPMG   A belt-fed 7.62mm machine-gun. Both sides in
                      the Falklands War used the FN MAG design.

H-Hour   The specific time at which an operation starts.

HE   High explosives.

Helly-Hansen   A popular brand of civilian-bought thermal
                      clothing much used in the British Army.

Illum   Starshells and flares used to light up a battlefield.

IO   Intelligence officer. A member of the battalion
                      staff – normally a captain or senior lieutenant –
                      responsible for disseminating intelligence
                      reports to the CO and company commanders, and
                      reporting intelligence information to superior
                      formations. In 3 Para, the appointment was held
                      by Captain Orpen-Smellie.

IWS   Individual weapon sight. A bulky nightsight that
                      can be mounted on a rifle or machine-gun, or
                      used like a telescope.

Kevlar   A fabric developed for the US space programme
                      which has proved resistant to low-velocity bullets
                      and shrapnel. Now used in body armour and
                      helmets.

Lance corporal   The first rung on the promotion ladder for
                      soldiers. Often carries with it the appointment of
                      2ic of a section of eight men.

Larkspur	Radio system superseded by the vastly superior 'Clansman'.
Lieutenant	Junior officer with at least two years' service (unless a university graduate). Will generally be commanding a platoon of thirty men.
Lieutenant colonel	A senior officer, normally commanding a battalion-sized unit or holding a senior staff appointment.
Lieutenant general	A three-star general under the British system, may command a corps.
Major	A 'field' grade officer, often commanding a company or equivalent-sized sub-unit.
Major general	A two-star general, often commanding a division.
Milan	A wire-guided anti-tank missile with a range of up to 1950 metres.
Mirage	A French-built fighter-bomber used by the Argentines.
MO	Medical officer.
Morphine	In combat, soldiers are issued with a dose of morphine-based painkiller to use on themselves if they are wounded. It comes in the form of a 'syrette', a small tube with attached hypodermic needle, for intramuscular injection.
MT	Mechanical transport.
MTO	Mechanical transport officer, an appointment usually held by an officer newly commissioned from the ranks.
ND	Negligent discharge (of a weapon). An ND is a serious occurrence in the British Army; aside from being highly dangerous, it is indicative of sloppy drills and lack of professionalism.
NOD	Night observation device.
'O' Group	The means by which detailed operational orders are passed down the chain of command. It is, necessarily, a formal event which is usually carefully stage-managed and controlled by the commander giving the orders. The sequence of events is as follows: the commander describes the ground over which the operation he is outlining will take place and follows this with a briefing on the situation (the intelligence picture, what 'friendly forces' are doing, who is attached and detached for the operation, etc.); once the situation has been described, the commander must then give a clear and simple mission

statement (for example: 'to capture Mount Longdon'); at this point, the commander gives an outline of his plan and then goes on to describe in detail what he wants of each individual sub-unit under his command; this is followed by co-ordinating instructions explaining such crucial matters as timings; these are followed by a round-up of essentially administrative points, and signals instructions. The formal structure and set format of an 'O' group should mean that subordinate commanders will not miss any relevant orders or instructions.

At the time of the Falklands War, the prevalent command doctrine of British land forces was essentially restrictive and, as a result, commanders were expected to provide their subordinates with intensely detailed orders, trying to cover every eventuality. This is a somewhat unrealistic approach to adopt in the chaos of all-out war (it can work very well in low-intensity conflicts) for a number of reasons, and the more able and intelligent commanders, like Hew Pike, allowed their subordinates a good measure of leeway.

OC	Officer commanding. The formal title of an officer in charge of a unit smaller than a battalion (ie a company or platoon).
OP	Observation post.
Ops Officer	Operations Officer. The battalion ops officer is responsible for the co-ordination and administration of the battalion's operational tasks and for assisting the CO in his planning process.
P-Company	A set of physical tests designed to assess an individual soldier's aptitude for serving with airborne forces. It occupies the most gruelling week of a Para recruit's basic training.
Padre	All infantry battalions and most other major units have an attached chaplain known as the padre. Although padres are given officer's rank, they do not use it when dealing with soldiers to whom they are expected to provide spiritual leadership and moral guidance.
PC	Platoon commander.
Platoon	Sub-unit of an infantry company, normally comprising about thirty men commanded by a

	lieutenant or second lieutenant.
Pucara	Argentine-built turboprop bomber designed for counter-insurgency and close air-support applications.
QM	Quartermaster. The officer, normally commissioned through the ranks, who is responsible for the battalion's logistics. In 3 Para, this role was fulfilled by Captain Norman Menzies ('Norman the Storeman').
R Group	Reconnaissance group. A small team led by the CO, normally including the adjutant, a signaller and some bodyguards, which may leave the battalion tactical HQ ('Tac') in order to allow the CO to make a personal assessment of the battlefield situation.
RAP	Regimental aid post. Battalion-level casualty clearing station where the wounded of both sides are assessed, stabilised and prepared for evacuation.
REMF	Rear echelon mother-fucker. A non-combatant soldier.
RSM	Regimental sergeant major.
RSO	Regimental signals officer.
Sangar	A defensive position constructed above ground using sandbags, earth, peat or rocks, as opposed to a trench which is dug into the ground.
SAS	Special Air Service. A multi-roled special forces unit of the British Army. The majority of its members are recruited from the Parachute Regiment.
SBS	Special Boat Squadron. A special forces unit recruited from the Royal Marine Commandos, with particular skills in amphibious and underwater infiltration of their targets. Now expanded, it is called the Special Boat Service.
Second lieutenant	The most junior officer's rank. A second lieutenant will normally be in command of a platoon.
Section	A sub-unit of a platoon, normally comprising eight to ten men commanded by a corporal.
Sergeant	Senior NCO, normally employed as 2ic of a platoon.
SLR	Self-loading rifle. Semi-automatic British variant of the fully-automatic 7.62mm FN FAL.
SMG	Submachine-gun. A small fully-automatic weapon which normally fires pistol ammunition.

In the British Army, this meant the 9mm Sterling-Patchett carbine.

Staff sergeant
Also known as a 'colour sergeant' in the infantry. Senior NCO, usually employed as CQMS or sometimes as a platoon commander.

Super Etendard
French-made naval fighter-bomber. Capable of carrying the air-launched version of the Exocet missile.

Tab
Tactical advance into battle. Paras' slang for a forced march ('like yomping only faster and harder').

Tom
Any private soldier in the Paras.

Webbing
The green canvas belt, harness and pouches used to carry ammunition, water and other essentials into battle. Also known as 'fighting order', 'belt-kit' and 'belt order'.

Windproof
High-quality camouflaged combat jacket.

Wombat
120mm recoilless anti-tank gun issued at battalion level. Superseded by the Milan system.

Zulu time
Greenwich Mean Time. Used in all military operations in order to avoid confusion.

Bibliography and Sources

The vast majority of this book is based on interviews conducted by the authors during 1994 and 1995 with veterans of the Falklands campaign, and these are noted in the text. Additionally some published and unpublished sources were consulted for background material, and the majority of these are listed below; when they are directly quoted, they are noted in the text.

Arthur, Max, *Men of the Red Beret* (Century Hutchinson, 1990)

Bramley, Vincent, *Excursion to Hell* (Bloomsbury, 1991)

Bramley, Vincent, *Two Sides of Hell* (Bloomsbury, 1994)

Fitz-Gibbon, Spencer, *Not Mentioned in Despatches* (Lutterworth, 1995)

Fox, Robert, *Eyewitness Falklands* (Mandarin, 1992)

Major General John Frost, *2 Para Falklands* (Buchan & Enright, 1983)

Robert McGowan and Jeremy Hands, *Don't Cry for Me Sergeant Major* (Futura, 1983)

Middlebrook, Martin, *Task Force: The Falklands War 1982* (Penguin, 1987)

Middlebrook, Martin, *The Fight for the Malvinas* (Viking, 1989)

Thompson, Julian, *No Picnic* (Leo Cooper, 1985)

van der Bijl, Nicholas, *Argentine Forces in the Falklands* (Osprey, 1992)

Walzer, Michael, *Just and Unjust Wars* (Allen Lane, 1978)

Index